A Boy of Good Breeding

Miriam Toews was born in Steinbach, Manitoba, and currently lives in Winnipeg with her family. Her novel *A Complicated Kindness* won – amongst many other accolades – the Governor General's Award, becoming an international bestseller.

by the same author

Summer of my Amazing Luck
Swing Low
A Complicated Kindness

A Boy of Good Breeding

Miriam Toews

First published in 1998 by Vintage Canada
First published in Great Britain in 2006
by Faber and Faber Limited
3 Queen Square London WC1N 3AU
This paperback edition published in 2008

Printed in Great Britain by Clays Ltd, St Ives plc

A CIP record for this book
is available from the British Library

ISBN 978-0-571-22949-9

2 4 6 8 10 9 7 5 3 1

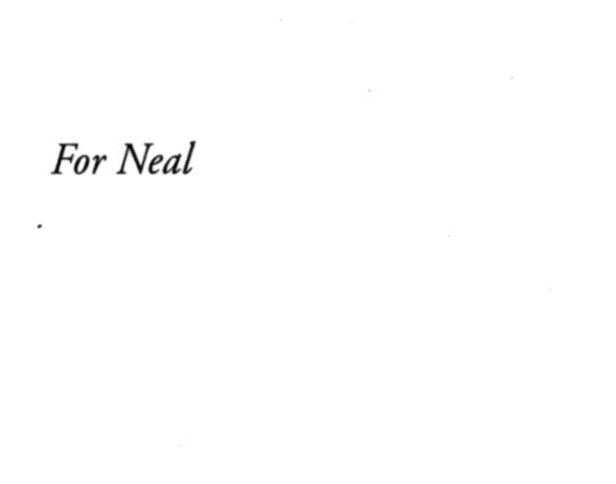

For Neal

one

Algren was Canada's smallest town. It really was. Canada's Smallest Town. It said so on a big old billboard right outside the town limits and Knute had checked with one of those government offices in the blue pages and they said fifteen hundred is what you need for a town. And that's what Algren had. If it had one less it would be a village and if it had just one more it would be a bigger town. Like all the rest of the small towns. Being the smallest was its claim to fame.

Knute had come to Algren, from the city of Winnipeg, to look after her dad who'd had a heart attack. And to relieve her mom who said if she spent one more day in the house she'd go insane.

She was twenty-four years old. Her mother, Dory, had intended her name to be pronounced "Noot uh," but nobody got it so it became just Knute, like "Noot." Even her mom had given up on the "uh" part but did from time to time call her Knutie or sometimes, and she hated this, Knuter.

Knute had a daughter, Summer Feelin', and Summer Feelin' had a strange way of shaking when she was excited. She flapped her arms, and her fingers moved quickly as though she were typing to save her life, and sometimes her head went back and her mouth opened wide and sounds like *aaah* and *uh-uh-uh* came out of it.

When she first started doing it, Knute thought it was cute. Summer Feelin' looked like she'd lift right off the ground. But then Knute started worrying about it and decided to take her to a specialist, a pediatric neurologist. He did a number of tests, including an encephalogram. Summer Feelin' liked the wires and enjoyed the attention but told the doctor that flapping was just something she was born to do.

Eventually after all the results came in and the charts had been read and analyzed, he agreed with her. She was born to flap. There was no sign of strange electrical activity in her brain, no reason to do a CAT scan, and all accounts of her birth indicated no trauma had occurred, nothing untoward as she had made her way through Knute's birth canal and into this world.

Every night Knute lay down with Summer Feelin'. That was the time S.F. told Knute stories and let her in on her big plans and Knute could feel her daughter's body tremble with excitement. It quivered. It shook. It was out of her control. Knute would hold Summer Feelin' until she stopped shaking, maybe a twitch or two or a shudder, and fell asleep. The specialist said S.F.'s condition, which wasn't really a condition, was very rare but nothing to worry about. Then he'd added, in a thoughtful way, that the condition or lack of condition might be the precipitator to that rare phenomenon known as spontaneous combustion. So Knute worried, from time to time, about S.F. bursting into flames for no apparent reason. And that was the type of concern she couldn't really explain to people, even close friends, without them asking her if she needed a nap or what she'd been reading lately or just plain laughing at her.

March was the month that Knute and Summer Feelin' arrived in Algren. Tom had had a heart attack (or *his* heart attack, as Dory called it) in December. He'd been putting up the last decorations on the tree and BAM, it happened. He fell over, and because he was sort of clutching at the tree it fell on top of him. Ten days later, in the sterile intensive care ward of the hospital, nurses were still finding tiny pine needles in his hair and in the many creases of his skin. He picked up a nasty infection called septicemia in the hospital and, as a result, his lungs malfunctioned and he was put on a respirator. Of course, he couldn't talk, but in his more lucid, pain-free moments he could write. Sort of. All he ever wrote, in a barely legible scrawl either stretched out over the whole page or sometimes scrunched up in the bottom corner, was "How is the tree?" Or "Is the tree okay?" Or "Is the tree up?" Or "I'm sorry about the tree."

One day in the hospital Dory told him, "Tom, it's Christmas Day today. Merry Christmas, sweetheart."

His eyes were closed but he squeezed her hand. She said, "Do you remember Christmas, darling?"

And he opened his eyes and looked up at her and shook his head. Yet the next day, again, he wrote about the tree. He couldn't remember Christmas, but he knew a tree should, for some reason, be erected in his living room.

Gradually he could remember a bit more and he could spell "world" backwards and count by sevens and all those things they'd asked him to do in the hospital when he was off the respirator and out of intensive care, but still he had a strange scattered memory, like, for instance, he knew he must, absolutely *must,* shave every morning, but he was unsure why. He reminded Dory to check the battery in the smoke detector, but when she said, "Oh, Tom, what's the worst that can happen if our battery is dead for a day or two?" he didn't have an answer. So he was caught in a bind where he was committed to doing what he'd always done but he couldn't remember why he was doing it. His life, some might have said, had no purpose.

Neither did Knute's, really. Summer Feelin' was in a day care that she hated and Knute was working full time as a hostess in a busy downtown restaurant where everybody was used to seating themselves. She wasn't aggressive enough to say, "Hey, can't you read the sign? It says 'wait to be seated,'" and so, pretty much, she just stood there all day smiling and feeling stupid. From time to time she moved the sign right in front of the door, but people would walk into it and then move it back out of their way. Sometimes the waitresses got mad at her because she wasn't seating anybody in their sections or because everybody was sitting in their section and they were run off their feet trying to keep up with the orders. Then, for a while, Knute would try to keep people from walking past her and she'd say things like, "Please follow me," or "A table will be ready in a minute," or "How many of you are there?" Usually there would be two and when she asked how many of them there were, they'd look at each other like she was nuts, then they'd hold up two fingers or point at each other and say, "one, two," in a loud voice.

"Two!" Knute would say, "okay, two, hmmm . . . two, you say," like she was trying to figure out how to seat twelve. Then she'd meander around and around the restaurant with them behind her, suggesting possible tables, and she'd say, "Oh no, I think, well, no, well, yes, okay, sure, right here is fine. Wherever you want, really, I guess."

Her boss's wife and all the waitresses and the dishwasher and the two cooks kept telling him to fire her, but her boss kept giving her more chances. He told Knute she'd get the hang of it in a while, just get in their faces and make them wait. "They're like pigs at the trough," he said. "You gotta keep 'em under control."

On her first day Knute had actually managed to lead an old couple to a table. But somehow they got their wires crossed, and Knute pulled a chair away from the table just as the man was going to sit on it. In slow motion he fell to the ground while Knute and his wife stared, horrified. As he fell, he knocked over the fake flower arrangement and the vase shattered.

Knute's boss came running out and picked the old man up, cleaned up the glass and told them lunch was on the house. Then he took Knute into the kitchen, made her a salami sandwich on a bagel, sat her down on a lettuce crate and told her not to worry, not to worry, this was her first day, she'd work out the kinks. But she never did. Anyway, it was a lot better than pumping gas. The one time Knute tried that she accidentally filled up a motor home with gas—not the gas tank, but the interior of the motor home itself. She had stuck the nozzle into the water-spout hole instead of the gas tank hole. The woman driving the van hadn't noticed until she lit up a cigarette and her motor home exploded, partially, and her leg ended up needing plastic surgery. Her husband sued the gas station and won a bunch of money, of course. Knute was let go and told, by her supervisor, that she should get tested for brain damage.

On her way home from the restaurant, Knute would pick up Summer Feelin' and listen to her tell lies about the day care. How Esther, one of the workers, had punched her six times in the face, how Justin, one of the twins, had made her put her tongue on the cold swing set and it had stuck and they left her out there all alone all day, how a terrible man with purple skin and horse feet had come and killed seven of the kids.

"Summer Feelin'," Knute would say, "I know how much you hate it, but for now you have to try to find something good about it. It can't be that bad."

Knute was tired from standing around stupidly all day. But she felt she had to make it up to Summer Feelin', so for an hour or two before bedtime the two of them would play in the park or get an ice cream, maybe rent a movie or walk to the library. And that wore Knute out even more. Her favourite days were when Summer Feelin' would relax and they could just sit at their little table and talk. Summer Feelin' would tell her funny stories and shake with excitement and then, in the evening, they'd curl up together with Summer Feelin's soft head under Knute's chin. Knute would try not to fall asleep because that would mean that was it, the day. If she didn't fall asleep she'd get up very quietly and make herself a cup of coffee and phone Dory, collect, or her buddy Marilyn, who just lived a couple of blocks away but had a kid and so was housebound like her in the evenings. Sometimes Marilyn and Knute watched TV together over the phone.

When Dory called and suggested Knute and Summer Feelin' come back to Algren and live with her and Tom for a while, Knute felt like someone had just injected her with a warm, fast-acting tranquilizer. It felt like she had just put her head on a soft feather pillow and been told to go to sleep, everything would be fine. Dory made it sound like she needed Knute desperately to help with Tom, to protect her sanity, and it's true she did. But Dory also had a sense that Knute was tired, really tired. That all she was doing was spinning her wheels. It took Knute about fifteen minutes to quit her job, cancel Summer Feelin's spot at the day care, tell her landlord she was moving, and pack their stuff. When she told Summer Feelin' that she could kiss her awful day care good-bye, she flapped like crazy, and Knute had to put her in a nice, warm bath to calm her down. She told Marilyn she was going to her mom and dad's for a while and Marilyn asked if she could go, too. The next day Summer Feelin' and Knute were on the road.

Not for long, though, because Algren was only about forty miles away from Winnipeg. Knute and Summer Feelin' peered out the car windows at the clumps of dirt and piles of melting snow and S.F. said it reminded her of the moon.

When they got to the outskirts of Algren, which was really the same thing as the town, they saw Hosea Funk, the mayor, standing in a ditch of water with hip waders, gazing soulfully at the billboard that said, Welcome to Algren, Canada's Smallest Town. Of course there's not a lot to be done when people die or when they're born. They come and go. They move away. They disappear. They *reappear.* But more or less, give or take a person or two, Algren was the reigning champ of small towns. Well, there was another famous thing about Algren but it wasn't as impressive (if you can call being a town whose population consistently hovers around fifteen hundred people *impressive*): Algren was also the original home of the Algren cockroach. The Algren cockroach was one of only three types of North American cockroaches. Apparently it was first brought to Algren on a plant or a sack of potatoes or something a hundred years ago from Europe and the rest was history. In the encyclopedia under "cockroach" it listed the Algren cockroach and mentioned Algren as a small town in southern Manitoba. No mention of its being *the* smallest town in Canada, much to Hosea Funk's chagrin.

As they passed Hosea standing in the ditch, Knute honked the horn and waved. "Who's that?" S.F. asked.

"The mayor," said Knute. "He's an old friend of Grandpa's."

The horn startled him out of his reverie and Hosea straightened his golf cap and started up the side of his ditch. He didn't wave back. He tugged for a second at the front of his jacket and then nodded his head, once. That's how the men in Algren greeted everyone, friend or foe.

As a kid Hosea Funk would say, "okay . . . okay . . . okay . . ." before leaving the house to walk to school, just sorting it out in his head and coming to terms with it. In the playground and at the skating rink he was very cautious. He would creep around the rink clinging to the boards, not caring what the other boys and girls thought. He was keeping himself alive, saving himself for something big. He wanted to make sure he was okay down the road because he knew he had things to do. And because he was all that his mother had.

Hosea Funk was born in the middle of a heat wave on June 11, 1943, in a machinery shed belonging to his mother's parents. The shed was long gone by now and in its place was a large rectangular-shaped patch of dead grass, discoloured and flattened and strewn with rocks and scraps of metal. Euphemia was eighteen years old when Hosea was born and sure her father would kill her, quite literally, if he found out she had had a baby. Getting pregnant in September was a lucky thing for her because all winter she was able to hide her body away in big coats and sweaters. But it was a good thing that Hosea was born when he was because if she'd had to have worn that huge woollen coat a day longer in that heat wave, she would have died for sure. As it was, her parents were so concerned about her health, thinking she must be very ill to need so many clothes in that heat, that they forbade her to leave the house and had a neighbour or a relative watching her just about every minute of the day. Getting to the machine shed to have her baby had not been easy.

Euphemia had had nothing to prepare her for Hosea's birth. Well, almost nothing. Once, as a girl, she had wandered into the barn where her father was helping a mare give birth to her foal. Just about his entire right arm was stuck inside the horse. His left arm he used to brace himself against the horse's buttocks. The mare was kicking him and screeching and her father was purple in the face, cursing the horse and the reluctant foal. Euphemia stood and stared in horror. Would it be possible to stick her own arm inside herself and pull the baby out? There was nobody else to help her, after all. Hadn't some of her father's mares given birth without any help? And hadn't she heard her friends talking about walking out to the field and finding a new calf or piglet or whatever happily sucking milk from its mother and nobody had even known the cow or the sow was pregnant? So, it could be done, Euphemia thought.

Euphemia lay in her bed, in the heat, in her sweaters and coats. She stared at the dark wood and flowered wallpaper of her bedroom. She could smell chicken noodle soup. She could hear her brothers hollering in the yard and things clanking. Her sisters had gone to town and her mother was rummaging around downstairs. Things were as they usually were and it all would have been comforting except for the sticky circle of blood staining Euphemia's cotton underwear. That evening she went into labour.

The pain had started after supper. By now Euphemia's meals were being brought to her in bed, to save her strength. How long would this mysterious fever last, anyway? her parents wondered. They asked her if she thought she might be feeling better and if perhaps she could join them at the supper table. But she said no, if anything she was feeling worse and really needed to be alone. One after another, her brothers and sisters came to her room and left again, shrugging their shoulders, going back to their business.

By nine o'clock the pain was almost unbearable. Euphemia's lower back, pelvis, stomach, and uterus together had turned into a rigid two-thousand-pound stick of dynamite going off at first intermittently and then continuously. Iron cannonballs were rocketing around inside her body, pounding and bashing, desperate for a way out. If anything, the dull warning pain that preceded each explosion terrified Euphemia the most. She whimpered and moaned. She dug her fingernails into her thighs and almost passed out holding her breath. She cried and prayed to God to help her survive. Beside her, in another twin bed, lay her younger sister, Minty, still asleep, but tossing and turning a bit more with each of Euphemia's muffled moans. Euphemia knew that somehow she had to get out of the house.

By this time it was ten-thirty. Her parents and her other brothers and sisters would be in bed, if not asleep, and if she was stealthy enough she could creep down the hall, down the stairs, and out the back door. If she had time she could make it to the machinery shed.

Euphemia managed to get out of her bed and tiptoe to the door, hunched over, in agony, in tears, but on her way. Just as she crossed the threshold, her little sister woke up. "Phemie?"

"Minty," said Euphemia, "I'm going to the john, go back to sleep. I'm coming right back."

But Minty said, "Wait, Phemie, take me with you. I gotta go, too."

Oh God, thought Euphemia. If she said no, Minty would start to cry and wake up her mother and her life would be over. But she couldn't bring her with her. Of course not. Euphemia clutched the door frame, trying not to cry. "Listen, Minty, if you promise to go back to sleep right now, tomorrow morning I will give you the best present in the whole wide world. Okay?"

Minty stared at Euphemia and asked excitedly, "What is it, what is it, Phemie?"

Euphemia put her finger to her lips. "Shhh, Minty, it's the best thing in the world, I told you, but I can't bring it to you until you go to sleep. Please, Minty?"

"You promise?" said Minty. "Yes, Minty, yes, I promise."

Euphemia made it out of the house. In the darkness she stumbled and lurched, cupping her belly with one hand, in an attempt to keep the baby in, until she could make it to the machine shed, to the little bundle of hay she had tossed in one corner months ago, before being confined to her bedroom.

The effort of opening the heavy shed door helped to break her water. Inside the shed, Euphemia ripped off her coat, her two sweaters, her wet woollen leotards, and stained cotton underwear and sank to the floor, naked, on her hands and knees. It was pitch-black inside the shed. Euphemia, her face twisted sideways on the cement floor, screamed into the darkness, and Hosea Funk was born.

two

When Knute and Summer Feelin' drove up to the house they could see Tom and Dory standing in the living room, staring out the picture window. Next to them were small bronze statues and clay busts that Tom had bought, and he and Dory seemed to blend in with these things. As soon as they saw Knute's beater pull up in the driveway, though, they came to life. Dory zipped to the front door and Tom smiled and waved. These days he stayed away from the doors when they were being opened. He couldn't afford to get a chill and get sick all over again. S.F. ran up to the picture window, flapping like crazy, and Tom gave her a high-five against the glass, smudging it up a bit. Dory came running out of the house saying, "Welcome, welcome, oh I'm sooooo glad you're both here." And she scooped up S.F. even though her heart wasn't in much better shape than Tom's and then, with her other free arm, wrapped herself around Knute. Tom beamed through the glass.

Dory had prepared a large meal. It consisted of boneless chicken breasts with a black bean sauce, steamed broccoli, slices of cucumbers, tomatoes, and carrots, brown rice, and a fruit salad. Knute could just barely pick out the grimace on Tom's face when he sat down at the table, rather ashamed and annoyed that all this dull stuff constituted a celebratory meal.

And that it was all made especially for him and his fragile heart. He would have preferred a big piece of red meat with lots of salt, some potatoes and thick gravy, cheese sauce to accompany his steamed broccoli, great slabs of bread with real butter to soak up the gravy and juice from the meat, a large wedge of apple pie and ice cream, and four cups of coffee to wash it down.

But, of course, Tom couldn't eat steak every day, or maybe he could have and it wouldn't have made any difference. Who knows? Anyway, Knute could tell that Dory felt very good about herself when she prepared the chicken and steamed vegetables, and the fact that they had hardly any taste made S.F., at least, happy.

After lunch Tom did a bit of walking up and down the hall, S.F. went down to the basement to play with the toys, and Dory and Knute had a cryptic conversation about Tom.

"So?" said Knute, and jerked her head in the direction of Tom and the hallway.

"Well," said Dory, "you know . . ."

"Mmmmm . . ."

And then Dory said, "One day at a time . . ." and Knute nodded and said, "Yup . . ."

They sat there and stared at their coffee cups for a bit and Dory added in a very hushed tone, "A bit more," she tapped at her chest, "these days."

Knute tapped her own chest. "Pain?" she asked.

Dory nodded and pursed her lips.

"Hmmm . . . well, what does the doctor say?"

"OH TOM, YOU'RE DONE?" Tom had finished his walk and Dory had been timing him. He had walked for eight minutes. Dory was trying to be extremely upbeat about the eight minutes. "Well, Tom, yesterday it was only seven," and that sort of thing. Tom went over to the picture window and stood with his back to Dory and Knute. He punched his fist into his palm once and then after about thirty seconds he did it again. He slowly walked back to the couch and lay down with a heavy sigh.

After supper (of leftovers), Dory and Knute played Scrabble. For weeks Dory had been playing with "Marie," a phantom Scrabble opponent whom she had given her own middle name to. Knute asked Dory how she felt when "Marie" won, and she said, "Divided." Summer Feelin' had wandered over to the neighbours' house to play with the little girl, Madison, who lived there. Dory could never remember Madison's name. "Montana?" she'd say. "Manhattan?" Which got them onto the subject of names, and Dory wondered if Knute had, perhaps, considered calling S.F. just "Summer" instead of "Summer Feelin'"? Knute knew Dory wasn't altogether enthusiastic about her granddaughter's name and she told her she'd think about it, although she wondered if Dory was really any authority on girls' names considering the choice she'd made when her own daughter was born.

"Summer," Dory said over and over. "If you say it enough times, you know, Knutie, you *get* that summer feeling. You don't have to actually *say* it. The Feelin' part becomes rather redundant, don't you think? Or maybe you could change the spelling of Feelin' to something, oh, I don't know, Irish, maybe, like Phaelan, or . . ."

Just then the doorbell rang. Tom woke up from his nap on the couch and Dory answered the door. A large man with a pale yellow golf cap tugged twice at the front of his coat before greeting Dory and stepping inside.

Tom was the first to speak. "Hosea Funk, c'mon in, c'mon in." And he nodded his head once, in the traditional male greeting, got up from the couch, and stood there in his polo pajamas looking a bit like William Shatner in the *Enterprise* and smoothed down his hair, which had become mussed from lying down. Dory said she'd make a fresh pot of coffee and told Hosea to have a seat.

"Hose, do you remember our Knutie?" Dory asked him, putting her arm around Knute's shoulder and grinning. Hosea's thumb and index finger went for the front of his shirt, but then, through some act of will on his part, he adjusted his golf hat instead and replied, "Why sure, Dory, I remember Knutie." Everybody smiled and nodded and finally Hosea broke the awkward silence. "So, are you here for a visit, Knutie, or . . ."

Knute was just about to answer when Dory said, "No, she and Summer Feelin' have moved back, for the time being."

"Oh, well," said Hosea, "that's great! Welcome back to Algren."

"Tha—" Knute was cut off by Hosea, who had suddenly sprung to life. "You still barrel-racin', Knute?"

Barrel-racing! thought Knute. The one time she had barrel-raced, badly, was in a 4-H rodeo and Hosea Funk had happened to be her timer. That was years ago, before he became the mayor. Back then he got involved in every event in town. If there was a parade, Hosea walked along throwing out candy to the kids. If there was a flood, Hosea organized a sandbag crew. If the hockey team made it to the playoffs in the city, Hosea offered to drive. Once, at a fall supper in a church basement, he was given a trophy by the main street businesses and it said, Hosea Funk, Algren's Number One Booster.

"Nah, I've given it up," said Knute. And she kind of buckled her knees to look bowlegged and horsey. Hosea Funk nodded and Knute could tell he was thinking of something else to say. She waited. A few seconds more. There. This time he couldn't help it. His fingers went to his shirt and tugged, not twice but three times. He was ready to speak.

"But that palomino could turn on a dime, couldn't he? He was something else. Now whose was he? Art Lemke, that's right, he was Art's. Wasn't he, Tom? You know the one I'm talking about? The palomino?"

"Yup, yup, I think you're right, Hose. Wait a minute, no, yeah, he would have had to have been Art's. Well . . . hang on, I'm trying to remember. Nope, he would have been Lenny's. Remember, Hose? Art sold the palomino to Lenny after his accident and Lenny couldn't keep the palomino from jumping the fence and hightailing it back to Art's barn. If I remember correctly . . . it's hard to say. I don't recall how it all turned out exactly, but I do know that horse loved Art all right. Never really took to Lenny . . ."

Hosea leaned back in his chair with his legs stretched out in front of him, his palms pushed against each other as if in prayer, his fingertips against puckered lips. He and Tom pondered the palomino while Dory and Knute slipped away into the kitchen to make the coffee.

Hosea and Tom were friends, in a way. Not like in the old days, when they were boys, but in the kind of way that you are in a small town with another man your age who has never done anything, really, to make you hate him or love him. They might as well be friendly, although Hosea visited Tom's house more often than Tom visited his. And, since his heart attack, Tom didn't go anywhere except to his doctor's appointments and those visits exhausted him.

Tom had been a veterinarian and knew about animals and that might have been one of the reasons Hosea brought up the subject of the palomino. Hosea might have felt inferior to Tom, being a professional, having a wife and a daughter and even a granddaughter, but Tom didn't think enough about Hosea to feel much of anything towards him other than a simple affection and a certain type of sympathy and from time to time, especially these days, a pang of nostalgia when he remembered himself and Hosea as boys. During all those years while Tom was busy working as a vet and living with Dory and Knute, and while Hosea was living with his mother and looking after just about everything in Algren, their paths had kind of veered away from each other.

Of course, now, with Tom's heart attack, the balance might have shifted. Tom was feeling fragile, while Hosea was still running around town taking care of business. Knute thought Tom was kind of uncomfortable with Hosea showing up like that, unannounced. He probably would have liked to have changed out of his polo pajamas at least and maybe shaved. But Hosea always just showed up. Making his rounds, enjoying a cup of coffee, passing the time. He liked to know what was going on in his town. People were used to Hosea dropping by for a visit.

"So, Hose, what are you up to these days?" asked Tom. Knute could hear him from the kitchen.

"Well, to tell you the truth, I've got a lot on the go right now. I've, uh . . . well, you could say I'm working on a major project, Tom."

"Good for you, good for you," said Tom, and Knute imagined him grimacing, wishing he had a major project besides staying alive, and Hosea tugging, wishing he had something more to say and quickly, too, like a great conversationalist, a real charismatic public figure.

Tom had begun to say something else, though. "Are you ready to divulge the nature of your major project, Hose, or—" But just then, Summer Feelin' came barrelling in through the front door, made a beeline for Tom's lap, leapt, and landed square on her target, knocking off Tom's glasses. Tom let out a big "oooph" and Dory came running from the kitchen thinking it was another heart attack, and Hosea stood there all nervous, tugging, tugging, tugging, until everyone realized what had happened and they began to laugh and S.F. tried on Tom's glasses and coffee was served and the conversation turned to gossip and did you know that so-and-so was let go at the bank, after thirty years? No one's saying why, and did you know that Sheila Whatsername has left her husband and is seeing a therapist in the city, but she looks great, she really does. And Hosea's major project was forgotten.

At the end of the visit, they all stood clustered around the door for what seemed like hours. This was what Tom and Dory always did with their guests. Knute wondered why Dory didn't serve another couple rounds of coffee or why they didn't just sit down there on the floor in the front entrance area. Coats would be done up, then undone slightly, undone completely, sweat would form on the upper lip, the coats would be taken off and slung over their arms, then a hand on the doorknob, the coats would be on again, all the way, then undone an inch, mittens would be slapped together purposefully, then removed, bodies would stand erect, close to the door, then one leg would buckle and they would slouch against the wall. Well, the visitor would say like he or she meant it this time, "I'm outta here," and then, "Oh! Did I tell you . . . ?"

Summer Feelin' fell asleep in the hallway on the floor between Dory's legs.

"Excuse me," said Knute, "I'm gonna take her to her bed."

And with that, the three of them, Tom, Dory, and Hosea, began to flutter, and Hosea said, "Okay, yes, the poor kid, here I am keeping her up, keeping you all up, really, I should go." This time Tom and Dory didn't say, "Oh, Hosea, there's no hurry." Tom reached for the door and opened it, not caring at this point whether he got a chill and risked his life.

But just before Tom could close the door gently on him, Hosea turned around and said, "Say, Knutie, if you need any part-time work while you're in town, let me know, I may be able to set you up with something." And then he was gone. Tom and Dory went running for Tom's evening medication, and Knute watched through the large picture window in the living room as Hosea walked away, into the night, through the few empty streets of his town, Canada's smallest.

The baby. Naturally Euphemia had a plan. She had had nine months to figure out elaborate plots, twists and turns, casts of characters, acts of God, all to explain the sudden arrival of this baby. In the end, however, she didn't use any of her fancy stories to explain the baby. Her family had always shrugged off any changes in their lives. If there was no explanation offered they couldn't be bothered to hunt it down or make one up. Of course, the mysterious arrival of a baby in the household was not a small deal. But Euphemia decided to take a chance. A chance on simplicity. Instead of coming up with a thousand details, which could be forgotten or repeated in the wrong order and arouse suspicion, she decided to give her family only one.

The beauty of it, too, was that it wasn't even really a lie.

"I went out late in the evening to use the outhouse and a mysterious man on a horse gave me his baby. All he said was 'Thank-you.' Then he was gone."

Well, that was more or less the situation that had occurred nine months earlier at the harvest dance at the Algren Community Dance Hall.

Euphemia hadn't planned to abandon herself to lust that evening. And it wasn't really lust she had abandoned herself to, anyway, but curiosity and maybe a bit of hope that the mysterious stranger might be her ticket off the farm. It was with the same shrug that her family used in almost all situations calling for decision that she allowed herself to be taken by the hand to the edge of the canola field behind the dance hall.

Euphemia was the last, well, maybe not the very last, girl in the area anyone would have called immoral. She did her chores, obeyed her parents, had lots of friends, and was pretty, a good runner, and playful. She won spelling bees and quilting bees, and had never even had a boyfriend in her life. In the forties girls like Euphemia Funk did not allow themselves to be led by the hand to dark fields behind dance halls.

She had stepped outside to use the outhouse. The little building was a ways from the dance hall, down a dirt path, towards the canola field. The stranger had been leaning against a tree, smoking a cigarette, and before she could even get to the outhouse, he had wandered over to her and put out his hand. She knew he had been at the dance. She and her friends had seen him and wondered who he was. Probably a relative of someone around there or a farm hand. He had nice eyes and a beautifully shaped back, they thought. "It tapers, it really does," said Euphemia's friend Lou. And he obviously bought his shoes in the city. No, he couldn't have been a farm hand. Not with shoes like that. Euphemia had seen him talking to Leander Hamm, so maybe he was a horse breeder or a horse buyer or maybe he owned racehorses in America. But he looked so young, just a few years older than she was. Euphemia liked the way his thighs filled out the tops of his pants and the way his legs were shaped, vaguely, like parentheses. There was a bit of a curl to his hair at the bottom and it was longer than the hair of any of the boys from around there. Euphemia liked those curls, at the bottom, the ones that rested against his neck.

She just hadn't said no. Nobody had come along to discover them. The night was very dark and warm. The stranger was handsome and sure of himself. Euphemia couldn't think of any reason not to take his hand. She had tried to come up with a reason, but couldn't. Afterwards, he retied the bow in Euphemia's hair and wiped the grass and leaves off of her skirt.

It had hurt, but she hadn't cried. She hadn't made a sound. And neither had he. She had kept one hand cupped firmly around the curls on his neck and her other hand beside her, on the ground. Afterwards they sat together, and Euphemia said, "well," and turned and smiled at him. And the stranger smiled back and squeezed her hand and said, "Thank-you." Then he walked over to where his horse was tied up, just on the other side of the dance hall, and rode away.

Euphemia hadn't told a soul about what happened. She hadn't felt a second of guilt. She was thrilled with herself.

"He said 'Thank-you,' and that's all, that was it?" asked Euphemia's mother, as she and Euphemia and Euphemia's brothers and sisters peered down at the baby, now resting in the Funks' old cradle.

"Yes, and then he rode away on his horse." Euphemia couldn't stop herself from smiling, but as she did so she widened her eyes for effect.

"Hmmmm, very odd. What a peculiar man. The boy is barely a day old, Phemie, are you sure he didn't say who he was or why he was giving you this child?"

"Yes, Mother."

Euphemia had successfully been delivered of the baby's placenta and had taken it and the clothes that had blood on them and buried them behind the machine shed. With trembling fingers she had tied a knot in the baby's umbilical cord and wrapped him in one of the sweaters she had been wearing just before he was born. The baby hadn't cried, not really. He had made a few creaking sounds, but nothing that could be called a real wail. By the light of the barn lantern, Euphemia saw the baby open one eye. The other wouldn't open for a few hours. The fingers on his hands moved almost constantly and his head, too, swivelled from left to right, back and forth, towards the lantern's light and away again.

Euphemia put her face to his. She breathed on him and felt his tiny puff of breath in return. She put her index finger against his lips and he tried for a moment to get it into his mouth. She moved her lips and her cheek against his damp head and prayed to God to keep him from all harm. Still, she was not afraid. She would protect him. At the time Euphemia hadn't noticed the baby's black hair curl on his neck and hadn't thought for a second about the stranger, the baby's father, at the dance hall. For the second time in a year she was thrilled with herself.

Euphemia knew that she could not breastfeed the baby. She would have to find a way to wrap her breasts and get rid of her milk. The postpartum bleeding could be explained as normal menstrual blood, if it was explained at all. Bleeding, women's bleeding, was another thing the Funk family shrugged off as one of those things, which it was.

For now she would wrap her breasts in strips of gunny sack and cotton and pray to God they wouldn't start to leak as she sat at the supper table with her family. She would, inconspicuously, drink a lot of black currant tea and if the pressure grew too great, she would squeeze the milk out herself in the john. Maybe she could even save some of it and mix it in with the formula when nobody was looking. Over time she would squeeze out less and less milk as though she were weaning a baby. Euphemia hoped her breasts could be fooled. When Flora Marsden's baby was born dead, she had drunk huge amounts of black currant tea to stem the flow of her milk. Euphemia remembered her mother talking about it to a friend of hers. Her mother and her mother's friend had been outraged that a neighbour of Flora's had suggested she hire herself out as a wet nurse to mothers too busy farming to feed their babies. "I know I was never too busy to feed my own baby, that's for sure," Euphemia's mother had said in a rather convoluted, self-serving indictment of Flora's neighbour.

"Well, he'll need a name, won't he, Phemie?" asked Minty. The sun was coming up now. Euphemia's mother went to the china cabinet and came back to the cradle with the black Bible. She yanked a bobby pin from her hair and stuck it into the shiny pages of the big book. It opened at Hosea. "There," she shrugged, "Welcome to the world, Hosea." And she stuck the bobby pin back into her hair.

Hosea Funk lay in his bed in his house on First Street, watching the sun come up over Algren. Thank God that health food store hadn't worked out, he thought. If the couple running it hadn't packed up their rice cakes and moved back to Vancouver Island last week, the recent arrival of Knute and her daughter would have put Algren's population at fifteen hundred and two, and that would have been two too many. Hosea closed his eyes and thought about his letter, the one from the Prime Minister. Well, okay, it wasn't a personal letter, it was a form letter, but Hosea's name was on it, and so was a photocopied signature of the Prime Minister's name, John Baert.

The Prime Minister had promised to visit Canada's smallest town on July first, and Algren, the letter had noted, was one of the preliminary qualifiers in the contest. Everybody in Algren knew it had been short-listed, why wouldn't it be? After all, check out the sign on the edge of town. Even the Winnipeg daily paper had mentioned, in one line, on a back page, that Algren had been picked as a nominee for the Prime Minister's visit. But the people in Algren went about their business with very little thought of July first, other than looking forward to the holiday from work, and the rides and the fireworks. If Algren had the smallest population at the time of the count, great. If not, who really cared? After all, they thought, the Prime Minister had made promises before. Of course, they knew Hosea Funk was extremely proud of Algren's smallest-town status, he was proud of everything about Algren. Good for him, they thought, usually with a smile or a raised eyebrow. Might as well be. But nobody in Algren knew what Hosea knew, or what he thought he knew, or just how determined he was to be the winner.

Hosea wanted to relax, to savour the early morning calm, to stretch out in bed, enjoy his nakedness, and happily welcome the new day. A small part of him wished his mornings resembled those in the orange juice commercials where healthy clean families bustle around making lunches and checking busy schedules, kissing and hugging and wishing each other well. But he was alone. And he hated orange juice. It stung his throat.

So Hosea lay quietly in his huge bed. For the last year or so he had been working on his panic attacks. Mornings were the worst time for them. And for heart attacks. His buddy Tom had had his in the morning just about an hour after waking up. Hosea suspected, however, that his determination to stay calm was a bit like overeating to stay thin and so he tried not to think about it too much. Instead he tried to relax his entire body starting from his toes and working his way to the top of his head. The alarm on his clock radio came on, as usual, ten minutes after he woke. It was set to a country station, and Emmylou Harris was wailing away, Heaven only knows just why lovin' you would make me cry, and Hosea thought, Ah Emmylou Harris, a voice as pure as the driven snow, a real class act, all that hair and those cowboy boots with the hand-painted roses . . .

Hosea lay naked in his bed and whispered Emmylou, Emmylou a few times and closed his eyes and mumbled along with her, Heaven only ever sees why love's made a fool of me, I guess that's how it's meant to be . . . He thought of Lorna and the last time they'd made love and then tallied up the days, and the weeks. Almost two months.

He tried to leap out of bed, just as his own personal joke, but ended up getting tangled in the sheet, knocking the radio off the bedside table, and yanking the cord out of the outlet, so that Emmylou Harris was cut off and fifty-two-year-old Hosea Funk, mayor of Algren, was left alone again and aching.

But not for long because by now the sun was up and he had work to do. Fifteen minutes on his exercise bike, a piece of whole wheat toast with honey, black coffee, half a grapefruit, a freshly ironed shirt, and a shave, and Hosea was out the door of his modest bungalow and driving down First Street in his Chevy Impala, humming the Emmylou tune on his way to the Charlie Orson Memorial Hospital.

The town of Algren had four long streets running north-south, one of them being Main Street, and ten short avenues running perpendicular to the streets. It was possible to walk anywhere in town in less than fifteen minutes, but Hosea almost always drove.

Driving down First Street towards Hospital Avenue, Hosea continued to think about Lorna. She had been his girlfriend for about three and a half years. About the same length of time it had been since Euphemia Funk had died. They had met at an auctioneers' convention in Denver. Auctioneering had been another thing Hosea was involved in, following Euphemia's death, but had since abandoned. For a guy who had trouble finding the right words to say hello, auctioneering wasn't the best hobby. Lorna had been wearing a name tag that had said, "Hi, my name's . . ." then nothing—she hadn't filled it in and Hosea was smitten by her for this reason. He looked at everybody else's properly filled-out name tags and thought how ridiculous they all were. And his, too, Hosea Funk, how absurd. Who was this mysterious Mona Lisa with the blank name tag, anyway?

Throughout the convention, Hosea stumbled about hoping to catch a glimpse of her, tugging fiendishly at his shirts and not giving a hoot about cattle calls or estate auctioneering protocol. He had been forty-nine at the time, but he felt like a sixteen-year-old-kid, creating impossible scenarios in his mind whereby he could prove himself worthy of this mysterious woman with the blank name tag.

On the plane home from the convention he had all but given up, when, to his amazement, he saw her stroll down the aisle towards him. She had stuck out her perfect hand and introduced herself. Lorna Garden. It turned out she lived in Winnipeg, was divorced with no children, worked as a medical secretary, and dabbled in auctioneering. The name-tag thing had been an oversight on her part. But Hosea was in love and Lorna thought he wasn't too bad and the rest is history.

"And my relationship with her may be history, too," thought Hosea, "if I don't get my act together."

Hosea couldn't make up his mind, it seemed. Did he want her to move out to Algren and live with him or not? He knew Lorna wanted to, but now, with Hosea's hemming and hawing, Lorna was starting to play it cool. "Whatever," she'd said the last time they'd talked about it. Hosea hated that word. Whatever. All through his childhood on the Funk farm and then in town living with his mother he had heard it being used, oh, almost daily. Whatever, Euphemia would say if Hosea asked if he could have ten cents. Whatever, she'd say if he told her the U.S. had invaded Korea.

It wasn't a question of damaging his public reputation, having Lorna live with him. The townspeople of Algren would have been happy for Hosea to have a woman living with him. And it wasn't a question of room or money. Hosea had enough of both. And it certainly wasn't a question of wavering commitment. He loved Lorna with all his heart. It was just . . . well, would she have been one person too many for Algren? For Algren's status as Canada's smallest town.

And soon Lorna might just give up on him, thought Hosea as he pulled into the parking lot of the hospital. But what could he do?

Hosea focused on the task at hand. He had a question to ask Veronica Epp—just one and he'd leave her alone. Veronica Epp was expecting her fifth child. This fact alone irked Hosea. But now there was some talk around town that she was expecting twins. If she had two babies instead of one, which he had figured on, Hosea would have to do some fancy footwork.

"Good morning, Jean Bonsoir," said Hosea, with one slight tug at his front, to the hospital's only doctor, an import from Quebec. His name was Jean François, but Hosea like to think his alternative pronunciation was funny and helped to break the ice.

"Hosea," the doctor returned with a nod. He was counting the days until he could leave Algren for Montreal, where he could do something other than minor surgery and routine obstetrics and where people would pronounce his name correctly. It still peeved him to think of Hosea Funk calling his girlfriend, Genvieve, who remained in Montreal, Jenny Quelque Chose.

"Uh, listen, Doctor, I need to talk to Mrs. Epp for a minute, tops. Then I'll be out of your hair. Fair enough?"

Jean François had understood the Mrs. Epp part and shrugged Hosea down the hall. "Room four, Hosea, but be quick because she needs to rest."

"Will do," said Hosea, already moving towards Veronica's room.

He had begun to walk into her room as if he was entering his own kitchen but stopped abruptly. Veronica Epp was lying with her back towards him and, unfortunately for Hosea, her blue hospital gown had come untied, exposing her buttocks and lower back. Before turning away, Hosea thought to himself how a woman could look, well, like normal, from the back, even while she was ballooning out in the front, and he wondered if he himself looked thinner from behind. It was something to consider. But now, he grabbed at his shirt and took three steps backwards, returning to the hallway and standing on the other side of the doorway.

This was the type of situation that completely unnerved Hosea. Was Veronica sleeping? Should he wake her up? How? Just then he heard a godawful moan coming from across the hall. A tiny tuft of white hair and an atrophied face poked out from beneath a blue sheet. The body attached to it looked like that of an eight-year-old girl. Hosea looked closer. Oh my God, he thought, it's Leander Hamm, Lawrence's dad. Nobody had told him old Mr. Hamm was in the hospital, and, from the sounds of it, he wasn't long for this world. Well, thought Hosea, it could be a good thing. Not that he invited death upon his townspeople regularly, but, after all, Leander Hamm would have had to have been almost ninety-five, and that's a good long life. If he were to buy the farm sometime soon, then Veronica Epp's alleged twins might not be as big a problem. Though it didn't bode well for having Lorna move in with him.

Which reminded him. He cleared his throat and stretched out his arm to knock on Veronica's door, keeping the rest of his body safely behind the wall. He had to find out from Veronica what the story was and he didn't want the doctor coming around and wondering what his problem was.

"Come in?" Veronica called out to the empty doorway. Hosea had quickly pulled back his arm after the knock and was still standing behind the wall next to her door.

"Uh, Mrs. Epp, it's, uh . . . Hosea Funk."

Dead silence then except for the swishing of stiff sheets.

"Oh, Mr. Funk? Well, come in."

Hosea had thought that Veronica Epp would have recognized the name right off the bat. He was the mayor, after all, but then again, she had just woken up and was in a somewhat groggy condition. He wouldn't let it bother him. And besides, as he stood there, far from her actual bed, a look of recognition came over her face and she smiled warmly.

She rolled over, on her back now, and Hosea was truly alarmed at how enormous her belly was. Darnit, he thought. That's gotta be twins.

"How are you feeling, Mrs. Epp?" Hosea planted his gaze on her face to avoid having to look at her stomach.

"Fine, thanks. The doctor just thought it would be a good idea to come in a bit before I go into labour, because I'm a high risk."

"I see," said Hosea. "Well, that's good."

Veronica Epp looked slightly puzzled.

"I mean it's good that you're here, being observed like this. It's a very good thing." Hosea coughed twice but resisted the urge to tug.

"Yes, Dr. Jean is very attentive, very good. And, love 'em dearly though I do, it's rather a nice break from my other kids, you know."

No, Hosea did not know. And what was this business with calling Dr. François Dr. Jean? That was rather personal, wasn't it? He knew he would have balked to be called Mayor Hosea instead of Mayor Funk, but then again that wasn't usually a problem in Algren as most people just called him Hosea or Hose. The few times someone like Tom had called him Mayor Funk he had detected just the slightest hint of sarcasm. But, of course, that might have been because Tom was his friend and why would friends be formal? But still.

"Hmmm . . ." Hosea nodded, trying to smile. He stepped towards Veronica and put his hand briefly on top of the mysterious machine making beeping noises and showing various squiggly lines on its screen.

"Handy contraption, this, eh?" Hosea stared at the lines in deep concentration as if he knew what they meant. What he was trying to do was figure out how he could best ask the question without appearing to be prying, that is, inappropriately curious about what was so obviously none of his business.

Veronica strained to turn her enormous body towards the machine to get a better look. The sight of her shifting startled Hosea and he stared, wide-eyed, hoping her gown would not slip off and expose her privates.

Hosea was beginning to feel very warm. Veronica looked uncomfortable. She grimaced slightly, then scratched her stomach. As she did so her gown shifted over a bit, and what was revealed to Hosea was just about the most gruesome thing he had ever seen. He thought he would be sick. What was it, he wondered, a scar? A birth defect? A smallish, round, bluish disk of smooth skin with what looked like lips in the centre of it stretched across the middle of her stomach. It wasn't a tiny head pushing through, was it? Hosea knew it couldn't be. He knew, of course, that babies did not just poke through the abdominal skin of their mothers for a look around or a bit of air. However, it looked like it would burst any second and Hosea did not want to be around when it did.

"Ha, would you look at that?" Veronica laughed. "Wouldn't know it was a belly button, would you?"

A belly button! thought Hosea. Of course! And suddenly Hosea felt very lonely. Something so simple, so tender and common as a belly button and he had not been able to identify it. He had been scared of Veronica Epp's belly button. He was fifty-two years old. He should know about these simple things by now. Old Leander Hamm, all shrivelled up and dying, he had a belly button, too. And Lorna Garden and Tom and Dory and Jean François. For some reason the thought made him sad, momentarily. He had to get on with the job here. He would have to get directly to the question, just simply ask it of Veronica and hope she wouldn't think it was strange.

"So you're high risk, are you? Why exactly is that?" There it was. He had popped the question. Hosea braced himself, waiting for the worst.

"Well, they think it's triplets." Veronica Epp now beamed up at Hosea. For her it was like winning the lottery. Hosea's gaze moved down to her mountain of a stomach and then out the window towards the tiny trickle that was Algren's Main Street. Lawrence Hamm's dad moaned from across the hall. Hosea felt like he had just been kicked in the groin.

"You mean three?" he whispered.

three

"Knutie!" Dory had said after a week of Knute's hanging around the house trying to help. "Didn't Hosea mention some kind of part-time job or something or other?"

"Ick," said Knute. She wasn't so resistant to the idea of working for Hosea Funk as to the idea of working, period. She was still licking her wounds from the awful experiences of her last two part-time jobs. And, of course, she was working. She was taking care of Summer Feelin', getting her acquainted with the few kids in the neighbourhood, organizing tea parties, trips to the park down the street, keeping her amused in her relatively new environment. Also, she was helping out around the house. She helped Tom with things like changing the oil in the car. He knew it needed to be changed but had forgotten why. She tried to explain as best she could. She helped him set a trap for a skunk that had been lurking around the back door. She hacked away all the ice on the sidewalk so he wouldn't slip when he went outside. She took him grocery shopping in the hope that they could find something healthy and delicious for him to eat. She experimented with new chicken and fish recipes and tried to spruce meals up for him with wine and candlelight and a red-and-white checkered tablecloth. And she was teaching him how to juggle.

He loved to juggle. So far he had two balls mastered. Summer Feelin' would scurry around picking up dropped balls and throw them back at Tom and he'd try again. "Remember, Dad," Knute would say, "one and then the other. The right goes over to the left, and the left to the right, okay? One, two, three, catch them. Good. Try again."

The time that she spent hanging out with Tom and Summer Feelin' was the time that Dory could escape. Tom was distracted and didn't mind as much if she left when he was busy. Usually she'd go out for coffee with her friends or to her office where she did some part-time bookkeeping for the farm labour pool. Or she'd shop at the Do-It Centre in Whithers for wallpaper and carpets and flooring and cupboard fixtures and curtains. She was re-doing the entire house, one room at a time. It had been twenty-five years since anything had been changed and now suddenly she was attacking every square inch of her house. She was getting rid of everything that was beige, brown, avocado, or moss green (which was everything) and replacing it with light sunny colours or pastels or white.

She had vowed she would not stop until the entire house was done. When she was tearing wallpaper off walls she'd wear an old pair of Tom's sweatpants, cut off at the bottom or rolled up, and a T-shirt that said SoHo, New York, on it. Tom would take a floor heater and down-filled sleeping bag and the paper or sometimes one of his veterinarian manuals and go and read in the garage while she worked. He hated the noise and mess but he loved Dory, and if Dory wanted to change the house around he wasn't about to stop her. He'd sit in the garage and wait until he heard the washing machine go on, which meant Dory was washing the sweatpants and SoHo shirt and all the rags and things she used and her work for the day was over.

Often, after Dory had removed the easier sheets of wallpaper and moved on to the next room, Knute would stay behind and finish off the tougher bits, steaming and soaking and, finally, scraping them off. Dory would yell to her from the next room, "Hey, Knutie, do you remember Mr. Pagliotti?" And Knute would say, "Uh, yeah . . ." just knowing something awful had happened to him because Dory seemed to be in a morbid mood these days and was constantly telling Knute about somebody or other who had died or been diagnosed with terminal cancer or had a leg amputated or lost her baby.

"His grandson found him dead in his car," she'd holler from the other room, from up on her ladder or stretched out on the floor with a hammer.

"Hmmm . . ." Knute would say bracing herself.

"Yeah, he and his grandson were taking a look at the field and apparently he had told his grandson that he was a bit tired and he was going to go and have a little nap in the car."

"Oh oh," Knute would say. She knew what was coming.

"The grandson came back to the car, found Mr. Pagliotti, well, you know, his grandpa, and then ran back to the house telling everyone Grandpa won't get up. He's sleeping and he won't get up."

"Yikes," was about all that Knute could muster. And she could imagine Dory in the other room sucking in her breath or shaking her head. Knute thought, maybe, that Dory was trying to prepare herself for Tom's death, for a sudden departure on his part. Or maybe she was trying to make herself feel better. After all, Tom was still alive. Or maybe she could only relate this type of gloomy information when Tom was safely tucked away in the garage. All Knute knew was that the telling of these morbid anecdotes was somehow related to the home renovations. And as soon as she'd positioned herself on the stepladder, holding a steaming kettle in one hand and a scraper in the other, she could expect Dory's "Hey, Knutie, do you remember so-and-so, something terrible's happened" stories to come floating over from the other rooms.

So, Knute was working. But then again she wasn't making any money. Not that she had a lot of expenses. No rent, no food, no utilities. Tom and Dory would never have thought to charge their own daughter room and board. But at her age, she figured, a little contribution to the general management of affairs might be in order.

She wondered just what Hosea Funk would pay her to do. It couldn't be that complicated being the mayor of a town with fifteen hundred people. Besides, nothing ever really changed in Algren. About the only thing she remembered Dory telling her was that Johnny Dranger's farm kept being rezoned. One week it would be in the town limits of Algren, the next it was, well, sort of in limbo. Somewhere in the municipality of Libreville, but not actually in any town. Which makes sense, Knute thought. What's a farm doing in a town? Last time she checked farms were in the country, not next to a 7 Eleven or a credit union. But she didn't think it was Hosea doing the rezoning anyway because mayors didn't have that privilege. It was a provincial government thing. She thought.

So after Johnny Dranger's being in and then out and then in again, the only other change in Algren was the new indoor arena and curling rink. Hosea had battled long and hard to get that built. None of the older people in Algren thought it was a good idea. They had always played hockey outdoors—why shouldn't their grandchildren? They would have liked to have seen the money spent on another doctor, an English one preferably, though nobody would have said it, or maybe new blacktop on some of the roads. In Algren the oldies lived for new blacktop. But, in the end, Hosea had managed to convince them. He promised that during the summer he would air-condition the indoor arena and curling rink and hold auctions and quilting bees and bake sales and have inspirational speakers and car shows and you name it, he'd get it. So that, in the summer, the seniors of Algren would have a sort of retirement club of their own.

Hosea had also managed to convince the townspeople to name it The Euphemia Funk Memorial Arena, Curling Club, and Recreational Complex. Of course, nobody called it that, they called it the rink, but it had raised a few eyebrows at the time. Mrs. Funk, as the kids of Algren knew her even though she wasn't married, had this aura of mystery about her. They all found out, at a certain age, that she wasn't really Hosea's mom, and different stories about how she got Hosea were always circulating. According to Tom and Dory, the truth was somebody, a man on a horse, had just come along and given him to her, barely a day old. Nobody knew who the man was or where Hosea came from, but Euphemia, from that day on, was Hosea's unofficial mother. So anyway, it wasn't like Mrs. Funk, Euphemia, had done anything wrong, it was just considered, by many people in Algren, a bit weird and maybe not entirely healthy for a single unmarried woman to suddenly become a boy's mother. And many people would have preferred Hosea and the arena committee to come up with a different name for the complex, a name that wouldn't have them shifting in their chairs, staring at the ceiling, or changing the subject every time one of their kids asked them who Euphemia Funk was.

But that's what it was called and that was the big news in Algren.

"There it is," thought Hosea. The scribbler was always there, in fact, in the top drawer of his desk, but Hosea would always repeat these words to himself, not so much as an obvious affirmation of what was there but as a sort of mantra, preparing him for his work, a simple prelude to the more complicated nature of his obsession. The scribbler was an orange Hilroy, the kind still available on dusty drugstore shelves in places like Algren. On the front of it, at the bottom, were spaces to fill in personal information. Hosea had filled in each space. Name: Mayor Funk. Subject: 1500. Classroom No.: Mayor's office, town of Algren, Canada's Smallest!

Hosea preferred to take out his scribbler when no one was around. Usually that wasn't a problem as there were only two very part-time employees working in the place. The old renovated house was a municipal government project. It contained the Mayor's Office, the Arts Council Office for Algren and the surrounding areas, the Recreation District Office, the Weed Control District, and the Cemetery Board. Two women, sisters, in fact, shuffled around between the various responsibilities. Hosea's Aunt Minty, Euphemia's younger sister, used to work in the office, but years ago she and her husband, Bert Seeger, had moved to Fresno, California, and Hosea didn't hear much from her anymore. She and Bert had come out for Euphemia's funeral, but most of their time had been taken up with the Seeger in-laws.

Hosea had enjoyed working with his Aunt Minty. Every time he came into work she'd have the coffee made and sometimes fresh pastry, and she'd smile and say to Hosea, "Good morning, sweetie, you're looking well." From time to time Hosea murmured those words to himself under his breath as he stomped the snow from his boots or took off his coat, hoping the sisters working behind the counter wouldn't hear him and look at each other in that way.

But now he was alone. And that was just fine because he needed to make a pertinent entry in his scribbler. Under the Dying and Potentially Dead column, he carefully printed the name Leander Hamm. Then he turned to the very back of the scribbler and, under the Newly Born and Rumoured to be Born he printed the name Veronica Epp and the notation, "expecting triplets," and then he added—"high risk." Drumming his pen against his desk for a moment, he returned the scribbler to its place in the drawer.

He glanced out his window and saw the dog. The same dog he had seen on his way to work after visiting Veronica Epp. A woman had been crouching down and holding the dog by its collar and had asked Hosea if he knew whose dog it was. Hosea had been concerned that the dog was not on a leash but running freely, unsupervised, all over Algren. He asked the woman if she would call the pound, or actually Phil Whryahha, the man in Algren who, proudly appointed by Hosea himself, was responsible for stray pets. And that's when John Funk (no relation to Hosea), the caretaker of St. Bartholomew's Church, had walked up and suggested to the woman that she simply let the dog go. That the dog would surely find its way home. There was hardly a car on Algren's streets that would run the risk of hitting it, he'd said, and the dog seemed friendly enough. Let it go, he'd said. It'll be fine.

Hosea had stood there, dumbfounded. Why hadn't he thought of that? Such a simple and obvious solution. The woman let go of the collar, the caretaker strolled back to St. Bart's, and the dog slowly walked away, towards the edge of town. Hosea stood there. He had said something. Something like "very good." Or "there you go." But he had felt unsure of himself. This dog business had jarred him.

He focussed on his plan to bring the Prime Minister to Algren. It could be a good thing for everybody in Algren, he thought. It would be an exciting day, a coup for a small prairie town, a psychological boost, and a surefire guarantee that Hosea would be re-elected, when the time came, as Algren's mayor.

Hosea whipped open the second drawer from the top of his desk and pulled out the letter from the House of Commons, dated February 12, 1996. "Dear Mayor," it began. Hosea had read and reread, folded and unfolded this letter so often that it had become slightly torn down the middle. He had carefully fixed it with a piece of Scotch tape so the tear was hardly noticeable. Hosea moved his finger across the photocopied signature, John Baert, Prime Minister. The contents of the letter were by now so familiar to him that he could sit back in his chair, close his eyes, and recite it from memory:

> *Dear Mayor,*
>
> *As part of the federal government's commitment to rural growth, I have promised to visit Canada's smallest town for 24 hours, on July 1, 1996. Algren may be one of our candidates. We will inform you of further plans at a later date, providing you are interested in participating in the aforementioned event.*
>
> *Sincerely, John Baert, Prime Minister*

Hosea sat at his desk and imagined the day the Prime Minister would come to Algren. Hosea would be there to greet him, with Lorna at his side. He'd have bought a new suit in Winnipeg, Lorna a new dress and maybe new shoes. The sun would be shining, the high school band would play some rousing march, little Tilly Bond, the cutest kid in town, would present the Prime Minister with a bouquet of flowers. The billboard announcing Algren to the world would be repainted and so would some of the storefronts along Main Street. He and the Prime Minister would shake hands warmly and the Prime Minister would pat him on the back and congratulate him, would take him into his confidence, and they would exchange jokes and leadership tips and anecdotes and discuss crisis management and possibly even correspond after the visit. At dinner, prepared by the Elks or the Kinettes and served in the

Euphemia Funk Memorial Arena, Curling Club, and Recreational Complex, Hosea and the Prime Minister would raise their glasses for the photographers and toast to hmmm, whatever, rural prosperity, perhaps. There would be stories written in the papers and pictures taken, bearing eternal witness to the event and to Hosea's and Algren's victory, to their reigning status as Canada's smallest town.

It would be a day like no other. Hosea now sat way back in his chair, his legs up on his desk, his hands clasped behind his head, his thumbs making circles on the nape of his neck. So lost in thought was he that he didn't notice his pen roll off his desk and onto the shiny hardwood floor. Even Hosea's sexual fantasies couldn't hold a candle to his fantasy of meeting the Prime Minister and having Algren shown off to the world. Yes, it would be a day like no other, that's for sure, thought Hosea and leaned back even farther so that his swivel chair almost fell over backwards and he had to lurch forward and grip the hard wooden edge of his desk to keep his balance. He must have slammed the palm of his right hand hard against the wood, because that pain triggered a flood of memories and now Hosea pictured another day that was full of pomp and circumstance and nervousness and . . . what? What was it about that day, anyway? Hosea wondered.

He had been outside playing in the small yard behind the house on First Street. He hadn't had a jacket on, or was it shoes he hadn't had on? Had it been March or July? Well, he had picked flowers later that day, so it must have been July. But hadn't he just come home from school? Yes, of course, he had walked home with Tom who had lived across the street. Well, actually they had run home because two older fellows were chasing them and one of them had taken Hosea's jacket. That was it. He wasn't wearing his jacket, because the older boy had taken it, and it must have been a day in May or June. Sometime when flowers could grow in Manitoba. Roses. He was sure they were roses because they had pricked the palm of his hand when he held them.

"Run, Hosea! Run!" Tom had already been caught as usual and managed to yell out the simple instructions to Hosea before a big hand was clamped over his mouth and he was taken away for his session. These sessions consisted of various activities. Tom and Hosea, for one year in particular, were the whipping boys for a group of older kids from school. Sometimes they were forced to crouch on their hands and knees right below Evangeline Goosen's bedroom window and the older boys would stand on their backs and watch Evangeline change from her school clothes to her play clothes.

Anyway, on this day they had managed to get his jacket but not him. Hosea didn't want to go inside his house, he remembered, because Euphemia might get mad at him for losing his jacket. He would never have told her what had really happened. Even now, at age fifty-two, Hosea shuddered to think of his mother marching over to the home of one of the big boys and telling his parents what he had done and demanding that her son's jacket be returned immediately. But Euphemia wouldn't have been angry, really, thought Hosea. She would have shrugged and said something like, "Well, easy come, easy go." And then she would have gone to the hall closet and pulled out one of her old curling sweaters and rolled up the sleeves and made Hosea try it on for size. "There you go, pumpkin, a new jacket."

She wouldn't have gotten into a flap over a jacket. She wouldn't have run over to the school to look for it, or asked Hosea to think back or retrace his steps. She wouldn't have asked why this was the third jacket he had lost in as many months or why his jackets always had grass stains and leaves and twigs and dirt on the back of them as though he'd been rolling around on the ground like a crazed horse with a bad case of ringworm. Why, thought Hosea, did he possess none of her insouciance? Why, Hosea thought further, did her laissez-faire attitude towards just about everything irritate him so?

Finally Hosea went inside the house. He remembered hoping his mother would act normally and be upset about the jacket, and yet knowing she wouldn't be upset comforted him. What Hosea got from his mother was what he wanted but what he didn't get was what he felt he needed. Euphemia would have disagreed with this, he knew. "Why shouldn't I do my best to make you happy, Hose?" And he would have said something like, "Well, it's just that maybe I need more discipline or maybe you should get mad at me more." And he'd tug at his shirt and stare at the ground and Euphemia would look at him and then pull his head to her bosom and rub her lips in his hair and laugh. "Oh, Hose. Don't make it harder than it has to be." He remembered the song she always sang exuberantly at full volume. "Man's life's a vapour, full of woes . . ."

Anyway, that day Hosea tiptoed inside hoping to make a silent detour of the kitchen and go directly to his bedroom. But Euphemia was right there, standing at the stove, her back to Hosea. He changed his mind and decided to surprise her instead. He crept up behind her and said "hello," clear as a bell, and Euphemia, startled by the sudden greeting, twirled around and knocked him against the stove. Hosea put his hand out, against the red-hot element, to break his fall and wound up with a large oval-shaped burn on his right palm. Euphemia had apologized profusely and rushed around getting butter and ice and ointment for Hosea's burn. Afterwards Euphemia and Hosea had sat at the table, the little white wooden table in the kitchen, and Euphemia had said, "Hosea, I want you to go outside and pick some roses. We're going to visit somebody very special later this evening." Hadn't that been it? thought Hosea.

Yes, that's what she had said. Because Hosea remembered the thorns from the roses pricking the burn on his palm, even after Euphemia had tied around it a beige piece of cotton from one of her aprons. Hosea even remembered thinking that he deserved the pain, that it was a token of his allegiance to Tom who had been caught by the big boys when Hosea hadn't and who was probably experiencing some pain right then, too.

This was the memory that had been triggered when he had banged his right palm against his desk, trying to keep himself from falling over backwards in his chair. Hosea looked at his right palm. There was a very faint trace of scar tissue. Unless it was bumped in a certain way, and it never had been until now, he felt no pain there. He brought his palm up towards his face. He stared at it. He moved his lips over it. Nothing. He couldn't remember anything else of that day. The roses had pricked his palm, so therefore he had picked them. And he would only have picked them if his mother had asked him to. And she would only have asked him to pick roses if they had been going to see someone very special. Like, for example, the future Prime Minister. "Your father," Hosea recalled the words Euphemia had spoken on her deathbed, "is the Prime Minister of Canada."

But why couldn't he remember what happened that day he picked the roses? Hosea sat at his desk now and slammed his fist against his thigh.

Who was the special person? Had Euphemia told him or hadn't she? Had he asked? Had he wanted to know then? Had the special person been the man who was now Prime Minister of Canada? Why had Euphemia, on her deathbed, told Hosea that his father was John Baert, the Prime Minister of Canada? Surely she had been hallucinating. She must have been crackers, substituting reality with good intentions. She had always wanted the best for Hosea, after all, and knowing Hosea's penchant for public office, his respect for politicians, and especially successful leaders, people who didn't shrug their lives away but made decisions and tried to change the world, she had made up this one final ridiculous story. This was her parting gift to Hosea, the words, "Your father, your father, is John Baert." And then, "Come back . . ." The words not spoken to Hosea or to Dory or to a doctor or to the Lord, but to John Baert, the stranger on the horse, the young man from long ago with the dark curls on his neck, her only lover, the father of her beloved Hosea.

But had she made it up? Hosea wondered. Or was it true? In any case, if he had met his father on that day, perhaps his father would see, in Hosea, a resemblance to himself? Hosea had, since the day Euphemia told him his father was the Prime Minister, stared long and hard at any photograph, any news footage of the Prime Minister trying to see some similarities. They both had blue eyes and dark hair, but then so did millions of people. Hosea remembered the rhyme the American people had chanted when Grover Cleveland was the president and news broke out he had fathered an illegitimate child somewhere along the line: "Ma, Ma, where's my pa? He's gone to the White House, ha ha ha." But what if what Euphemia had said was a lie? Or simply morphine-induced rambling? Hosea didn't want to think about that. He had the letter, the form letter with the photocopied copy of the Prime Minister's signature promising to visit Canada's smallest town. Hosea had always been interested in maintaining Algren's status as smallest town. It had kept the town on the map and given the folks in Algren a dose of civic pride, of recognition beyond being the birthplace of the Algren cockroach.

But now, since the arrival of the letter three months ago, Hosea's job became clear. It was more than a job, though: it was his mission in life and his only dream. He must bring the Prime

Minister to Algren. He must. "John Baert." Hosea murmured the name quietly, his eyes tightly closed, his mind trying to batter down the door that blocked his memory of that day he burned his hand and picked the roses.

four

"I think he's dead," Summer Feelin' whispered.

"I doubt it. His lips are moving," Knute whispered back. "Say something, Mom."

Knute cleared her throat. "Excuse me?"

Hosea, for the second time that afternoon, lurched forward in his chair and banged his scarred palm against the edge of his desk, sending a few paper clips skittering off the side.

"Caught you sleeping on the job, eh? Ha ha," Knute said. Summer Feelin' stood beside Knute, holding her hand and staring at Hosea, who was now tugging at his shirt with one hand and smoothing the already smooth surface of his desk with the other.

"Oh no, oh no, I wasn't sleeping. I was just, thinking, so how are you, Knutie? Hi there, uh . . . Autumn . . . uh, May?"

"Summer Feelin'. Say hi, S.F."

"Hi, S.F."

"Ha, ha, that's her little joke."

"Oh yes, that's, uh . . ." Hosea felt his hand go to his shirt again but this time he stopped himself from tugging by lunging towards the floor and picking up the fallen paper clips.

"Well, I just thought I'd take you up on that job offer,

remember, when you came by to visit my folks you mentioned that—"

"Yes. Yes, I remember. I do, well, I will have work for you. Quite a bit of work, actually, very soon. Well, what I'll need you to do, mainly, is, you know, answer phones, write letters, make appointments, that sort of thing. Generally, keep the place in order."

Hosea hadn't expected Knute to show up quite so soon. Actually, he hadn't expected her to show up at all. And now he was having a hard time explaining what it was he wanted from her. He could have kicked himself for not being prepared. He needed a young, attractive woman at his side, plain and simple, if he was going to impress the Prime Minister. Look at all the politicians. They all had attractive aides and writers and handlers, not to mention young, beautiful wives. Lorna would do just fine as the wife, Hosea figured. Granted, she wasn't that young, and she did stoop slightly and forget to do little things like lay down her collar or straighten her necklace so that the diamond Hosea had given her was often draped over her shoulder instead of hanging down towards her cleavage, but Hosea loved her and was confident she would pass muster with the Prime Minister. Who knows, by then she might even be living with him in Algren? And Knute would be his lovely and capable assistant, provided she wore something other than torn jeans and police boots. Hosea could picture it now. There he'd be with Lorna on one side and Knute on the other, waiting for John Baert to emerge from the limousine, to offer Hosea his hand and—

"So when do I start?" asked Knute. She could sense Hosea was nervous about this whole thing. Summer Feelin' was trying to drag her out of the room so she was trying to get it over with as fast as she could.

"Start. Well. Tomorrow. Tomorrow morning. Say about ten o'clock."

"Okay," said Knute. "Sounds good."

"Oh, Knute?"

"Yeah?"

"How's your father's health?"

"Oh, comme ci comme ça, you know . . ."

"Hmmm . . . Do you think his heart is getting stronger?"

"I think so, yeah. He's learning to juggle."

"Juggle? Really?" For a brief moment Hosea was nine again and he heard Tom's voice. "Run, Hosea, run!" It seemed like just the other day. "Juggling, well, what do you know?" said Hosea.

By then Summer Feelin' had dragged Knute out of the room and halfway down the hall. Knute managed to yell over her shoulder to Hosea who was still sitting at his desk tapping a paper clip against his teeth, "See ya tomorrow!"

The snow was melting and the sun was hot, so Knute and Summer Feelin' walked home with their jackets tied around their waists and this was enough to make S.F. flap. Normally when she flapped in public Knute tried to calm her down. She'd take her hand or rub her back or say her name or get S.F. to look at her and tell her what she was so excited about. But this time Knute thought she'd just let S.F. get it out of her system. They stood right in front of the big windows of the Wagon Wheel Café and S.F. stood on one spot, her head back, mouth open, and flapped like she was about to lift right off the ground. Knute was excited, too. The world is full of possibility at that precise moment when winter jackets are taken off for the first time in Manitoba. Things were okay. Living with Tom and Dory, working for Hosea, hanging out with S.F. She wouldn't be featured in *Vanity Fair*, but . . .

A couple of men in the café noticed S.F. and pointed at her and stared for a while and then went back to their coffee.

When she and S.F. got back to the house they saw Combine Jo lying on the ground in front of the front door. Tom was sitting in a lawn chair beside her wearing a tuque and a down-filled jacket and reading a Dick Francis novel.

"Hello, ladies, how'd the interview go?" asked Tom.

"What the hell is she doing here?" said Knute.

"Do you mean what the hell is *she* doing here?" said Tom, "or what the hell is she doing *here*?"

S.F. crawled onto Tom's lap and peered down at Combine Jo. "Is she dead?" she asked Tom, who looked at Knute and winked.

"No, she's just resting." Tom put his head back and swallowed a couple of times for the benefit of S.F. who had, recently, become intrigued with his Adam's apple and liked to follow its course with her fingertips. "Aack, not so hard, S.F. I'll choke." He bulged his eyes and Summer Feelin' giggled.

"This is ridiculous," Knute said and went inside the house. She had to step over Combine Jo's right arm, which was stretched out as a pillow for her head. She had almost made it into the house. Her bloated fingers grazed the sill of the door and, as Knute stepped over her, lifted slightly as if she were waving.

Knute stormed into the house and flung her jacket onto the floor.

"Why the hell is Combine Jo here and what the hell is she doing lying on the ground?" she yelled in the general direction of the den, where Dory had been painting for the past few days.

"Oh, Knutie?" came Dory's reply. "I'm glad you're here. Jo fainted and she's too heavy for Tom and me to move so I just sent Tom out to sit beside her and keep an eye on her 'til she woke up. You know, it's warm enough out there today for her to lie there, and anyway he'd likely have another heart attack if he tried to lift her, you know, and my back isn't—"

"She did not faint, Mother, she passed out. She's drunk. I'm not a child. I know when somebody is drunk. You know, I've been drunk myself, I realize when something like this is happening."

By now Dory had come out to the kitchen. She was covered in paint and wearing her SoHo T-shirt. Knute was sitting on the counter, swinging her legs like a kid and drinking milk directly from the carton.

"I'm not hauling her inside if that's what you think," she sputtered through a mouthful of milk. "Forget it."

"Okay, okay, Knutie, calm down, okay? Just calm down." Dory put her hands on Knute's thighs and looked at her imploringly in very much the same way Knute looked at S.F. when she flapped.

Just then Combine Jo came thrashing through the door holding S.F. in her arms with Tom behind her, invisible except for his arms moving wildly around her trying to make sure she didn't drop S.F. or smash any part of her against the walls of the front entrance. As Combine Jo and S.F. ricocheted from wall to wall one of Jo's sleeves caught on the hall mirror, which yanked it right off, sending bits of glass and plaster flying and Tom, still in his tuque, started doing a sort of jig to avoid stepping on it, saying, "Dory? Dory? Dory, you gotta help me here."

"Goddamn it!" Combine Jo slurred as one of her feet involuntarily slid out in front of her like Fred Astaire and then began to plow her way to the living room couch. "Christ, girl, hang on! We're almost there!" she told S.F., who answered meekly, "I am. I am." By this time Tom and Dory were flanking her like two tugs bringing in the *Queen Mary,* and Knute was frozen to the spot, livid.

"Ho!" Combine Jo belched out as she fell onto the couch. S.F. kind of dropped beside her and then attempted to climb off the couch, but before she could escape Combine Jo grabbed her by the shirt and said, "Not so fast, you little devil. I want to have a good look at you."

At this point Knute intervened. "Leave her alone, Jo. S.F., come here, sweetie."

"S.F., come here, sweetie," Combine Jo mimicked, moving her head back and forth. "Jesus, Knuter, I'm not gonna kill the kid. When the hell are you gonna bury the hatchet, eh, Knute? I've apologized until I'm fucking blue in the face."

"Coffee, Jo?" Dory asked.

"Thanks, honey." Combine Jo sat on the couch. She was wearing giant Hush Puppies and a tent dress with tiny anchors all over it. She stared at S.F. "God, she's an angel, Knute. She's an angel made in heaven. Aw c'mon, let me have her. Let her sit with me for a second. Doncha want to, eh, Summer Feelin'?"

"No." S.F. tightened her grip on Knute's hand. Tom was busy sweeping up the broken glass in the hallway. He asked S.F. if she would like to do a puzzle with him in the den and she nodded and flew out of the room.

"Lookit her go. Runnin' like the goddamn dickens. How old is she, anyway, Knuter? Five, six?"

"Four."

Combine Jo sighed heavily. "I heard you two were in town, Knute. I had to come and see you. See her. You know I've got no way of getting to the city to see you. How was I gonna see you and S.F.?"

"Nobody invited you."

At this Combine Jo slapped her thigh and barked, "Ha! You haven't changed at all, Knute. Not one iota. Still a spark plug, you crazy kid. You and I should have a drink together some day. But, you know I like your spunk. I've always loved your spunk. And you know what? So did Max. Of all Max's girlfriends you were my goddamn favourite and that's no lie. The rest were pffhh . . . In fact, that's another reason why I'm here."

Dory handed Combine Jo her coffee and immediately Jo spilled a few drops on her anchor dress. "Whoops. Shit." Then Jo did it again. "I'll be goddamned!" she said. Dory attempted a tortured smile. Knute stood a ways away with her arms folded across her chest. The thought of a drink wasn't a bad one. But not with her. Knute looked at her and raised her eyebrows placidly in an unfriendly gesture, egging her on.

"Max called me. Finally, the little bastard, and he's coming home. He's broke and tired of Europe. Who wouldn't be? He's coming back, Knuter. And he wants to see his goddamned daughter!"

"Are you serious?" Marilyn muttered over the phone later that evening. "That's what she said? Just like that?"

"Yeah. Can you believe it?" Knute was soaking in a tub of hot water and talking to Marilyn on Tom's new cordless phone. Tom and Dory and S.F. were all in bed together eating popcorn and watching TV. She could hear an occasional laugh track through the bathroom wall.

"I can believe that he's broke," said Marilyn.

"Some things never change," Knute answered.

"What are you gonna do?" she asked.

"I don't know. What can I do? I can't keep him from coming back. I'm not gonna leave just because he's coming back. And besides, he's not a terrible person or anything, he's just completely hopeless. I don't know."

"Well, he's an asshole, Knute. He knew you were pregnant and he took off."

"Well, I kind of told him to get lost."

"Yeah, but that doesn't mean get lost, *get lost* like for five years. It means just fuck off for a while and don't bug you."

"Yeah, but he might have figured that out himself if he

wasn't such a slave to his mother. She's the one who told him his life would be ruined forever if he became a father and stayed in Algren."

"Well, that's probably true."

"Thanks, Marilyn."

"Well, for Christ's sake. He'd have to be a total moron to believe her."

"Yeah, shhh, I know. I know. Actually I think he just wanted to leave. He couldn't deal with it. I don't think he ever listened to his mom."

"Oh, so he's Leonard Cohen all of a sudden, moping around Europe in a big black coat all grim and sad-faced because it's what he has to do? Gimme a break. So now you're just gonna forgive him and let him see S.F. and waltz right back into your life, just like that? Have some self-respect, for Pete's sake, Knute."

"Yeah, but what about S.F.? He is her father, after all. If he wants to see her, shouldn't I let him? Just because he's a moron doesn't mean she wouldn't want to see him, right? She knows about him and everything. I mean, she can decide later if she hates him enough never to see him again. I can't really decide that for her, you know."

"Why not? Lots of parents do that. If you think she's better off without him in her life, then that's that. You decide."

"Well, you let Ron see Josh even though Ron's an idiot."

"Yeah, but he pays me, Knute. You know, child support? I'm forced to let him see Josh."

"But don't you think you'd want Josh to know Ron even if he wasn't paying you?"

"Absolutely not. Ron's a twit. Josh can do better than him for a father."

"Well, Marilyn, that doesn't make any sense. He *is* his father. *You're* the one who could have done better than him for a boyfriend. There's nothing you can do about him being Josh's dad. And just because he's a twit doesn't mean Josh doesn't like him."

"Hmm, I don't know, Knute. You know what I think? I think you're still hot for Max."

"Wrong-o."

"You are! I can tell. I can always tell. You definitely are still hot for Mighty Max."

"Oh God, Marilyn. I don't even *know* him anymore."

"Yeah? So what's your point? Welcome to—"

S.F. came into the bathroom and asked if she could join Knute in the tub. Marilyn heard S.F. asking and said, "Oh God, don't you hate that?"

"Yeah. I have to add more cold. Okay, I gotta go."

"You know what you have to do, Knute?" said Marilyn.

"What."

"You have to learn how to make pudding. It says on the box you have to stir constantly, *constantly*, and it takes a good twenty or thirty minutes before the stuff boils. So if S.F. is bugging you, you know, asking for this and that, you say, Sorry ma'am, do you want pudding or not? I cannot leave this pudding for a second."

"Yeah?" said Knute.

"Yeah," said Marilyn, "it's great. I make tons of pudding, and while I stir I read. Thin, light books 'cause you only have one hand to hold 'em. Josh can't do a thing about it, so he actually amuses himself and I get a decent break. All hell can break loose around me. I don't care, I'm making pudding."

"That's a great idea, Marilyn," said Knute. "What happens when he gets sick of pudding?"

"I don't know, I hadn't thought of that. I'll think of something when that time comes, though. Something less fattening."

"Yeah. Marilyn, you have to come and visit me here soon, okay?"

"Definitely," said Marilyn, and they put off saying good-bye for a while and then eventually hung up.

That night just before Knute went to bed she watched S.F. sleep. A strand of hair was stuck in her mouth. Knute removed it. S.F. put it back in. She was beautiful. An angel made in heaven, as Combine Jo had said. God, thought Knute, that woman was S.F.'s paternal grandmother! Not that it mattered. In Knute's opinion, Combine Jo was more interested in her next drink and her piles of money than she was in S.F. Or even Max.

Dory had told Knute, when she was pregnant with S.F., that Combine Jo hadn't always been the way she was now. Years and years ago, she had been the wife of the wealthiest farmer in Algren. She had been beautiful and serene. Before Max was even a year old, she had had an affair with a farmer from Whithers. One stormy spring night she had stayed at her lover's place under the pretext that the roads were too treacherous to get back to Algren. The next day she returned home to find Max, her baby, just about frozen to death, lying unconscious and bruised on the kitchen floor—her husband beside him, dead and covered with logs. Apparently he had had an epileptic seizure while trying to fire up the woodstove, dropped Max, whom he had been carrying in one arm, fallen down and died right there. After that Combine Jo started eating and drinking and swearing and generally raising hell all over Algren, until she became too fat and alcoholic to easily make her way out of her house.

With all the money left to her and Max in her husband's will, and by selling most of the farm, Combine Jo was able to hire enough people to look after Max when he was little, and bring her food and booze. She got the name Combine Jo not because she was as big as one, but because each spring she would take her husband's old combine out of the barn and drive it up and down Algren's Main Street as a personal spring-seeding celebration. Dory thought that Combine Jo might carry a sawed-off rifle in the cab of the combine, but nobody knew for sure. She would career down the street, one hand on the wheel, the other clamped around her bottle of Wild Turkey. She would then drive the combine to her husband's grave, often right up over it, and enjoy a toast with him. She'd pour half a bottle of bourbon into the grass on top of his grave, light a cigarette and prop it up, as best she could, in the grass around where his head would have been, six feet under, and then she'd lie there beside him, where she felt she belonged.

Combine Jo had loved her husband deeply. The affair had been a stupid distraction, a way to pass the time while her husband farmed night and day. Knute wondered if Jo had ever given Max any advice on love. Maybe she'd told Max to leave town when she found out Knute was pregnant. Maybe it wasn't his idea at all. Maybe Jo gave Max a million bucks to leave. Maybe I'm a complete idiot, thought Knute.

If she thought he had left because Jo had told him to, she was fooling herself. And her telling him to get lost the day that she found out she was pregnant and he hadn't seemed happy enough—happy at all, really—wouldn't have been enough for him to leave, either. Knute was always telling him to get lost, knowing he'd come back.

No, Max had left because he'd wanted to leave. And now he was coming back because he wanted to come back, and he wanted to see his "goddamned daughter."

"Well," Knute concluded, "Fuck him."

That same evening, Lorna had come out to Algren on the bus to visit Hosea. When Hosea got home from work he had listened to her message on the machine. And then he had listened to it again, sitting on his couch, still in his coat and dripping water from his boots on to the living room carpet. "Hi, Hose," she'd said. "Are you there? If you're there, pick up the phone." Hosea smiled. Doesn't she know me better? he thought. Hosea had nearly killed himself a couple of times running for the phone when he'd heard Lorna's voice coming over the machine. "Okay, I guess you're not there." Lorna wouldn't call Hosea at work. She used to, at the beginning of their relationship, but after a while she had told him he always sounded distracted at work and she didn't need to call long distance to get the cold shoulder. Hosea had pleaded with her to understand. He was the mayor, after all, of Canada's smallest town. He had work to do. He loved her more than life itself but . . . But no, Lorna was unmoved. And since then had called him only at home. "Our office is closed tomorrow so I thought I'd come on the bus and stay over and you could take me home the next day or the next, or I'll just take the bus again. Okay. Whatever. You're really not there, are you? Hmmm. Okay, call me, but if you get this message after six o'clock, don't bother because I'll be on the bus. I should—"

Damn, thought Hosea. He still hadn't installed one of those endless-tape answering machines. She should what? he thought. She always seemed to forget about the length of the tape. Sometimes she'd call back—sometimes two or three times—and just carry on with her monologue, entirely unruffled by the fact that she'd been abruptly cut off. This time she hadn't called back to continue. Why not? Details like this could give Hosea chest pain. Did it mean she was angry at being cut off? Or if not angry, then (and this was worse), oh God, offended? Had she been suddenly incapacitated by an aneurism? Or was she simply in a hurry to get on the bus to see her sugarbaby, her man, Hosea? Hosea would just have to wait and see. But oh, how he hated to wait. Why hadn't old Granny

Funk stuck her bobby pin in the book of Job when they were naming him, instead of at Hosea? Hosea! Could Lorna really love a man she called Hose? He glanced at his watch, a Christmas present from Lorna before she knew him well enough to know that he was never late for anything, and in fact already owned five working watches. Okay, if she takes the 6:15 bus, thought Hosea, she'll be here at 7:15. That gave him exactly half an hour to get things ready, maybe call the doctor and still make it to the bus depot to pick Lorna up. Hosea decided to make the call first.

"Dr. Bonsoir?"

"Hosea?"

"Yes, Doctor, Hosea Funk here. Yes, I know. Well then, okay. Any news over there?"

"News?" said the doctor.

"Yes, news. Has Mrs. Epp—"

"No, she has not. Hosea, I'm a busy man. I'm sure you understand."

"Why yes, yes, indeed I do, but then, quickly, before I go, how's, uh . . . Leander?"

"Do you mean Mr. Hamm?"

"Yes, yes, that's the one. How's he doing? Not good. I see. Any prognosis or—"

"No, I do not have a prognosis, nor would I be giving it out over the phone to . . . non-family members."

"I see, but—"

"Hosea?"

"Yes?"

"I have to see to a patient."

"Of course, well then, thank-you, Doctor."

"Mmmmm," said the doctor in reply.

"Au revoir, Doctor," said Hosea cheerfully.

"Good-bye, Hosea."

Well, of course he was busy, he was a doctor, thought Hosea. No problem. He'd go back to the hospital and see for himself how things were. Hosea checked his watch. Lorna would be pulling up in front of the pool hall, which doubled as a bus depot, in a few minutes. He grabbed two old tablecloths of Euphemia's. One he threw over the dining room table and the other he draped over his shoulder. He lugged his exercise bike downstairs and put it into its usual hiding place, behind the furnace next to the hot water tank. He yanked the tablecloth that was on his shoulder and threw it over the bike. One time Lorna had said, "You know, Hosea, you're in great shape for a man your age and you don't even care. That's what I like about you."

Since then, Hosea had pedalled furiously every morning on his bicycle to nowhere—as Euphemia had called it—and had hid it in the basement each time Lorna came to visit.

Hosea checked his watch. Damn, he thought. The tape!

"You're late," said Lorna.

"I know. I'm sorry," said Hosea. He couldn't tell Lorna the real reason he was late, and he hadn't had time to make one up, so he stood there, thumping his breast with his big green Thinsulate glove (because he couldn't get a proper pincer grip to tug), and hoping her love for him would sweep this latest infraction right under the rug. It had taken Hosea twenty minutes to set his new Emmylou Harris tape to exactly the right song. Fast forward, oops too far—rewind. Too far, fast forward again. Darn! Too far *again*! He had planned to rush into the house ahead of Lorna and push play on his tape deck so that as she entered the house she would hear Emmylou singing "Two More Bottles of Wine," at which point Hosea would produce two bottles of wine, red for the heart, one in each hand, and they would sit down and have a drink.

None of this happened. The tape hadn't played when he'd pushed play because he had, in his haste, unplugged the tape deck to plug in his tri-light desk lamp to create more of a mood. He hadn't been able to find his corkscrew for the wine and so, while Lorna roamed around the house switching lights on and wondering out loud why it was so dark in there, he had rammed the cork down the neck of one of the bottles with his ballpoint pen and then spilled the wine all over himself when it splurched out around the cork. He used the tea towel hanging on the fridge handle to wipe up the wine and then, pushing the cork way down with his pen, managed to pour two glasses without much spillage.

He brought the wine to Lorna and sat down beside her on the couch. "Oh thanks, Hose," she said.

"Lorna?" said Hosea. "Are you mad at me?"

Lorna shifted around to look at him. "Why would I be mad at you?"

Hosea jerked his head towards the answering machine. "Well, because of your message. You didn't call back to finish it. Usually you do."

Lorna put her wine down and took Hosea's hand in hers. She slung one of her legs over his and stroked the top of his hand with her thumb. "Hosea," she said, "you really are something, you know that?"

Hosea used his remaining free hand to flatten her hand over his and stop her from stroking. He longed for his glass of wine, but now his hands were busy. He smiled at Lorna. "You're something, too," he said.

"I suppose I am," said Lorna.

Hosea shifted slightly and smiled again. He stared at their hands, tangled together and resting on Lorna's thigh. He noticed that the middle knuckles on Lorna's fingers were wider than the other parts of her fingers, whereas his own fingers tapered to a point. He wished his fingers were more like Lorna's.

"Hmmmm," murmured Lorna.

"Lorna?" said Hosea.

"Yeah?"

"Are you mad at me?"

"No, Hosea, I am not mad at you. Look at me here. I'm trying to get closer to you. Jesus, Hose, can't you figure it out?"

"But what about the message on the—"

"I was in a hurry, okay? I love you, I'm not mad at you. I love you."

"Well, what were you going to say, I should what, you should what? You know, you were going to say you should do something and I . . ."

"I was going to say, 'I should go if I'm gonna make the bus.' That's what I should do, go. Okay? Go so I could make the bus to get to *you*!"

Lorna sighed, removed her hands from Hosea's, and used one of them to reach for her glass of wine.

"Well, now you're mad then, aren't you?" asked Hosea.

"Hosea, what the hell is your problem? Why do you have to derail every romantic moment in our lives with your paranoid worrying? Do you do it on purpose? Maybe you don't love me, maybe you're mad at *me* and you don't know how to tell me, and you turn it around to make it look like I'm mad at you and then you won't feel so bad, and you'll be the martyr. Great. Now I *am* mad at you."

"I knew it," said Hosea. "And I do love you." He looked at his hands, at his tapered fingers. They were pudgy, he thought. Why? The rest of him wasn't fat. Could he lose weight in his fingers? They looked childish to him. He slipped them under his thighs for a few seconds, then pulled them up and folded them behind his head. Just a minute ago Lorna had been stroking one of his hands and he had wanted her to quit. Now he wanted her to continue, more than anything. He reached for his glass of wine.

"No, you do not know it, Hose, I'm not really mad at you. Can't we just have a normal time together?"

"That's what I really want, Lorna."

"Okay, then why don't you just shut up and relax," said Lorna.

"Oh. Well," said Hosea. And quickly put his glass back on the coffee table.

"Oh God, Lorna, I've missed you," said Hosea.

"Yeah?" said Lorna.

"You know, I've missed you, too, Hose," sighed Lorna about thirty minutes later.

Hosea hated lying around and talking after having sex. He preferred to go outside, flushed and happy, and feel the earth and the sky, and himself sandwiched between them, and know that as things go in the universe, he had just been blessed. But he knew from experience this was not Lorna's first choice. One time he had dragged her outside in the dark, naked and sweaty, and she had started to cough and complain about mosquitoes, and had not said she felt blessed when Hosea had asked her. And so this time he decided he would just get up and get that Emmylou Harris song playing, finally. He brought the tape box back to the floor with him and lay down beside Lorna so that his head was right under the coffee table. Together they listened to the music and looked at the box, at the picture of Emmylou folded up inside it.

"God, does she have long toes, eh?" said Hosea.

"Wow. They're kinda creepy-looking, don't you think?" asked Lorna. Hosea didn't think so. He imagined Emmylou's toes contained in her painted cowboy boots, slightly splayed, planting her body onstage while she belted out "Born to Run."

"Yeah they are, aren't they?" said Hosea.

"Hmmm," said Lorna. "Is this song about heartbreak?" Lorna put her head on Hosea's chest. He patted her head and stared up at the underside of the coffee table. Made in Manitoba, it had stamped on it.

five

Hosea had told on himself. It was eleven-year-old Minty who had spilled the beans to Hosea about where he had come from, but she had made him promise not to tell anyone or she'd be in trouble. "Cross your heart and hope to die?" she'd said to him.

"Cross my heart and hope to die," he'd said and moved his tapered little index finger in the shape of an X over the general vicinity of his heart on the outside of his sweater.

"Okay," said Minty. "Good boy."

They were sitting together in the back seat of a rusted-out car that somebody had abandoned on the edge of Grandpa Funk's alfalfa field.

Minty looked out the windows on each side of the car to make sure nobody was watching. Hosea did the same.

"Lookie," said Minty.

Hosea stared. Minty spread her skinny bare legs, making sure her dress didn't ride up and thumped on her flat stomach a couple of times with the bottom of her fist like she was checking a soccer ball for air. Hosea's eyes widened and Minty nodded.

"Yessir," she said. "But not me. Euphemia. You came right out of her . . ." Minty thumped her belly again.

"You're lying," said Hosea.

And then Minty panicked and saw her chance at redemption at the same time.

"Yeah, I am," she said. She smiled, relieved.

"Are you?" said Hosea.

"Yeah, I am," she said.

"Are you sure?" said Hosea.

"Yeah, I'm sure," said Minty.

"Good," said Hosea.

They were both relieved. They smiled and giggled and Hosea thumped lightly on his stomach, too, just to try it out.

"Punch me as hard as you can," said Minty.

"No," said Hosea.

"C'mon, Hose, just do it. I've tightened it up so it won't hurt." She put her chin down to her chest and moved her arms behind her back.

"No," said Hosea. He started kicking the back of the dusty seat in front of him.

"Don't you want to?" asked Minty.

"I don't want to," he said. He was four years old.

The next evening at the supper table Hosea sat on Euphemia's lap finishing off his potatoes. From time to time he would thump on Euphemia's stomach and she, irritated and trying to finish her own potatoes, would tell him to stop. Minty noticed this and tried to get Hosea's attention. Hosea ignored Minty. He was grinning and he continued to thump Euphemia's stomach. Minty was afraid Hosea was going to say something to get her in trouble, so she suggested that they go outside and play catch.

"Uh-uh," said Hosea. Finally, Euphemia had had enough.

"Hosea!" she said. "Stop it, you're hurting me!" By now all the Funks were looking at Hosea and Euphemia, sternly, curiously, amusedly, in a number of ways. There were a lot of them.

"Let me in, let me in," said Hosea. "I want to get back in!" He laughed and scrunched up his face and put it next to Euphemia's stomach.

"Minty told me I lived in your stomach, Mom, then I came out, right, Minty? Right, Minty?" Euphemia, horrified, stood up and marched out of the room with Hosea on her hip. But not without first noticing the look on her father's face and the way his head swivelled ever so slowly to meet her mother's own incredulous stare.

The Funks had, actually, considered the possibility of Euphemia being Hosea's natural mother before this (five months of sickness, huge coats in the summertime, a man on a horse? The Funks might have been complacent but they weren't stupid), but hadn't wanted to make the situation worse. They had decided, without speaking about it or agreeing to it, to leave well enough alone. Euphemia's honour would remain intact, and so would their reputation as decent people. But now, for some reason, Euphemia's father broke their unspoken pact and opened a can of worms. Had he kept his mouth shut and his eyes on his plate and allowed Euphemia and Hosea to leave the table without further ado, they would have gone on for another four or ten or fifty years, swallowing their suspicions and not rocking the boat. Maybe Euphemia's father wanted some drama in his life. Maybe he was tired of shrugging everything off. Maybe he wanted to get angry at something. Who knows? His gaze said it all. His wife knew it. She panicked. The jig was up.

Euphemia flung Hosea onto his bed upstairs and asked him just what the heck he was talking about, wanting to get back in? Just then Minty came flying through the door, white as a sheet, and said, "Phemie, Phemie, I didn't tell him anything. I was just joking." Hosea lay on his back in his bed.

"She said I came out of your stomach," he said, starting to cry.

"But I said I was lying, you little shit. You know I did," said Minty. Now she began to cry.

"Shut up, Mint, and lock the door," said Euphemia. She knew her parents and her other brothers and sisters would be upstairs and in the room in no time.

"You promised me, Minty, you fat liar," said Euphemia. She shoved Minty onto the bed next to Hosea.

"Let us in, Phemie!" Euphemia's father roared from the hallway. Her mother was begging him to calm down. Euphemia stared at Hosea. He had put his pillow over his head to muffle his sobs. The back of his neck poked out, soft and very narrow. It looks like somebody's wrist, thought Euphemia. Two brown curls framed the tiny nape of Hosea's neck. Euphemia kicked Minty's leg, gently. She didn't care. Not really. It was probably a good thing. She walked over to the door and let the rest of her family in.

"What's this all about, Euphemia? What does Minty have to do with this? What the hell is going on?" Euphemia's father looked from one girl to the other, barely acknowledging the small, heaving lump on the bed.

Euphemia couldn't believe it. Her parents had accepted, cared for, and even loved Hosea when they believed he wasn't hers. Now that they knew the truth, or suspected it—she was Hosea's real mother, he was their flesh and blood, their own real little grandson—they were ready to reject him. And her. And maybe even Minty for keeping the secret. She'd had to tell Minty. She'd had to tell someone. She had been thrilled. And still was.

Euphemia sat down on the bed beside Hosea. She stroked his back. She didn't try to remove the pillow. She moved her thumb up and down the back of his neck, dipping in and out of its soft hollow and feeling his hairline begin just above it. She put her mouth to his curls and kissed them.

"C'mon, Hosea," she whispered, "we're going."

———

Euphemia's parents had tried, in the end, to get them to stay. They had been angry and shocked and hurt and embarrassed, but they weren't the kind of people to throw their daughter and grandson out on to the street. Why hadn't she told them the truth? they asked Euphemia, to which she responded with a shrug. Euphemia's father had told her she was a tramp, but had then apologized. Minty had been grounded for two weeks, which, after a day, was modified to one week, and had told Euphemia a thousand times she was sorry. Euphemia's mother had asked her who the father was and Euphemia said she had no idea, a man on a horse. "Oh, Phemie, not that old cock and bull story," her mother would say. "Your mother's right, Phemie, that dog won't hunt," her father would echo, and Euphemia said calmly, "It's true, that part of it is true." Euphemia's father would rise from the table and slam his fist down and curse Euphemia up one side and down the other and would then lie on the couch, spent and despondent.

But all the while Euphemia was packing her bags. In her mind she had already moved on. She had left. She had locked up this part of her life and thrown away the key. She had turned the page. The next morning she and Hosea were standing on the side of the road, hitching a ride to town.

Hosea would miss the farm. He'd miss Minty. He had planned to marry her when he was older. He was sorry he hadn't punched her in the stomach when she had begged him to. But he didn't really know why they had to go. He had crossed his heart and hoped to die in that old car, in the field with Minty. He had bothered his mother at the supper table. He had pretended to crawl into her stomach. He had thought it was funny but his grandpa and grandma were very angry and Minty was crying and now he and his mother were moving to town. He had heard his grandpa yell, "She's his mother, for God's sake," and he hadn't known why that was suddenly a problem. She had always been his mother and Grandpa had been happy. He had offered to play catch with Minty, thinking that might be it, but she said it was no use, it didn't matter anymore.

Hosea stood at the side of the road and tugged at his shirt.

"Please," said Euphemia and straightened out his arm. "C'mon, Hosea, let's walk for a while."

"But what about our boxes?" Hosea said.

"Hmmm," said Euphemia, "we'll just leave them right here and when we get a ride, we'll ask the driver to come back and pick them up."

They walked together towards town. Euphemia asked Hosea if his boots were pinching his toes yet, and he said no.

"That's good," she said. Hosea asked Euphemia if she'd give him a piggyback ride. She hoisted him up onto her back, and reminded him every twenty yards or so to put his arms around her shoulders and not her neck. After about half an hour they stopped and walked into the ditch and through it and up the other side and sat in the grass and leaned against a farmer's fence.

"Hosea," said Euphemia.

"What?" said Hosea.

"You did come from me, from inside me, inside my stomach."

"Oh," said Hosea. He pulled out some grass and started to make a pile.

"I'm your mother, Hosea, your real honest-to-goodness mother."

Hosea looked up at her briefly and smiled and nodded.

"Do I got a dad?"

"He's a cowboy."

"Where is he?"

"Well, I suppose he's riding the range. Cowboy's can't stay put, Hose."

"That's good," said Hosea. He threw a piece of grass into Euphemia's lap. And then another and another until he had made himself a pillow, and he put his head down on it and had a little nap.

"Why can't I come along?" Summer Feelin' wanted to go with Knute to work. Every time Knute made a move to get dressed, brush her teeth, eat breakfast, Summer Feelin' made exactly the same move. She wasn't letting Knute out of her sight.

"Because. I'll be working."

"So?"

"Well, I'm working for the mayor."

"So?"

"So, it's . . . detailed work."

Summer Feelin' was quiet for about ten seconds. Dory gave Knute a look (raised eyebrows, chin on chest) from the sink indicating she could have done better with the explanation.

"Grandma and Grandpa are boring," said S.F. finally.

"Summer Feelin'!"

"Well, goodness, Knutie, it's true, isn't it?" said Dory, staring directly at Tom.

"No, no," Knute began to say, glaring at S.F. and wondering if the question was actually intended for Tom. Dory was still staring at him.

"Well, I don't know," he said. "Boring? I suppose we are."

"I suppose we are," said Dory. She slammed down the milk in front of Tom and got up for her toast.

Tom and Knute looked at each other and shrugged their shoulders.

"Please don't do that," said Dory.

"Don't do what?" Knute asked.

"Don't shrug your shoulders like that," said Dory. "I'm not crazy, you know."

She left the room then, and Tom and S.F. and Knute sat in silence for a while. One half of Dory's toast had fallen off the plate and onto the table when she slammed it down. Tom put the toast back on her plate, lining it up perfectly alongside the other half. S.F. went over to the fridge and tried to open the door as fast as she could to catch the light coming on. Then, when that didn't work, she opened it slowly, slowly, slowly. Tom and Knute watched, curious to know if it would work.

"C'mon, Summer Feelin'," sighed Tom. "Let's do some juggling. Your mom's gotta go. Hosea's a stickler for punctuality."

Knute walked along Third Avenue towards Hosea's office. She knew she had to make some other kind of babysitting arrangements for S.F. Dory had been getting more work, lately, at the farm labour pool and Tom couldn't look after S.F. all day, every day, by himself. Later on, she might be able to bring S.F. to work with her occasionally, but not right then at the beginning. Her old friend Judy Klampp from high school had a couple of little kids, but Knute didn't think she'd want to look after Summer Feelin' as well. And about a hundred years ago Knute had gone to a party with Judy Klampp's husband, before he was her husband, and had left with his brother and . . . no. Forget Judy Klampp.

Knute told herself she would not think of Max. As far as she was concerned, he was yesterday's news. S.F. thought it was cool that he was coming back to Algren. She thought he would be very happy to see her do her cartwheels and spell her name. She wondered if he'd have a present for her.

"Not bloody likely," Knute thought. She moved the hair out of S.F.'s eyes and said, "Of course he will, sweetie." Max, she supposed, could take care of S.F. while she worked. But no, he couldn't, because he'd be living with Combine Jo and she would maul S.F. every chance she got and who knows? thought Knute, S.F. might hate Max.

Well, she thought, she'd have a cigarette and worry about all that later. She walked along Third Avenue and a dog in a hurry passed by without glancing up at her. She heard the sound of someone practising a violin. Must be spring, she thought.

When she got to the office Hosea was sitting in his chair with his hands folded on his desk in front of him as if he were waiting for a cue from the director to spring into action. His chin jutted out slightly and his face was flushed. His hair was fluffier than usual.

"Ho! You scared me. How are you, Knute?"

"Fine, thank-you. How are you?"

"Whoosh, whoosh, whoosh, very busy," said Hosea, making chopping motions with his hands. "All over town. In fact, I've gotta fly."

"Okay . . ." said Knute. She wasn't sure what she should be doing. Staying. Going. She could see this job shaping up to be another one of her colossal failures at meaningful employment.

"All you have to do, Knute, is answer the phone, take messages, maybe think of ways to spruce up Algren: flowers along Main Street, new lettering on the water tower, some new blacktop, maybe check into the price of a new Zamboni, that sort of thing. Okey-dokey? At about noon you can go and get my mail from the post office. Just tell 'em who you are. Fair enough?"

"Okay," she said again. She nodded and smiled. She was about to ask Hosea if she could smoke in his office, in their office, in the office, but he was gone.

Hosea Funk hurried up the steps of the Charlie Orson Memorial Hospital. The hospital was perched on top of a small hill, and from its front doors Hosea could just see the smoke coming out of the chimney of his house, a block away. Man's life's a vapour, full of woes, he thought, seeing the smoke twist in the sky and disappear. He cuts a caper and down he goes. But then he remembered his beloved Lorna, probably still asleep, warm and soft, her hands curled up like a baby's beside her head, her dark eyelashes . . . and Hosea's thoughts flip-flopped from one end of the spectrum to the other in a matter of seconds: from life's woes to passion's throes. Then, looking once again at the smoke escaping from the chimney, his thoughts tumbled back towards the woes, lodging themselves somewhere in the humdrum middle of the spectrum with thoughts of Knute and his work, and Knute's ripped jeans in conjunction with his mayoral status, and would it all work out—should he mention the jeans, should he not?

"Ello, Hosea, you're looking . . . sound."

"Good morning, Dr. Bonsoir, I'm feeling . . . sound." Hosea smiled.

"Well then," said the doctor. "If you are so sound, what can I possibly do for you? I am a physician. Wait. Don't tell me. You're here to check up on my patients. On my quality of care? Perhaps you could check Mr. Hamm's IV levels, or inspect Mrs. Epp for signs of dilation, or maybe you would like to discuss the radical new treatment for enlarged polyps recently making its debut in the *New England Journal of Medicine,* eh? Mr. Hosea Funk, why do you feel you have the right to 'check in' as you call it, on my patients? You are not a priest or a funeral home director. You are not family. You are not an intern practising for the real thing, you are not a hospital administrator or the CMA.

You are not even a florist or a pizza delivery person, not that our patients order pizza every day. So, what do you want? Mayors do not, as far as I know, make hospital rounds every few days. It is not part of their job and you are irritating the hell out of me, do you know that?"

"Well, Dr. Bonsoir, I—"

"And my name is not Bonsoir, it's François. Bon soir, for your information, means good evening. Dr. Good Evening? Have you ever heard of anything so ridiculous? Think about it. Would you like me to call you Mayor . . . Hello? Hello, Mayor Hello. Or Mayor Good Night?"

"Well no, gosh, I'm sorry, Doctor . . . Doctor—"

"François!"

Hosea looked around the room, then down at his shoes. His hand went to his chest, but instead of tugging he flattened his hand over his heart.

"What? Are you having chest pain, Hosea? Sit down there, in that chair. Come on. I'm sorry. Clearly I've upset you. I apologize. Here now, let's loosen your coat."

"Dr. François, I'm sorry, I—"

"Shhhh, I'm taking your pulse. I need to count. Please, shhh." The doctor bent over Hosea, holding his wrist between his thumb and forefinger, looking sternly at the second hand of his watch. Hosea sat there, feeling foolish. His heart was fine. How could he tell the doctor he had a nervous condition, not a heart condition? Hosea felt bad for the doctor, who was feeling bad for Hosea. He looked at the curved back of the doctor, at his dark brown hair just grazing the back of his collar. Such care, such professionalism. For a moment Hosea wished the doctor was his own son. Lorna would have a delicious lunch prepared. He and the doctor would enter the warm kitchen slapping each other on the back, each kindly ribbing the other and gazing at Lorna with mutual tenderness.

The doctor let go of Hosea's wrist and stood up.

"You've got the pulse of a nine-year-old girl, Hosea. Nothing to worry about."

"Thank-you, Dr. François. I'm sorry I irritate you."

"Oh, it's nothing. I realize there isn't that much for you to do, a small town like Algren isn't exactly—"

"But that's not true, Doctor," said Hosea. He stood up.

"I have a lot of work to do. Algren isn't just a small town, it's *the* smallest. You know, just today I've hired a girl—a woman—Tom McCloud's daughter, Knute, to take care of some of the details so I can work on the bigger projects. I'm sure your work is never done even though you work in a small hospital and not one in the city."

"Well, I suppose so. I didn't mean to offend you, Hosea, I was simply trying to shed some light on the subject. Listen, everything is very much as it was three days ago when you were last here. Monsieur Hamm is very ill. His organs are shutting down. He has begun to hemorrhage internally. It is very difficult to find a vein in which to insert his IV tubes. The members of his family are coming around to say good-bye. Unless you are a good friend, I would suggest you maintain a respectful distance. As far as Mrs. Epp goes, if she does not go into labour soon, we will have to induce her. I have discussed over the phone, with some of my colleagues in Winnipeg, the possibility of transferring her to one of the larger prenatal wards in the city. She is very uncomfortable. Okay, Hosea? Is that what you wanted to know? You know, this information is generally regarded as confidential. Are you happy?"

"Yes. Thank-you, Dr. François."

"Don't mention it."

Hosea put out his hand to shake the doctor's. He truly was grateful. That was exactly what he needed to know. But before the doctor could extend his own hand in return, the hospital's head nurse, Mrs. Barnes, came careering around the corner. A clean white blur. "Dr. François? Dr. François, Mrs. Epp is leaking amniotic fluid and having contractions one and a half minutes apart. I'm afraid one of the babies is not in position. I'm only getting two pulses. A C-section may be necessary."

In a second, Dr. François was gone. Hosea watched him and Nurse Barnes run down the hall, their white coats flying behind them like twin pillow cases on a washline. Hosea wanted to run after them, run with them. For one semi-unconscious moment Hosea envied the uncooperative baby, the one who was stuck, the one who would have the gentle, capable hands of Dr. François guiding him, or her? towards the light, out and up. Towards safety, towards home, towards his mother and his father. Such tenderness, such concern. For something so small as a baby, one of three, a triplet. Hosea's mind almost capsized as he began to imagine the younger Dr. François as his own father, as the cowboy on the range, as the leader of the country, as the . . . Cut it out, Hosea, said Hosea to himself. Dr. Bon-François is busy, so are the nurses, I'll have a quick peek at old Leander before I go. Thank God for my rubbers, thought Hosea, as he padded softly down the hall, away from the commotion in Mrs. Epp's room.

Hosea peered around the door of room 3. He jumped when his eyes met Leander Hamm's. They were open wide and staring directly at Hosea.

"Mr. Hamm?" whispered Hosea.

"Susie? Susie?" Leander Hamm's eyes didn't leave Hosea's face. Hosea stood, frozen, in the doorway. He knew that Susie had been the name of Leander's wife, long gone now.

"No . . ." whispered Hosea.

"Cut the crap, Suse. Take me . . . with you," Leander Hamm managed to say. He had always been a cantankerous man. He preferred horses to people.

"I can't. I—"

And then Leander Hamm let out a howl that terrified Hosea.

"Shhh, shh . . ." said Hosea. He was worried that the doctor would come running. He would be so angry with Hosea if he saw him in Mr. Hamm's room.

"Okay, I'll take you with me . . . dear. Let's go right now. But please be quiet." And Hosea went over to Leander Hamm and took his hand. He thought of taking Mr. Hamm's pulse, the way the doctor had taken his. He stared at his thumb and tapered forefinger holding Leander Hamm's tiny wrist. Hosea couldn't believe that this narrow piece of bone had held down wild horses, broken savage stallions, held off the powerful hindquarters of a bucking bronc intent on squashing him between the stable boards. But Leander Hamm tightened his grip and, with more surprising strength, pulled Hosea to him so that Hosea's face was touching his. Hosea wasn't quite sure where Leander Hamm wanted to go, or how they'd get there. He just wanted the old man to simmer down.

"Susie. Susie," said Leander Hamm. He moved his sunken cheek gently against Hosea's.

"Susie, I'm . . . I'm . . . going now. I'm . . ." But Leander Hamm was sobbing. And Hosea Funk was gasping, speechless, as Mr. Hamm tried to guide Hosea's hand down towards his legs.

"No, no, my darling . . . my love," said Hosea. But it didn't matter. Leander Hamm had released his grip on Hosea's hand. He had released his grip on all of it. Man's life's a vapour. Leander Hamm was dead.

About thirty-five years earlier, when Leander Hamm was only sixty years old, and Hosea was an awkward teenager, Leander had meant to tell Hosea that he thought he knew something about his father. That old story about the Funk girl being handed a baby one night by a man on a horse didn't wash with him. Leander knew that was the official story, and he'd done enough stupid things in his day that he wasn't about to blow the whistle on somebody else, but, gee whiz, you couldn't lead Leander Hamm down the garden path that easily. Besides, he had seen them together in the field. And years later, he had felt something for Hosea, loping around town, so eager to please. He wanted to mention to Hosea that he had been there, at the dance in Whithers, when the man on the horse had left the hall and met Euphemia in the canola field. Leander had noticed that the stranger had left his hat behind, and he ran out to tell him. But when he saw young Euphemia and the cowboy together in the field, he turned around and quickly walked back to the dance hall. "Two kids in heat," he'd muttered to himself at the time.

The cowboy never came back for his hat. It was a Biltmore, a good hat. Leander decided to keep it for himself. Now, he wasn't sure, of course, that this cowboy was Hosea's dad. But he knew, like everybody else in the area did, that Euphemia was no tramp, that she came from a pretty good family and wouldn't have been the kind of girl to sleep with every Tom, Dick, and Harry. So chances were it was the cowboy. He seemed like a healthy boy to Leander, but of course Leander Hamm was partial to anybody who was partial to horses. The only thing that had confused him over the years was how nervous Hosea could be the son of that confident cowboy. But it happens. Anyway, the fact that Euphemia had gone out back with this stranger didn't upset Leander. The stranger was a good boy. They had talked for a few minutes. Was he from Alberta or was he an American, maybe Montana? Leander couldn't remember. And he hadn't gotten around to telling the story to Hosea when he'd thought about it, and then the thought was gone.

He had taken the hat. After all, the cowboy had left and never returned. And who better to wear a quality Biltmore than Leander Hamm? In fact, he had worn that hat every day since he'd acquired it. He never saw a dentist or a doctor but twice a year he'd brought that hat into the city to have it steamed and blocked. Horses had trampled on it, shat on it, his kids had misplaced it, his grandchildren had mocked it, his wife had thrown it in the garbage half a dozen times, and not one, but two, cats had had kittens in it. Just about nightly Leander used that hat to cover his privates when he would walk, naked except for the Biltmore, to the outhouse. One time it made a journey to the Holy Land when Oberon Gonne, a man from Leander's church, had grabbed it from the men's hat rack after one Sunday service and flown off to Jerusalem for six months. When he came back and returned the hat to Leander it had a strange smell and Leander was pissed off.

Instead of leaving his hat at home when he went to church, he decided to leave himself at home with his hat while his wife, Susie, went to church alone. That was that.

And so, on the day that Leander's son Lawrence had taken him to the Charlie Orson Memorial Hospital, he had been wearing the hat. And, when the nurse had told him that she would put all his belongings, including the hat, into the hospital safe while he was a patient there, Leander had managed to grab the hat and say, "Oh no, you don't, Florence Nightingale, I've had that hat longer 'n dogs have been lickin' their balls."

Lawrence had smiled sweetly at the nurse. "That's really not too much to ask, is it?" he'd said. Without a word, the nurse tossed the hat over Leander's shrunken body, to Lawrence, and stalked out.

"You don't throw it, either, it's a Biltmore, you goddamn . . . Nazi!" Leander had yelled after her.

Leander had wanted to wear it, of course, but Lawrence had convinced him that it would be better if he hung it on the IV contraption. That way Leander would be able to see it and to reach out and touch it, but it wouldn't get flattened in bed.

And this was where the hat was hanging when Leander died. Hosea saw it and thought it was a very nice hat. It was a Biltmore, he noted. It felt like flour but was as tough as a pig's hide. He wanted it. Oh God, what would the doctor think if he saw him, first going into Leander's room, then killing him in a convoluted way, and now stealing his hat? He wanted that hat. He didn't know why, but he had to have it. The doctor was busy with Mrs. Epp and the babies. Hosea reached out and grabbed it. Thankfully, Leander's eyes were closed and his hands forever still. Sorry, said Hosea to Leander. And he left with his hat.

six

Knute sat on the large windowsill in Hosea's office looking out at that dog. The same dirty black one that had passed her in such a hurry. It looked like he was panhandling or something. He sat in front of the Wagon Wheel, looking up at everybody who passed, then back down the street to see if anybody else was coming. Not very many people were. Smallest town and everything. He reminded Knute of the dog who lived in the apartment block across from hers in the city. He would hang out his fourth floor window, front legs on the windowsill, and if he saw somebody wave he'd sort of wave back. Once Knute saw him on a leash going for a walk with his owner and he looked sheepish, like, Okay, yes, now you know, I'm a dog, that's all there is to it.

Knute opened the window and stuck her head out.

"Hey!" she said to the dog. He looked up and nodded in a dog way but then returned to business. Somebody was coming down the street. Knute hadn't done any of the things Hosea had asked her to do, except get the mail.

She sat on the windowsill and smoked and looked outside.

"Uh, hello," she heard someone say.

"Can I help you?" she muttered and quickly butted her cigarette against the windowsill and threw it down to the street.

She turned around and there was Hosea, wearing a hat. He looked vaguely stricken.

"Oh hell-*o,*" she said. "It's you. Sorry. I hope you don't mind me smoking in here." Hosea put up his hand like a cop saying stop and shook his head. Knute wasn't sure he was shaking his head no, he didn't mind, or no, she shouldn't smoke.

"Any luck?" he said. Again, Knute wasn't sure what he meant exactly, so she said, "No. No luck. But I got your mail."

"Oh. Thank-you," said Hosea.

"No problem." Knute thought Hosea's hat looked good on him. It looked like it must have been a longtime favourite of his.

"So. Thanks again," said Hosea. "Um, I think you'll work out well. Did you, uh, have any problems?"

"No, nope, no problems," said Knute. And she thought how Hosea must be wondering because first she didn't have any luck and now she didn't have any problems, so what exactly did she have?

"Well, then, you may as well go home," said Hosea. "Thanks very much for your help. Well, not your help," he said, "I mean your services, your time. How does two hundred and fifty dollars a week sound? For, oh, a few hours a day, if that's, if that suits you."

"Two hundred and fifty bucks?" Knute said. "That's great. That's fine."

"Because, like I say," said Hosea, "if you need more or if you think it's not enough, just tell me."

"Fine, yeah, I will, but it sounds okay to me. It sounds good."

"Say hi to Tom," said Hosea. He sat in his chair and smoothed out the surface of his desk. "I should really drop in again soon. We had a very nice visit the last time I did."

"Yeah," Knute said. "You should." She smiled. Hosea smiled.

"Listen," he said. "Here's a key. To the office. In case I'm not around when you need to come in to work."

"Okay." Knute took the key. Need to come in to work, she thought. For what?

"Well, see ya," she said.

"See ya. See ya . . . Knutie. Knute."

She smiled as if to say whatever, call me whatever. "See ya," she said again.

The dog was still sitting there. Dusk was falling in around him. The sky was the colour of raw meat. Knute walked past the dog.

"Hey, you desperado," she said, "what are you waiting for?" No reply. She wondered if Summer Feelin' would like a dog. But no, not with all of Dory's redecorating. She kept walking. Past Darlene's Unisex Salon, past Jim and Brenda's Floral Boutique, past the Style-Rite, past Kowalski Back Hoe Services and Catering, past Willie Wiebe's Western Wear, past the only set of lights in town.

Hosea's hands were shaking. He opened his top right drawer and took out the orange Hilroy scribbler. His memory of what had just happened was, what was that colour, a dusty rose, a throbbing dusty rose? It took him to the doorway of Leander's room, but not beyond. Thank God for my rubbers, he had thought. The babies, a problem with one of them. Go back, Hosea, he had told himself. Go back into the room. You stole the hat. You killed a man and stole his hat. No, I didn't, thought Hosea. I didn't kill him. He just died and I happened to be there. Shouldn't you have told someone? Should I have? Yes, I should have. I know it. But then the doctor would have been angry with me. But this man died! I know, but surely someone will notice very soon. But the hat. Nobody saw me go in and nobody saw me go out, so nobody will know that I took his hat. And that makes it okay? People might think I killed him for his hat. Why did I take the hat? It's a beautiful hat. Because I'm no good. I stole the hat of a dead man. I can't be any good. That's right, that's right. You're no cowboy, Hosea Funk. You're a horse's ass. So I am. So I am.

Hosea sat still in his chair. His head hurt. He opened his scribbler and turned to the Dead column and carefully entered the name Leander Hamm, and the date March 23, 1996. Then he put the scribbler back into the drawer and took out the letter from the Prime Minister and read it twice. He also took out the newspaper photo that showed the Prime Minister sleeping on a plane to Geneva. It was Hosea's favourite. He had a full photo album of newspaper clippings and pictures of the Prime Minister. Shaking hands, singing the national anthem, talking into a reporter's microphone, speaking in the House of Commons, kissing his beautiful wife, playing with his grandchildren, unveiling some monument or another, riding away in a chauffeur-driven limousine. But the one of the Prime Minister sleeping was his favourite. It was the only one of them all in which Hosea could see himself.

"Three babies," Hosea whispered to himself. Three babies. If the third survives. Hmmmm. That's three more people in Algren, one less, Leander Hamm, that makes two, fifteen hundred and two. That's two too many, thought Hosea. But he still had a bit of time. The Prime Minister had promised to visit on July first, Canada Day. Hosea had a few months to work it out. He felt his hat. He took it off and put it back on. He phoned Lorna at his place. No answer. Where was she? There was nowhere for her to go in Algren. And she had said she'd be staying a couple of days. "Damn Damn *damn,*" said Hosea, and began to wonder if he was supposed to know anything.

Where was Lorna, anyway? He decided to go home and find out. As he was getting into his car, Combine Jo walked by and looked hard at him, as if she had seen that hat somewhere before, but where?

"La dee dah, Mr. Mayor with the fancy hat," she said. "Going to a party?"

"No," said Hosea. "No, I'm not. I'm going home."

"Ha ha," said Combine Jo. "I'm kidding, Hose, it's a nice hat, suits you. You should wear it on July first if buddy boy in Ottawa comes to town. You know, you look like . . . Oscar Wilde. Hey, didja hear my kid, Max, is coming home? Pretty good, eh?"

"Is it?" said Hosea.

And Combine Jo said, "Well, I think it is."

"Yes, well . . . good," said Hosea. He knew that Max had left town when Knute was pregnant with his child. So many cowboys, thought Hosea. He also knew all about Combine Jo and her craziness and the cause of it and it was no wonder Max flew the coop. He wondered if Knute and Summer Feelin' knew Max was coming back. Then again, maybe he wasn't coming back. Maybe Combine Jo was just talking. But then again, maybe it was true. "Oh, Jo?" he called out to her as she meandered down the sidewalk.

"Yes, m'dear?" she yelled without looking over her shoulder.

"Is he coming back for good? Like, uh, to live here?" he said.

"That's how it's lookin', sweetie. That's how the odds are stackin' up," she said, and she saluted the old black dog as she passed the Wagon Wheel Café.

"Three babies and Max," whispered Hosea to himself as he drove the two blocks back home. Three babies and Max. But Leander's gone, he thought and glanced at himself and his hat in the rearview mirror. Four more residents of Algren, minus one, equals three. And no potentially dead or dying at the moment either, thought Hosea. He drummed his fingers on top of the steering wheel and told himself not to worry, not to worry. He parked the car in the garage and went into his house through the kitchen door. He hoped Lorna was there, in bed where he had left her. He would put his cold hands on her warm thighs and she would say—

"Hosea! You're too early!" screeched Lorna. She had flour all over her face and hair and the kitchen smelled wonderful.

"Oops," said Hosea. "I am?"

"Yes, you are, and where did you get that hat? You know, it actually looks good on you! But what the hell are you doing home so early?" She'd said *urr-lee.* Hosea stopped for a brief second to reflect on that question. What the hell was he doing home so early? She said it as though it was their home, not just his. Home. She said it like she lived there, too. What with the flour on her face and everything, and barefoot! She could have said, What are you doing back so early? Or just, You're early! Three babies and Max and no potentially dead other than Leander and now Lorna's hinting at his home being hers, too, which would mean three babies, Max, and Lorna, as new residents of Algren, which would be next to impossible to level off before July first, the day the Prime Minister, his father, the man his mother had said, on her deathbed, was his father, had promised to come and see him—well, see Algren. All of Algren. Well, he had promised to see Canada's smallest town and Hosea hoped that would be Algren. But. Grrr.

"I'm home early because . . . I love you. And what are you doing?"

"I'm baking, Hose, what does it look like?" Lorna was dragging one finger down a page of a recipe book and moving her lips.

"What are you baking?" asked Hosea.

"I'm baking cinnamon buns, Hosea. The smell of cinnamon buns, for a guy, is an aphrodisiac more powerful than all the perfumes on the market, did you know that?"

Oh, Lorna, thought Hosea. I don't need an aphrodisiac with you. Just the mention of your name and I melt. I . . . melt.

"No, I didn't know that," said Hosea. "Well, good. That should help."

Lorna turned around and put one hand on her hip and the other held the recipe book with her middle finger stuck in at the right place.

"What do you mean that will *help,* Hosea?" she said. "Help with what?"

"With us?" he said, knowing, just knowing it was all wrong.

"What do we need help with, exactly?" asked Lorna.

"Um . . . I don't know. I mean, with nothing. We're fine. Right?"

"What are you trying to say, I don't make you hot anymore? You need a fucking cinnamon bun to get turned on?"

"No! You said it. I didn't say that. You said cinnamon buns were more of an aphro—"

"I know what the fuck I said, okay, Hosea?"

"Okay. Let's go back to it then. Say it again. Please? Please?"

"God, you're hopeless, Hosea. Okay, did you know that cinnamon buns are a more powerful aphrodisiac than all the perfumes in the world?" Lorna spoke in a bored singsong voice and moved her head back and forth as if she were reciting something. Hosea was ready now.

"To hell with all the perfumes and all the cinnamon buns in the world, baby," he said. "I don't need any aphrodisiac but you!"

Lorna was laughing now with her hands on her hips and saying, "Yeah, yeah. Not gonna happen. My timer's going off in about four minutes."

Knute and Summer Feelin' were sitting on the bed and talking.

S.F. was leaning against the wall with her feet sticking out over the edge of the bed and Knute was sitting on the edge of the bed with her feet on the floor and her hands stretched out on her thighs. Summer Feelin' lifted each of Knute's fingers painfully high, while she talked, and let them drop. From the pinkie on Knute's left hand to the pinkie on her right and back again.

"Is Joey a girl or a boy?" she asked. Joey was the neighbour's yappy dog. Knute hated that dog but Summer Feelin' thought he was cute.

"A boy," said Knute.

"What if he's not?" S.F. asked.

"Then he's a girl."

S.F. stared at Knute, gravely, for a few seconds.

"Do you know what I'm gonna use this stuff for when it gets goopy like nail polish?" She pointed to a container of old liquid blush Dory had given her.

"Uh . . ." Knute said, pretending to rack her brain. "Nail polish?"

"Right, Mom, how'd you know?" said S.F., climbing onto Knute's lap. Knute could feel S.F. starting to quake inside. Soon her head would be back and her arms would be flapping. What's so exciting? Knute wondered. Joey? Nail polish?

"Is he coming back just to see me?" S.F. asked. She shook. Knute knew who S.F. meant. She'd been wondering the same thing. No, she thought to herself, he's run out of money and probably has some type of venereal disease that requires antibiotics and that's why he's coming back.

"Yes, my darling," she said and wrapped her arms around S.F. "You're the main reason he's coming back."

"I knew it," said S.F. Knute fell over like a tree and her head hit Summer Feelin's pillow. She couldn't stop it from happening any longer. She closed her eyes and remembered Max. His hair, his smile, the way he talked, the way he smoked, the way he became maudlin when he drank too much wine, how he hardly ever took anything seriously, the passionate promises he made, how he took care of Combine Jo, how he hardly ever lost his temper, his hands, his stupid jokes, his laugh, his voice, his letters that stopped coming.

"Mom, Mom, don't sleep."

"I'm not sleeping, S.F."

"What are you doing?"

"I'm resting."

"Don't rest."

"Summer Feelin'," Knute said. "Do you think it's kind of selfish of Max just to come and go whenever he pleases? Do you wonder why he hasn't come to see you at all and you're already four years old?"

"I dunno," S.F. said. She shrugged.

Knute sat up and S.F. pulled her off the bed. It was time to make another heart-smart low-fat, low-sodium, low-cholesterol, low-excitement meal, probably of chicken breasts and rice.

"Oh, Knutie?" Dory called from some cubbyhole she was painting in another room.

Oh no, thought Knute. Another morbid anecdote. "Yeah?"

"Did you hear that old Mr. Leander Hamm died?"

"The guy with the hat?" Knute called out.

"The guy with the hat. Yes. But he was very old. It's a blessing, really."

"Well then!" Knute yelled. "Bless us each and every one and pass the whiskey."

"I just thought you might be interested!" said Dory. "For Pete's sake!"

"Hey, Mom!" Knute yelled. "Why don't you crawl out of that hole and come and hang out in the kitchen with us while I make supper."

"I'll be right there," Dory yelled back. "Put the coffee on!"

"Will do," said Knute, chasing S.F. into the kitchen with wild eyes and singing into the back of her neck, quietly, "He's dead, he's dead, he's given up his bed, he's said all that he's said, away his life has sped, his body's left his head, give us his daily bread," and Summer Feelin' had to laugh in spite of herself. Thank God, thought Knute.

Lorna was on her way home. Everything had gone quite well, thought Hosea, very well really, except for the end when she had said, "Oh, Hosea, you know I think about living with you, having a nice easy life together, you know, just . . . being together."

Nice? *Easy*? Could life be that way, Hosea thought, nice and easy?

Could it? And the two of them together? Obviously she meant in Algren. How could the mayor of the smallest town up and move to the big city? Well, he couldn't, thought Hosea. And after she'd said what she'd said, Hosea had pawed his chest a few times, and said, "Oh you." "Oh *you*?" Lorna had said. "Oh *you*? That's all you can say, Hosea? Oh *you*?" But he hadn't meant it that way. He hadn't meant it to sound like Oh you, you're such a silly kid. But oh you, oh you, oh YOU, my Lorna, my love. Hosea understood how Lorna might have misunderstood. He'd mumbled it into his tugging hand and looked down when he'd said it and had wanted to carry her back to his car, to his house, their house, to their bed, to bring the exercise bike out into the open and have Lorna's sexy, lively colourful stuff all over the place, instead of sad things like Euphemia's tablecloths and ancient jars of Dippity-Do, and forget about his stupid plan and live in honesty, the two of them, day to day, with July first coming and going like just another hot summer memory and not a looming deadline.

God knows how long it would be before Lorna came for another visit, or called to invite him over there, which was always exciting to think about but when he actually got there, to the city, to her apartment, to the cafés and bars and theatres and universities and health food stores and bookstores, he always felt like an idiot, like a big goofy farmboy on a school field trip, riding a big orange bus that said Algren Municipality Elementary School, and Lorna saying "Hi, hi there, how *are* you" to people he had never met, and introducing him and should he stick out his hand, and is this rough-looking guy hugging Lorna because he's what they call New Age, or . . . Or the time he had driven to the city for that Emmylou Harris concert and his car had started on fire at a red light. He remembered running into a little grocery store and asking to use the telephone and the guy said, "No, no, sorry no." Then, when he got back to his burning car, some kids in the neighbourhood had pelted him with hard, wet snowballs, laughing and yelling at him, "Let it burn! Let it burn!" No, he much preferred to have Lorna in his little house in Algren, baking cinnamon buns, just the two of them. And then, oh stupid me, he thought, that's just what Lorna had said she wanted, too, and he'd said, "Oh you," which she decided he meant as Oh you, that's a crazy romantic notion that really has no place in our lives, when he'd meant the opposite, and wanted the very same thing, but how could he tell her Algren didn't have room for her? She would have to be counted and he didn't have enough dying people to level it off. How could someone tell somebody else something like that? Could Lorna wait until after July first? Hosea shook his head slowly. She would have to, oh please.

Hosea had tried to get her attention but the bus just drove away under a sky the colour of glue and Lorna stared straight ahead. Hosea picked up a piece of hard snow and chucked it at her window and smiled and waved, but she had looked at him with one of those withering looks, a look that said, Chucking hard pieces of snow against my section of bus window will not thaw my frozen heart.

Hosea walked over to the chunk of snow, the one he had chucked at Lorna's window, and looked at it. The snow around it was dusty from the exhaust fumes of the bus. Hosea gently kicked the chunk of snow towards the sidewalk. He walked up to it and kicked it again, a little harder, to get over the ridge of snow that lined the sidewalk. Up and over, there it went. Hosea continued kicking the chunk of snow towards home. It was getting smaller and smaller. He hoped he could get it home before it disappeared. Gentle kicks, but long distances. Scoop it from underneath with the top of your foot. That was the trick. He shouldn't be doing this, he thought. What if somebody saw him, the mayor of Algren, kicking a piece of snow down the sidewalk? Well, it wasn't far to his house, and besides he'd done it as a boy, with Tom. They'd pick their chunks, inspecting them closely to make sure they were pretty much exactly the same size and weight, and then home they'd go. When they got home, if their chunks of snow hadn't disappeared or been kicked so far they got lost, they'd play hockey with one of them until it did disappear and then, for a big laugh, they'd continue to play with it. It wasn't there but they'd play with it anyway, taking slapshots, scoring goals, having it dropped by imaginary referees at centre ice, skating like crazy down the ice to catch the rebound off their sticks. Often, they would argue about goals, the puck being offside, illegal penalty shots, all that stuff, and they'd have huge hockey fights, throwing their woollen mittens down on the ground and trying to pull each other's jackets off over their heads.

One day Euphemia came out of the house with an empty whipping cream carton. "Here, you boys," she'd said. "Why don't you use this?" And she had put it down in the snow and stomped on it once for all she was worth and then picked the flattish thing up and tossed it over to them. They'd used it for a while, and Euphemia stood washing dishes looking out at them in the back lane and smiling, and then they'd gone to the front of the house, to the street, where Euphemia wasn't as sure to watch them, and went back to their imaginary puck.

It was Sunday. Algren was dead. Hosea slowly made his way home. As he walked past the back of the Wagon Wheel Café, Mrs. Cherniski, the owner of the café, poked her head out of the kitchen and said, "Hey, Hosea!" Hosea's head snapped up like a fish on a line, but not before he made a mental note of where his chunk of ice had stopped.

"Hello, Mrs. Cherniski, how goes the battle?" said Hosea.

"So that is you, I was wondering," said Mrs. Cherniski, "with that hat and everything. Looks like old Leander gave you his hat before he passed on. Nice of him. But I'd have it cleaned, if I was you."

"Yes, I should, I suppose," said Hosea, thinking that all its filth and wear was what he loved about it.

"Well," said Mrs. Cherniski, "I'll tell you something. If you don't get rid of that damn black dog out there, the one hanging around the front of my shop, I'll shoot the damn thing myself, not a word of a lie."

"Oh no," said Hosea, "don't do that. I'll find out who owns that dog and make sure they keep him on a line from now on."

"Well good, you better," said Mrs. Cherniski. "Last night I had thirty people in my store, you know the Whryahha clan up for the son's wedding, a private booking. I was serving roast beef and lobster bisque and damned if that dog isn't sitting outside right there on the sidewalk, his rear end twitching in the wind. Then, dammit, he's hunkering down in front of all the Whryahha's in their Sunday best, and I see he's having a shit right there on the path."

Hosea adjusted his hat and glanced at his chunk of ice. He shook his head in mock alarm for Mrs. Cherniski's sake and said, "Hmmmph, that's not very good."

"No it isn't," said Mrs. Cherniski. "A tableful of those Whryahhas just up and left, they couldn't finish their meals and they weren't about to pay for them, having to eat while a mangy mutt craps away right there in front of them. I damn well lost close to two hundred dollars last night, not to mention my reputation. Thank God I'm the only café in town, but Jesus, Hosea, you have to do something about that dog."

"You're absolutely right, Mrs. Cherniski. I'll see to it pronto. In the meantime, you might want to try shooing it away, maybe a little kick."

"A little kick, my ass," muttered Mrs. Cherniski. "I'll plug the goddamn thing right between the—" but she was back inside. Slam went the back door of her café in Hosea's face.

Adjusting his hat, he went over to his ice chunk and gave it another kick towards home. He looked up at the water tower and wondered what colour to paint it when and if he ever found the money for paint. Bright red would be nice, maybe with a huge decal of a white horse that would wind itself around the tower's entire circular top. He looked at the boarded-up feed mill and thought of turning it into a type of make-work project for the youth of Algren during the summer months. Perhaps they could turn it into a junior summer stock theatre for tourists passing through, on their way west to Vancouver, or east to Toronto. A quaint prairie play, maybe Lawrence Hamm could donate an old thresher that they could paint and put in the front of the theatre as a symbolic monument to a bucolic past. Now Hosea's mind began to spin.

He passed a couple of kids walking down the street. Their jackets were open and they were wearing rubber boots. "Hello there," he said, "beautiful spring day, isn't it?" The kids smiled and said, "Hi." They knew who he was but they didn't respond to his comment about the beautiful day. As a rule, thought Hosea, and he must remember this in the future, kids do not respond to comments about the weather. He stole a glance over his shoulder, making sure the kids weren't looking back at him, and then quickly retrieved his chunk of ice from the gutter of the road. He had overkicked. Suddenly Hosea wondered to himself what Euphemia had done all day when he was away in school.

"Penny for your thoughts," she'd say to him when he came home from school, and he'd smile and make something up and she'd give him a nickel or a dime but he never asked her what she was thinking about.

One day Hosea came home early because he had an earache, and he found Euphemia doing a handstand on a kitchen chair, gripping the nubby edge of it with her fingers and bicycling her legs around and around up in the air above her head. When she noticed him staring at her, she slowly brought her legs down to the floor and put the chair back beside the table. Then she'd laughed. "You know how it is, Hosea," she'd said. No, he didn't. He had not been amused. He was uncomfortable and alarmed. Why was his mother doing handstands on the kitchen chair? Had she lost her mind? Was she planning to run away and join the circus? Was she a freak? A Buddhist?

He had not been too impressed with that display of athleticism, yet later that evening he tried to do the same thing and could not. Therefore, he surmised at the time, it wasn't something someone could just do on command, and so she must spend her days practising this sort of thing. This is what she must do while I'm in school, he'd concluded. His question answered. But why?

You know how it is, Hosea, she'd said. Now, as Hosea walked along kicking his piece of snow, he understood. Handstands on kitchen chairs, chunks of ice we can't let disappear until we're home. That's how it is at a certain age. We're forced to create a challenge for ourselves and meet it. It doesn't matter what it is.

Actually, Euphemia didn't have as hard a time living in Algren as might have been expected. Nobody in the Funk family had told anyone about Euphemia being Hosea's real mother, not even Minty with her big, flapping, eleven-year-old mouth. Even if one of her little brothers had paid attention to the whole brouhaha the night the truth was revealed and then, innocently, mentioned to one of their friends' mothers, "You know what, my sister Phemie is Hosie's real mom," the friend's mother would have said sweetly, "that's right, dear, she is, of course she is, now run along and play."

Euphemia's father had made arrangements for Euphemia to live in the house on First Street rent free. The owner of the house, in exchange, was given a few acres of land by Euphemia's father. Euphemia's father farmed the land but anything reaped from those acres was sold and the money given to the owner of the house.

Just about everybody in Algren, except Leander Hamm—but he didn't really give it much thought—was under the impression that Euphemia had taken it upon herself to raise this child, Hosea. She was an unmarried so-called mother of a mystery boy. She had committed no sin, of course, because the boy wasn't hers biologically, they thought. The people of Algren were moved by her generosity and her devotion to the boy. It was a simple story with a familiar heroine, one of their own. A mysterious man on a horse gives Euphemia Funk a newborn baby when she's outside using the biffy, and Euphemia, a trooper from the start, accepts her lot, smiles at her fate, and raises the boy. Not only does she raise the boy, she raises him to be the mayor of Algren and the man responsible for its claim to fame, a fame that overshadows that unfortunate cockroach story laid out in the encyclopedia, a fame that makes the Prime Minister and the entire nation take note, a fame that comes with being the smallest town in the country.

But at the beginning, when Hosea was a little boy, the townspeople had no idea he would become their mayor. All they knew was that Euphemia Funk, a girl with so much going for her, had sacrificed it all to raise a child alone. And, furthermore, she didn't seem to mind.

The local churches brought her meals two or three times a week, the wealthier folks in town brought her their ironing and had her do their Christmas baking and sew their curtains and babysit their kids when they went to the city for a night out. Euphemia was almost always paid extravagantly for these jobs and was always promised more work in the future. Euphemia's neighbours would shovel her walk and trim her hedges and clean her eavestrough and mow her lawn in the summertime. Tom's mom gave Hosea all of Tom's old clothes and some new ones, and baked Hosea's favourite meal, Pork Diablo, whenever he stayed for supper.

At first, when Euphemia's parents and brothers and sisters would come to visit, her father would stay outside in his truck, picking his teeth, taking apart some tool or another, or having a nap. He would set Euphemia and Hosea up with a house to live in and drive by at night from time to time just to see what he could see, but he would not go inside and pretend nothing had happened. He missed Hosea more than he thought he would, and a very small and non-verbal part of him admired Euphemia for her spunk and her amazing lie that wasn't really a lie. But he would not set foot in that house. After all, he could make a statement, too. Let Euphemia's mother and Minty and the boys traipse in like they were going to a Sunday school picnic and not the quarters of an unmarried mother and her bastard son, arms full of cookies and sweetmeat pies and strong coffee, table games and crokinole, good cheer and hugs and kisses. He would sit in his truck. Until one day Tom's mother who lived right across the street came by and poked her head into Mr. Funk's cab.

"Have you got an aversion to family gatherings, Mr. Funk? Or are you afraid someone will steal your truck if you leave it alone for a minute? You know, I could have my boy Thomas watch it for you, ha ha ha. Like New York City. You know, where you pay a little boy from the ghetto a nickel to make sure nobody nicks your automobile, or strips the hubcaps—"

"I was just going in," Mr. Funk growled. "Thank-you for your consideration."

From that day forward, Mr. Funk dutifully entered Euphemia's house along with his wife and the kids and set himself up in the dining room as the king of crokinole. He taught the kids, including Hosea and Tom, the combination shot, the straight-to-the-gonads shot, the right-between-the-eyes shot, and the triple lutz. It was the perfect appointment for him. He could avoid conversation and, at the same time, could release his frustration and self-righteous indignation each and every time he curled his middle finger to his thumb and let fire another crokinole rock.

Euphemia and Minty and Mrs. Funk drank coffee in the kitchen and talked and laughed and the words "oh well," "one more cup," "what's the rush" were always punctuated with the vicious crack of a crokinole piece from the next room.

Well, thought Hosea as he walked along kicking his piece of ice, she must have done more than handstands on kitchen chairs. He was just about home now and Lorna's face came pushing and shoving into his thoughts and the picture of Euphemia upside down churning her long thin legs in the air was gone. Hello, Lorna, I'm sorry, Hosea said to the image of her face in his mind. His piece of ice had made it and just before he went into his house he gave it one last kick up and over his little fence into his neighbour's yard.

"Hey, Hosea, didja hear?" He whirled around to face his other neighbour, Jeannie, who had appeared on her front steps from out of nowhere.

"What's that, Jeannie?"

"Veronica Epp," she said. "She's had her triplets."

"Oh?" said Hosea.

"That's right, three," said Jeannie. "And they're all okay. All boys. The last one had to be delivered C-section, you know, but he's okay, too. Can you imagine giving birth vaginally to not one but two babies, and then on top of all that having to be cut open to have the third?" Jeannie shook her head and stared at the ground.

"No. No, I can't," said Hosea.

"Who could?" muttered Jeannie, still staring at the ground and shaking her head. Hosea was about to say Well, can't be easy or something like that and go inside but Jeannie wasn't finished. "They were going to rush her to the city, but, you know, they didn't. No time."

"Ah," said Hosea. "Well."

"So Veronica says seeing as how she went to so much work to have these three babies, she should at least be able to name one of them. Makes sense to me, right, but you know Gord her husband always does the naming, he's that kind of a guy. And he likes names like Ed and Chuck and Dirk and Todd, you know, names that sound like farts. So Gord says, Well, maybe one of them. I heard all this from Rita, you know Rita from the labour pool, she works with Dory, Tom's wife?"

"Hmmmm," said Hosea.

"So he says, Well, maybe one of them, right? And she says, Then again, maybe I should name them all, seeing as I'm the one who says their names the most, like all day every day and I like to say names I like, if I'm going to say them over and over again, she says to Gord, right, according to Rita. And Gord says, No way, you can name one, the one with the slow start because he'll probably turn out to be a mama's boy, anyway. Okay, so this makes Veronica really mad, right, and she says What do you mean by that? And he says Well, you know, kids with lung problems, wheezing and clinging and skinny, the slow starter had some lung problems, the doctor says. But that's all taken care of, she says, and she's really mad, right, and tells Gord to leave the hospital."

"Right," said Hosea.

"In the meantime, she names all three of the boys, fills out the forms for vital stats and gives them to the nurse to mail to the city and get this, Hosea, their names are . . . are you ready?"

"Uh, yeah," said Hosea.

"Their names are, now let's see if I remember, their names are Finbar, you know after that saint of lost souls or whatever he is, Callemachus, after I don't know who, somebody Greek, and Indigo. Like the colour, you know, of jeans?"

Hosea was quiet for a moment. Jeannie was staring at him with her mouth open in one of those frozen poses of suspended laughter and shock where the one suspended waits for the other to twig and then they both collapse in hysterics. Hosea didn't understand this type of gesture, however, and said, "Um, is there more?" His hand moved to his chest and he managed to tug at his jacket with his Thinsulate gloves.

"No, Hosea, that's it. I thought it was funny. You know, Gord will freak when he hears their names, of course he'll probably illegally rename them or something or refuse to call them by name at all, but Rita told me—"

"Wait," said Hosea. "It is, you know? Now that I think of it, it's very funny. Very funny." Hosea tried to laugh. "Ih, ih.

Boy, thanks for telling me, Jeannie, that's rich, Finbar, Callesomething, and, uh . . . well, good-bye."

"Say," said Jeannie, "hold on, where'd you get that hat? Isn't that whatsisname's, the—"

Hosea let the door slam behind him.

Hosea hung up his jacket and laid his gloves and Leander's old hat on the bench in the hallway. He heard the fridge heave and shudder. The kitchen lights flickered for a second while the fridge sucked every available bit of energy in the house. Hosea looked inside his fridge. Half an onion, dry and curled at the edges, a tub of expired sour cream, and the leftovers of the last meal he had shared with Lorna. There's something wrong with my fridge, he thought. All this energy for a rotting onion and love's leftovers. The phone rang. Lorna, thought Hosea. He picked up the phone and said hello.

"Jeannie here," said Jeannie. "One more thing. Apparently the Epps aren't thrilled with Dr. François. They say Veronica should have been transferred to the city and they're just lucky all three boys survived. So, are you there?"

"Yes," said Hosea.

"So anyway, Rita told me they might sue and Dr. François is getting riled by the whole thing, because the point is, of course, that the boys are all okay. He says even if he had transferred her, the problems she was having would have occurred in the city, too, and the procedure would have been exactly the same. So . . . anyway."

"Okay, then, thanks," said Hosea.

"Hey, by the way," said Jeannie, "when do you find out about Baert's visit? Is he coming?"

"Yes," said Hosea, giving his middle finger to the receiver. "Well, maybe. I don't know at this point. Good-bye." And he hung up the phone. Well, he thought to himself. Hmmm . . . if Dr. François is getting riled he just might leave Algren. He's always hated it here, after all. That would be one less, let's see, that might work . . . and Hosea went through the numbers dance in his head. But how could the hospital function without a doctor? Well maybe it could, just until after the Prime Minister's visit, thought Hosea. Obviously he had work to do. Tomorrow he would have to drive out to Johnny Dranger's farm and tell him he was outside the town limits, again. He would call Lorna and beg her to forgive him for his stupid remarks and maybe he could even explain what it was he was trying to do. That he had a good reason for not asking her to move in with him, and that very soon, in the fall, after the Prime Minister's visit, it would all be different. And he'd have to ask Knute to do something about that black dog. And check into renovating that old feed mill, and painting the water tower. And he'd have to ask her if she'd heard from Max. Fair enough. He could relax. He poured himself a glass of wine and put on his new Emmylou Harris tape. He sat down on the couch and looked around his house. He looked at his tapered fingers and then touched the faint scar tissue on his right palm, but this time he didn't feel a thing. No tingling, no pain. He rubbed it harder and felt a small ping. Good. Hosea raised his glass and thought, To the babies, Indigo and whatever their names are. And he had a sip of the wine. He remembered his exercise bike, hidden behind the furnace. What was it that mattered most in a man's life? He just didn't know. And he didn't know how to find out and he didn't know if ever he did find out he would know what it was he was finding out. Hosea had another sip of wine from his glass. Now his hand was on his forehead. Okay, Hosea, he thought, time to pull your wagons in a circle, time to cut bait, time to, whatever, something, for Christ's sake, the tears were streaming down his face now as Emmylou's voice, pure and high, settled in around him, sweet as mother's milk.

seven

The TV in Tom and Dory's room droned on, accompanying Tom and Dory's prodigious snoring routine. Summer Feelin' creaked in her bed and sighed, dreaming of who knew what, and the moon outside was portentous. Knute opened her window for the first time that spring. The screens were still stored for the winter so she could stick her head right out into the darkness. Everything was wet and shiny. The snow fell like chunks of warm cake. She lay down on her narrow bed and fell asleep.

"Hey," Max whispered, "hey, Knute? Knutie? Are you there? It's me."

He had his head in her room, sticking through the open window like a bear trying to get his face into somebody's tent. But Knute couldn't see him in the dark, she could only hear him. Then she felt his hand kind of batting at her blanket down around her feet and he was saying quietly, "Oh God, I hope it's you, Knutie, and not Tom. Knute. Knute. I am an asshole, I know it. Talk to me, please? Knutie, my ribs are breaking on this windowsill, say something to me. C'mon, Knutie, just say hello or something, or fuck off, Max, whatever you feel like.

C'mon, Knutie. My ass is getting soaked out here, you know it's raining, Knute? Spring is here. I'm here. What are you, dead? Talk to me . . ."

Knute hadn't actually been conscious for most of that. She thought she was dreaming and she was finding the whole thing funny. Until he said, "Spring is here. I'm here," and it dawned on her and she was awake. And then she didn't know what to say. She lay perfectly still. "Hi," she said.

And he said quietly, "Hey, Knutie, how are you?"

"All right, yourself?"

"Well," he said, "I can't see you and I'm kinda stuck . . . Where is she?"

"In the next room."

"Really? In the next room?" was all Max said for a long time. And they listened to each other breathe for a minute or two.

"Why don't you come out here?" he said, and he batted at the blanket again. Knute sighed heavily.

"I guess she's sleeping?" whispered Max. Knute didn't know what to say. "Knute?" said Max. "Will you come out and talk to me?"

"Okay, hang on," said Knute. "It's raining?"

"Yeah," said Max.

"Okay, hang on."

And then there they were, outside in the rain, standing and staring at each other, not really knowing what to say or how to act. Smiling, then frowning, then smiling again, looking off into the distance, looking at each other, wiping rain off their faces. Finally, Max asked, "What's she like, Knutie?" and Knute started to cry, she couldn't help it, and he, the favourite fuckster from afar, just stood and from time to time put his hand out towards her without touching her.

Finally he put his arm around her shoulder and she said something like "Don't you fucking put your arm around me."

And he said, "Fine," and dropped it, lit a cigarette and stood there, looking off towards the neighbours'.

"Here," he said. He gave her his lit cigarette and then lit another one for himself. Then they kind of blurted out at the same time, Knute with "You're such a fuck-up," and him with "I know, I know." Then more staring off and smoking.

"Well, Knute, it's been really nice chatting with you."

"Fuck off."

"Hey."

"What."

"Knute?"

"What."

"You're gonna let me see her, aren't you?"

"Oh, well . . ." Knute said, and Max smiled. "Actually, no," Knute continued, "no I'm not, never, well, maybe in four years, you kept her waiting, now it's her turn to keep you waiting."

"Hey, good one. I could wait longer, you know, five, six, twenty-five years, it's up to you, I'll just wait. Starting now. Okay. I'm waiting. You just let me know, give me a sign. I'm here. I'm waiting." Max leaned up against the brick next to the front door and stood there, arms folded, looking down at his wet boots.

"Okay," said Knute, "you wait right here. I'm going in to call the cops."

"All right," said Max, and he tipped an imaginary hat. "Buenas noches." A few minutes later Knute came back outside.

"Well?" said Max.

"There aren't any cops in Algren."

"C'mon, Knutie, let me see her, just let me have one peek at her now and I'll leave you alone, you can talk to her and call me at my mom's when she's ready, couple of days, tomorrow, four years, whatever. C'mon, Knutie, please?"

What was Knute supposed to do? She wasn't Isak Dinesen armed and living alone in the savannah or wherever. Blow his head off and nobody would ever know. She wasn't a member of Shining Path. She wasn't Camille Paglia. She let him in and they tiptoed, in their huge combat boots, down the hall to Summer Feelin's room. Max kneeled at S.F.'s bed and stared at her for about ten minutes, like he was at a viewing in a funeral home. The reverent Max. Knute sat at the kitchen table praying Tom and Dory wouldn't wake up.

"I think you should go now," Knute whispered to Max after the ten minutes or so were up. He stood up then but he didn't leave. He swallowed. Knute didn't want to look at him because she thought he might be crying. She hoped he was. Then he said, "So you think . . . you know you think she's warm enough and . . ." He kept his eyes on S.F. and didn't look at Knute.

"Yeah," she said, "I think she'll live through the night." Max smiled.

Outside they shared another cigarette. "I quit for a while," he said.

"Yeah?" said Knute. "That's good." Then Max was grinning, then laughing. "What are you laughing at?" Knute asked.

"Summer Feeling," he said, and he was laughing and coughing, rain falling all over his face, "Oh excuse me, Feelin'. Fee-Lin. Oh God, Knute, you kill me," he said.

Knute sat in the living room and stared out the window for a while after he had left. The rain had stopped. She watched the moon move towards the other end of Algren, somewhere over Hosea Funk's house, probably, or it could have been the other side of the world for all she knew. "Summer Feelin'," she said a few times. "Summer Feelin', Summer Feelin'." Pretty stupid, she thought, shaking her head. She couldn't stop grinning.

All right, I'm up. I'm up. I'm up! I'll fight Tyson. I'll fight Ali, I'll fight, that's it, I'm fighting, thought Hosea. Cassius Clay. I could change my name, he thought. Hosea Ali. Mohammed Funk. Mo Funk. Hosea sighed. Lorna, he thought. Lorna Funk. Lorna Funk, Lorna Funk. He was alone. "Listen to me," he said out loud. The telephone rang. "I got it," said Hosea. The phone quit after one ring. Hosea sighed again. And got up to make some coffee.

First thing that morning, after exercising, he was off to see Johnny Dranger. He would just tell it like it was. Lay it on the table. Let Johnny know he was out again. I'm sorry, Johnny, he'd say. There's been yet another mix-up at the top. They say your farm is outside the town limits of Algren. Johnny wouldn't be happy about it, he knew. Johnny had one passion in life. Putting out fires. He had worked himself up to assistant chief of the Algren volunteer fire department, and was hankering after the number one position. It was his dream. But he couldn't be a volunteer—let alone fire chief—with the Algren fire department if he didn't live within the town limits. It was a provincial policy having to do with something called response time. A team of firefighters couldn't be waiting around for volunteers to commute from all over the place. They had to be in the town. Besides, thought Hosea, there were too many men living right in Algren and a couple of women, including Jeannie, Hosea's next-door neighbour, wanting to be put on the roster. I like to help out where I can, she'd told Hosea. Occasionally, there'd be a major house fire—once there was a tragedy involving some drunken teenagers—but mostly it was putting out burning outhouses, overheated cars, kitchen fires, and stubble fires. That was Johnny Dranger's specialty. He had it in for stubble burners. But, thought Hosea, the farmers around here don't start burning their stubble until harvest time, and by then he could be back in. I'll make it up to him, thought Hosea, I'll crown him fire chief of Algren after July first, and he'll be in charge just in time to get those darn stubble burners.

Hosea drove down First Street, turned onto Main Street, crossed over the tracks, and began driving down the service road that ran alongside the dike that surrounded Algren. The dike was supposed to protect Algren from the raging flood-waters of the Rat River. The Rat River, thought Hosea. My ancestors landed in Halifax, hopped on a train going west, then crept up the Rat River and settled in Algren, Manitoba. My mother's dead, my father is the Prime Minister of the country, I think, and I am the mayor of Canada's smallest town and the spurned lover of the bold and beautiful Lorna Garden.

Hosea peered around the countryside. Dirt everywhere and grey snow, dog shit, ugly cows, puffs of steam coming out of their snouts and their rear ends, the smell of wet hay, and the sky that brilliant blue, the colour of toilet bowl cleanser. Hosea heard a screech, a voice. "Hosea, stop, stop!" Mrs. Cherniski the café owner was running down her long driveway wearing what looked like Shaquille O'Neal's basketball shoes and waving a rake around her head. "Get him, Hosea, get that motherfucking dog away from my Pat, goddamn it if he . . . that's it, he's mounting her, Hosea, get him, get him . . ."

Hosea scrambled out of his car and stood there for a minute, straightening his hat, trying to figure out what was going on. "Stop him, Hosea, for Christ's sake!" Mrs. Cherniski had slowed down by now and had her hand on her chest. The last part of her command to Hosea seemed to be swallowed up by tears and rage. She threw her rake as far as she could, spluttering and moaning, "Stop him, oh God, please stop him," and then crumpled into a heap on her driveway.

Hosea stood, frozen to the spot. Was she dead? A heart attack? For a split second he thought of his plan. Wouldn't that be a stroke of luck, after all, if Mrs. Cherniski was dead? He glanced at the dogs and ran over to Mrs. Cherniski who, by this point, was sitting on the driveway cross-legged and catatonic, shaking her head and muttering, "Bill Quinn, his name is Bill Quinn."

"What's that, Mrs. Cherniski?" said Hosea. "Who's Bill Quinn?"

"The dog," said Mrs. Cherniski, "the dog screwing the living daylights outta my Pat right over there, that's who Bill Quinn is. He may not be the original Bill Quinn, he may be Bill Quinn the Second or even the Third, but, mark my words, Hosea Funk, that dog's got bad blood coursing through his veins. That dog's the devil's best friend, loyal to the end . . ." Mrs. Cherniski stared straight ahead and spoke in a monotone. "I should have known when I saw him hanging around my café, driving my customers away with his disgusting antics. I should have known he'd be after my Pat next."

"How do you know his name?" asked Hosea.

"I know," said Mrs. Cherniski. "I just know."

"But," said Hosea."I don't mean to upset you further, Mrs. Cherniski, but isn't it sort of a natural thing for dogs to do, especially now that spring is here?" Hosea couldn't help but steal another peek at the dogs. He turned back to look at Mrs. Cherniski but she was asleep or dead, not moving, anyway—laid out flat now on the wet driveway, basketball shoes pointing up to Polaris, up towards the brilliant blue sky.

Okay, what? thought Hosea. What do I do? "Mrs. Cherniski?" he said, without touching her. "Mrs. Cherniski?" Nothing. Not a peep. She can't be dead, thought Hosea. Just because of . . . of Bill Quinn? Hosea got up and began to run. He ran up the driveway and across the yard and into Mrs. Cherniski's house. The TV was on and the room smelled like vanilla. He found the phone in the hallway and called the hospital.

"Charlie Orson Memorial Hospital, how may I direct your call?"

"What?" said Hosea. Is this a joke? he thought.

"How may I help you? Hello? Hello?"

"It's Hosea Funk."

"Oh God, Hosea, not you again. Now what? Do you want to know what we're serving for lunch? Or maybe—"

"No, no, Dr. Bon—sorry, François—it's Mrs. Cherniski. You know, the woman who owns the Wagon Wheel."

"Yes? What about her?"

"She's lying in her driveway," said Hosea. "I don't know if she's dead or alive. She just collapsed. There's this dog and—"

"Wait. In her driveway?"

"Yes."

"At her house or at the Wagon Wheel?"

"House."

"Okay, I'll be right there. Go back to her and loosen her clothing and see if you can get her to talk to you. You could try doing artificial respiration. I'll be there in three minutes."

Five minutes later Dr. François and Nurse Barnes and Lawrence Hamm, who happened to be the volunteer driver, had Mrs. Cherniski strapped to a gurney and ready to be loaded into the back of the ambulance. The doctor had found her pulse but it was weak and her breathing was irregular and shallow. Thankfully, Hosea had thrown his hat into his car before Lawrence Hamm had driven up. Surely he would have recognized his dead father's hat and accused Hosea of stealing it right there on the spot. Hosea stood by the side of the road and waved as they drove back to town and then was happy that nobody had looked up at him to see him wave good-bye to an ambulance. "Yes," whispered Hosea under his breath, and then, "no, no."

What kind of a . . . Hosea thought. Well, say she died, say Mrs. Cherniski didn't make it, at least she'd be rid of that Bill Quinn character. But then again, he didn't want to wish death upon her, not really, that is. Maybe she won't die but she'll be incapable of looking after herself and she'll have to move in with her daughter in the city. Even if just until July first. By then she'll be fit as a fiddle and she'll be able to come back to Algren and work in the café. Hosea looked over at the dogs. Pat was snapping at some flying thing and Bill Quinn was lying in a puddle, asleep. Bill Quinn, thought Hosea. In a strange and stupid way he admired Bill Quinn.

This is ridiculous, he thought. Bill Quinn has got to go. And I have to get to Johnny Dranger's place and give him the news. Three babies and Max, if he gets here, that's four in; Leander dead and Johnny Dranger put outside town limits, that's two out. Two more out and we're even-steven. If Mrs. Cherniski dies, just one. And Bill Quinn doesn't count, thought Hosea. He tugged at his chest and gazed up at the sky. He'd stay on course. Things would fall into place. He'd see to it. "Prime Minister Baert," he rehearsed, "I'm your son, Hosea Funk, Euphemia's boy. Welcome to Algren, Canada's smallest town."

Bill Quinn, roused by Hosea's voice, lifted his head and stared at Hosea. One watery brown eye closed for a split second and then opened again. But Hosea missed it. He was a million miles away and it didn't matter how many dirty dogs winked at him from wet ditches. He wasn't kidding about his plan. It was on.

"Catch a falling star and put it in your pocket," Hosea sang as he drove up Johnny's driveway. He'd put his hat back on. "Save it for a rainy day." He looked up and noticed that the sky had changed. From the colour of toilet bowl cleanser to the colour of dust. Johnny will know what's up before I even open my mouth, thought Hosea. And it was true. Before Hosea could properly park the Impala in the tiny driveway, Johnny was out of the house and trotting towards him. "So!" he shouted at Hosea from about twenty yards away. "Don't tell me, I'm out. Or am I in? Was I out or am I out now? In or out? Out or in? What's it gonna be this time, Your Excellency?"

Hosea smiled and got out of his car. He was about to shake his head and say, "I'm sorry, John, there's been another mix-up at the top" when Johnny began to shake his head and clear his throat. "I'm sorry, John," said Johnny, "there's been another mix-up at the top." Hosea tried to speak again but Johnny spoke first. "I don't get it, Hosea, who's the Mickey Mouse at the top? And at the top of what? The idiot list? I feel like a Fisher-Price farmer with a Fisher-Price barn and animals. Some moron kid plops me onto the little tractor, stuffs me inside the barn, clicks it shut, and moves me to another municipality. Do I look like a little toy, Hosea? Look, look, I bend at the joints. I've got arms, for crying out loud, and a hat that comes off."

Speaking of hats that come off, thought Hosea, and removed his quickly and put it inside his car. He still hadn't figured out a way of explaining to people why he was wearing dead Leander Hamm's hat.

"No, I know you're not, John," said Hosea. "You're not a toy." Hosea didn't know what else to say. Johnny stood there glaring at him.

"But I'm out, right?" he said. "Out again, isn't that so, Hosea? Isn't that what you're trying to tell me?"

"It's just that this particular piece of land is, well, has always been, a real trouble spot. It goes back a long way, and the province is still trying to figure out just where it belongs." Hosea's hand went to his chest.

"That's bullshit, Hosea, and you know it. You just haven't got enough to do, that's the real problem."

"Enough to do?" said Hosea. "Enough to do?"

Just then it started to pour.

"Look, Hosea," said John, "why don't you come in for a cup of coffee and I'll tell you what's wrong with this country. Guess there's no way you could put me right *out* of the country, eh, Hosea? Why quit at the municipal level? I've always wanted to live in a hot place, Myanmar, say. Or Burma, or is that the same thing? Anyway, why don't you get your pooh-bah at the top to make a really big mistake and move me and my toy barn and silo and tractor and little horses and cows all the way over to Myanmar?" Hosea looked at Johnny. He noticed Johnny had a strange way of speaking. What should have been the last word of a sentence seemed to become the first word of the sentence after it. Like, I'll tell you what's wrong with this. Country guess there's no way you could—

"I'm just kidding, Hose. C'mon in. You're not allergic to cats, are you?"

"No. No, I'm not," said Hosea. I'm just kidding, Hose. C'mon. In you're not allergic to cats, are you? Hosea repeated in his mind. Maybe he was asthmatic. Maybe it was a breathing problem. Hosea was intrigued with the way that Johnny spoke. Why hadn't he noticed it before?

"Good. I've been having problems with those damn. Cockroaches ever since Yusef. Died Tiny's not a roach eater so. I'm trying cats."

By this time they were inside and Johnny had pointed to a kitchen chair. Hosea sat on it. Johnny went over to the counter to make some coffee.

"You mean the Algren cockroach?" Hosea asked.

"The one and only," said Johnny. "Are there. Others, I mean around here?"

"I don't know," said Hosea. His shoulders slumped and he felt depressed. "I guess there could be," he said.

"Yeah," said Johnny, "there could be."

"Johnny," said Hosea. "I know you want to be the fire chief. I'm sorry, I . . ."

John turned around. "Hosea," he said. "I'm a farmer and a widower since the age of. Nineteen I've learned not to rely on. Anything, not my cows, not my horses, not my dogs, not my crops, not the weather, not my health, not my friends, not you, not women, not love, not the fire chief. Job I've been in and out of this damn town so many times it's a. Joke I don't know what the problem is at the top, as you say, Hose, but, you know, I've stopped. Caring I think you must have some kind of a plan but what that plan is I cannot begin to imagine. Hosea, in, out, what difference does it make. Anymore, I'm here in the same. Place so I can't be the fire. Chief I'll keep putting out fires just the. Same it's what I have to do doesn't. Matter what anyone calls me, chief or. Johnny I'm gonna put out fires and if some government pantywaist tells me I can't, that won't matter to me. Either a man's gotta do what a man's gotta. Do do you understand what I'm talking about, Hosea?"

"Yes," said Hosea. "Yes, I do."

"Okay," said Johnny.

"I didn't know you were ever married, John," said Hosea.

"Well, I was."

"To who?"

"Whom, you mean. To Caroline Russo."

Hosea thought for a second. "Caroline Russo?" he said. "But she was the girl who died in that house fire years ago, wasn't she? She was our age?" And then Hosea stopped. "Oh, I'm sorry, Johnny. Caroline Russo? I had no idea. Nobody knew you two were married. I'm sorry, Johnny."

"Thanks, it's. Okay it was a long time ago."

Hosea and Johnny were quiet. Both men had sips of their coffee. Hosea remembered Caroline Russo. She was wild. She was very funny.

"We took the train to the city and got married at City Hall I," said Johnny. He smiled at some memory. "Guess we eloped."

"Oh," said Hosea. He smiled too. "She was a beautiful girl."

"Oh yeah," said Johnny. He smiled again. So did Hosea. "So I put out fires."

"Yeah," said Hosea. "Yup." They smiled at each other again. There was no reason to say anything more about it. It was a neighbour's stubble fire that started it. The fire just got out of control and spread. The kids in the house were drunk and didn't have a chance. Hosea knew that Caroline Russo was five months pregnant when she died in the fire. Everybody did. Well, everybody did after the coroner's report. Nobody knew before that. Except Johnny, I guess, thought Hosea. And Hosea knew that Johnny had been one of the lucky ones. He had gone outside to piss or puke, that detail wasn't ever really clear, and then had passed out in the yard behind the house. But nobody knew Caroline was pregnant with Johnny's baby. Nobody knew they had married.

"I wanted to tell. People but I didn't at the. Beginning and then it just sort of got too late to," said Johnny. "I'm sorry."

"You don't have to be sorry, Johnny," said Hosea.

"Well, I may not have to be sorry about it, Hose, but I am sorry about. It I'm as sorry as they come."

Hosea put his head into his hands. By moving Johnny out of the town limits he was destroying Johnny's chance at redemption. And for what? For his own personal gain. For a kid's dream of meeting his dad. Johnny never got to see his kid, never got to hold him in his arms and protect him from harm, never got to show him off and call him son and sweetheart. Hosea's head hurt. He would put Johnny back.

Somehow. And before July first. Maybe tomorrow. He knew Johnny would just laugh if he said, Oh, by the way you're back in. He'd have to do it soon, though. And he'd have to get Johnny the job of fire chief of Algren. He was the only man for the job. It was his destiny. And I, thought Hosea, am not God. He took a deep breath.

"So," said Johnny, "more coffee?"

"You were going to tell me what's wrong with this country," said Hosea.

"Right," said John. "Remember Yusef, my. Lab, the garbage eater?"

"Big, black . . ." said Hosea.

"Yeah," said John. "He died in the fall, sudden. Death from lead poisoning." He smiled.

"Lead poisoning?" said Hosea.

"I shot him," said John.

Hosea smiled and nodded. "Why?"

"Cancer of the. Throat I gave him two Big Macs, his favourite, put the rifle to his head and . . . Bam Yusef's. Gone didn't even know what hit. Him far as he knew he was eating a Big Mac with special sauce, box and everything." John shook his head and had a sip of his coffee. "He was a good dog, Yusef."

"Mmmmm," said Hosea. He had a sip of his coffee.

"So a couple of months before Yusef died I got Tiny, another black lab, as a. Replacement they became really good. Friends I hoped Tiny would kill cockroaches the way Yusef. Had but no. Dice Tiny's all right. Not like Yusef, mind you, but Tiny's got a head on his shoulders and his heart's in the right place."

Where had Yusef's head and heart been? thought Hosea. He had another sip and said, "Well, that's good."

"After Yusef died I buried him out. Back it was a hell of a job because the ground was beginning to freeze, but I got him in there and I said good-bye."

But what's wrong with this country? thought Hosea. "That's too bad," he said. His thoughts turned to Caroline Russo. He remembered her orange lunch box. She had called the colour eldorado nights or eldorado sunset or something like that.

"So about a week ago, when we had the first big thaw, I'm riding in the truck with Tiny and I smell something weird and I look over at him and he's got blood and hair hanging off his. Snout sure enough we get home, I go out back, and I see that Tiny's been digging at Yusef's grave and then I get closer and I see that he's actually dug him right up and I see that parts of Yusef have been eaten."

"He's been eating Yusef?" asked Hosea.

"Yeah! And then I thought back to the day I buried. Yusef had Tiny been hanging around? Watching I knew he was shook up about Yusef. Dying they were good friends there towards the end."

"But he ate him," said Hosea.

"Yeah," said Johnny, and he began to laugh. He sat there laughing and Hosea stared at him. Johnny began to laugh harder and finally Hosea got it. He grinned. He rubbed his hands on his thighs and began to laugh.

eight

Max and Knute had worked out a sort of arrangement. He looked after Summer Feelin' from quarter to ten in the morning 'til quarter after two in the afternoon. Those were the hours that Knute worked for Hosea. Although calling it work was a bit of an exaggeration. Mostly it just gave her a break from Tom and Dory and Summer Feelin'. Tom was having more chest pain lately and was feeling depressed. He had quit practising his juggling. He had quit going to the garage to read his veterinarian journals. Dory was worried about him but at the same time she was restless and annoyed. The wallpaper was coming down in sheets all over the house and she'd bought herself a new hammer. Summer Feelin' was giddy with excitement over Max's return and was doing a lot of shaking and flapping. Max and Knute hadn't really talked much about anything. They'd had coffee at the Wagon Wheel together but it was just like always. It was fun at first but then Knute would get a thought in her head and she'd start getting more and more pissed off. The more pissed off she got, the more he joked around. He joked and she glared. And then she got tired of being the sullen, injured one and she said, "Fuck this noise," and left. She really wanted to hurt him the same way he had hurt her, but she didn't know how to. The rest of the time, whenever Max and Knute were together, Summer Feelin' was with them and then, of course, everything was kind of strained. Summer Feelin' and Max adored each other and Knute hung around saying things like "Watch her head" or "She should eat lunch first." Tom and Dory were wondering if Max was going to give Knute regular child support money and they also wondered if Summer Feelin' was going to be safe over at Combine Jo's place with all her drinking and lumbering around. The one time Max had been in the same room as Tom, Tom had said, "So, Max, are you still . . . putting pen to paper? Still looking for someone to publish your . . . jottings?" And Dory had given Tom a look and said, "It's called poetry, Tom." And he had said, "Oh really," and walked away.

Once Max had asked Dory if all kids flapped as much as Summer Feelin' did and she had said, "Oh, well, that's just something she does."

He had said, "What do you mean that's just something she does? Shouldn't it be checked out or something? Has she seen a doctor about it? She looks like a hummingbird, man, she could lift off anytime." Then Dory had become irritated.

"Max," she said, "Knutie has been taking very good care of Summer Feelin' with no help from you. Of course she's been checked out. She's fine. And nobody appreciates you, of all people, second-guessing Knute's efforts." She paused and then she said, "You can just keep your mouth shut, Buster."

Max and Knute looked at her. Buster? Knute thought to herself, Dory's mad.

"Really, Knute, he has no right to come in here and question your ability to parent, I mean . . ."

And Knute had said, "I know, I know."

And Max had said, "Sorry, Dory, you're right. It was just all that fluttering and flapping, you know, I was expecting a back door to open up on her and a battalion of soldiers to jump out with flak jackets and camouflage, with somebody giving her hand signals for lift-off—"

"Oh shut up," Dory had said and then, "Excuse me," as she stalked out of the room with her hammer and a pail of plaster.

Just then Summer Feelin' came running into the room. Max said, "Hey, Summer Feelin', it's a beautiful day for collecting bottles. Get your rubber boots on and we'll hit the ditches around the dike. They're full of 'em." This idea got Summer Feelin' flapping and Max started beating his chest to make helicopter noises and saying things like "incoming," "over," "prepare troops for landing," "all clear." Knute looked at Max. At his mouth and his hands, his boots, his narrow hips.

Knute said good-bye to no one in particular and left for work. There was a lot to do. Hosea said he wanted to concentrate on painting the water tower. "Red, with a white horse running right around it," he said. And something about turning the old feed mill into a theatre for young people. Neither of these ideas seemed feasible to Knute. Maybe a red water tower, okay, but how would they get a huge white horse painted on the top of it? "Why a horse?" she'd said. "Why not just the name Algren?"

"No," Hosea said, "it should be a horse, a white horse." She told him that if they painted a horse right around the top of it, it would look like the horse was chasing its butt, like a dog with worms. Then she mentioned that even though the feed mill might make a great theatre, the youth of Algren seemed more interested in playing pool at Norm's and going to the city whenever they got the chance. Maybe Hosea could turn the feed mill into an arcade, or a shooting range, but a theatre? Summer stock? In Algren? "Well, then," Hosea said, "see what you can do about getting rid of that black dog." This she could handle, she thought. No problem. She could find some farmer outside town, maybe in Whithers, who would want a dog, or she'd just take it into the city, to the Humane Society, and let them find a home for it.

"By the way," Hosea said, "his name's Bill Quinn."

"Bill Quinn?" said Knute. "You mean, he has a first and a last name? Bill Quinn? If he has a name, doesn't he have an owner?"

"Nope," Hosea said. "No, he doesn't. He's his own dog."

"Oh, Bill's a lone wolf, eh?"

"Yes, he is," said Hosea.

Knute was about to say, "Friend of yours?" But Hosea wasn't finished.

"Knute?" he'd said, just before walking out the door, "Please don't let him get hurt. Just get him out of town in one piece."

Knute said she'd do what she could and then sat for a minute and looked out the window on to Main Street. She saw Combine Jo sitting cross-legged on the hood of her car and looking at a magazine. She was wearing a fishing hat with hooks in it. God, she thought, that woman is S.F.'s grandmother. Knute looked the other way down Main Street and there were Marilyn and Josh! She opened the window and stuck her head out. "Marilyn! Hello!" she yelled. "What are you doing here?" Before she could answer Combine Jo yelled up at Knute.

"Hey, Knutie! I'm looking at my Canadian Tire book here, and kids' bikes are cheap! Do you think Summer Feelin' would want one? Does she ride a two-wheeler yet, or a trike? Max could teach her how to ride a two-wheeler, or we could get a two-wheeler and put the, what do you call 'em, training wheels on it. What do you think? Why don't you come down here and have a look! There is one in here with a very sharp racing stripe, and it's purple, did you know purple is S.F.'s favourite colour? And a basket would be nice, too, don't you think?"

Combine Jo pushed her fishing hat back on her head and peered up at Knute's window. She pointed to her catalogue and yelled, "It's all in here, in here!" Marilyn and Josh, by this time, were standing beside Jo's car, looking at her and up at Knute and back at Jo, and Marilyn was grinning.

"Hello," said Combine Jo.

"Marilyn!" Knute yelled from the window. "This is Jo, Max's mom, and Jo, this is Marilyn, my friend, and her son, Josh." Knute felt like throwing herself out the window onto the pavement below.

"Is he here?" asked Marilyn.

"Is who here?" Knute yelled.

"Max!" she said.

"Yes, he is," said Jo. "He's got S.F. at home with him right now, or they're somewhere around, who knows, he looks after S.F. while Knutie works for the mayor."

"Well," said Marilyn. "There have been developments." She and Knute looked at each other and smiled. Combine Jo went back to her catalogue.

"Jo," said Knute, "go ahead and get her a bike, with training wheels if you want. And, uh, thanks."

"Hear that?" said Jo to Marilyn. "That's the sound of ice breaking. Have a good time, you two," Jo said to Marilyn. "Knutie needs a friend, you know. We all do from time to time."

"That's true," said Marilyn, smiling, and disappeared into the building.

"Hey!" Jo yelled up to the window. "Knutie! Why don't you bring your friend's kid over to my house and Max can look after both of 'em? It would be good for S.F. to have a playmate for a change and then you two gals can have a real good talk, maybe a drink, Hosea wouldn't mind if you called it a day. Tell him I told you to punch out."

Knute felt like saying to Jo, "Would you shut the fuck up, please?" But instead she said, "Yeah maybe, maybe," and slammed the window shut.

Marilyn and Josh came into the office. Marilyn and Knute, both laughing by then, gave each other a big hug. "How's it going, buddy?" said Knute to Josh.

"Fine," he said. "Can I play with Summer Feelin'?"

Marilyn and Knute looked at each other. "Why didn't you tell me he was here?" Marilyn asked. "I can't believe you didn't tell me."

"I don't know," said Knute. "Because I know you would have told me to ignore him totally, or kill him, or have mad passionate et cetera, et cetera [Josh was in the room] with him, and none of those things has happened. It's all been just, you know, ordinary, really. I thought I'd be letting you down."

"Ordinary?" said Marilyn. "Well, that is too bad. But you could have told me, anyway. I need to know these things. We're best friends! You should have told me."

"I know, I know," Knute said.

"So that's Combine Jo, eh?" said Marilyn.

"Yeah." Knute rolled her eyes.

"She's cool," said Marilyn.

"Cool? Combine Jo? You gotta be kidding. She's nuts."

"Well," said Marilyn, "she wants to buy S.F. a bike, that's cool. She's nice."

"God, Marilyn, you have no idea. She's a drunk. She's crazy."

"Well," said Marilyn. "I would be, too, if I was Max's mom and if I lived in this weird town and everybody was pissed off at me for something I did a hundred years ago."

"I'm not pissed off at her for what she did way back then, I'm pissed off at her for telling Max to leave me when I was pregnant," said Knute.

"Well," said Marilyn. "I hate to tell you this, beautiful dreamer, but she didn't put a gun to his head."

"Oh, don't be so sure," Knute said. "Anyway, you're here.

Why didn't you tell me you were coming? I need to know these things. We're best friends."

Marilyn smiled. "I didn't know we were coming. Josh and I were walking around downtown 'cause it's nice out and there was the bus station, and there was my cheque in my pocket, and there was the bus to Algren, and there you go. Here we are."

"Here we are," said Knute, smiling.

"When can I play with Summer Feelin'?" Josh asked. Knute looked over at Marilyn.

"Do you want to bring him over to Max's?"

"Sure, what the heck. I'm dying to meet him, actually. Has he changed?"

"No."

"Too bad."

"I guess."

"You're still hot for him, I can tell. Aren't you, Knute?"

Before Knute could say anything, Marilyn said, "What about this guy, this mayor dude, is he cute?"

"Cute?" Knute said. "He's old."

"So?"

"I don't think he's cute. Well, maybe. Naah. And he's got some kind of a girlfriend, her last name's Garden."

"Garden?" said Marilyn. "Weird name. Garden of Eden, forbidden fruit. What's his name? Hosea? Strange biblical setup if you ask me. Can I meet him?"

"Maybe, he's all over the place, usually. I don't know what he does most of the time."

"He could be dealing drugs," said Marilyn.

"I doubt it."

"Oh yeah," said Marilyn, "drugs to farmers. They're a very stressed-out bunch of people."

"He wants me to get rid of a dog, actually. Bill Quinn. Do you want to help me?"

"Excuse me?"

"Bill Quinn's gotta go."

"The dog?"

"Yeah."

"Sure, I'll help. How old exactly is he, Knute? Eighty, ninety?"

"Bill Quinn?"

"Hosea."

"No, no, around fifty, I think."

"Oh, pfft," said Marilyn. "That's nothing."

Knute and Marilyn liked Combine Jo's idea about the talk and the drink. While Knute was leaving a note for Hosea telling him her friend was in town and they were off to see what they could do about Bill Quinn, Marilyn opened one of his drawers and pulled out an old orange Hilroy scribbler. "Look at this. Remember these?" she said.

"Marilyn!" said Knute. "Don't go snooping around in his drawers. Put that thing back."

"Wow," said Marilyn. "Hosea's really on the cutting edge, isn't he? He doesn't even have an electric typewriter."

"Let's go," said Knute. "C'mon, Josh. S.F. will be very happy to see you." And they left.

"Bye-bye!" said Combine Jo. "You girls enjoy yourselves. And don't worry about your boy there, he'll be fine with Max. Hell, I might go home myself in a while, see if my goddamn bike's in one piece. First I'll order this little purple one for S.F. and then she and I could go bike riding together around the dike or around town, somewhere. Wouldn't that be a hoot?"

Oh wonderful, thought Knute, cycling on a steep embankment with a crazy old drunk woman. Great. "Okay, Jo, just make sure it has training wheels on it. It needs training wheels."

"Righto!" said Jo. She ripped out the page from the catalogue and smiled. "Have a good time, ladies," she said, and waved them away.

"Did you see her looking at us?" said Marilyn.

"What do you mean?"

"The way she was looking at us. Wistfully like. I bet she'd like to join us for a drink. Does she have any friends, Knute, or what?"

"Oh, I don't know. Probably. Somewhere."

They walked along Main Street towards the dike road and the hatchery and Max's place. They took turns giving Josh a piggyback ride.

"You know, it really smells bad in this town," said Marilyn.

"Well, it's spring," said Knute, "that's all the fertilizer thawing, you know, shit on the fields."

"Oh. Real shit?"

"Yeah. Well, not human shit—animal."

"But real shit, not processed or packaged or anything?"

"Right. Raw animal shit. It might be liquidized or something, I don't know. Because they spray it on. You know, like hose it on."

"For fertilizer, eh?"

"Yup. It's the best thing. Crops, crops, crops. This high."

"Wow. But what about afterwards? You know, when we eat them, the crops. Fecal residue."

"We can't tell."

"Really? We're eating animal shit and we don't know it?"

"Well, we know it, I guess, we just don't think about it."

"But that doesn't make sense. It shouldn't stink now. There should be no fertilizer on the fields now because it would have been cut down with the crops, you know, reaped, in the fall. Wouldn't the farmers wait until spring has really sprung to put fresh shit on the fields? Like just before they plant or sow or whatever it's called?"

"Seed," said Knute. "And it's not reaped, it's harvested."

"Seed, yeah," said Marilyn.

"I don't know when they do it," said Knute.

"Well, spring, obviously, Knute, that's when crops are planted. That's when they need to be fertilized."

"I don't know, they could be perennials. Maybe they just come up at the same time every year. Like tulips."

"I don't think so," said Marilyn.

"I don't know," said Knute.

Over at Combine Jo's, Marilyn wandered around the house saying, "Holy moly, three bathrooms!" and "She lives here all alone?" and things like that. Max kissed her on both cheeks when Knute introduced them and said, "Pleased to meet you, Marilyn, Joshua, S.F.'s been telling me all about you."

"Joshua's allergic to dairy products," she finally managed to say. Knute told Max that Joshua was there to play with S.F. and she and Marilyn were going out. They'd be back around three. Max gave them a bottle of fine wine from Combine Jo's stash and half a pack of cigarettes, and suggested they go out to Johnny Dranger's rotting pile of hay bales, sit on top of it, and get hammered. They'd be able to see for miles and miles, he said. It was covered with orange plastic and sagging in the middle so if they got cold, he added, they could just hunker down in the centre and be protected from the wind.

Good idea, thought Knute, but how the hell did he know about Johnny Dranger's pile of hay?

"I go there to write," he said, grinning. Knute and Marilyn left and as soon as they were out of the house they looked at each other and said, "Yeah, right." Then Marilyn started laughing and telling Knute that Max was foxy, shorter than she had expected, nice eyes, all the stuff Knute already knew. Write, my ass, she thought. "Hang on," she said to Marilyn. She went back to the house and a few minutes later came back with another bottle—Jack Daniel's—and Marilyn said, "What about that dog? Bill Whatshisname, how're we gonna get rid of a dog from on top of a pile of hay?"

"Screw Bill Quinn," Knute said. "Let's go."

nine

Hosea Funk had spent the past few days cleaning out his house, getting rid of all the old sad things of Euphemia's, her Noxema, her Dippity-Do, her alum powder for canker sores, her old winter boots, the half-finished bags of scotch mints, and all her old clothes. He fixed his fridge and cleaned out the grout from behind the taps on the bathroom and kitchen sinks. He had planned to remove all of Euphemia's *Reader's Digest* condensed books from the small pantry in the basement. That's when he found out someone in his house had been drinking rye whiskey, and lots of it. Boxes and boxes of empty bottles had been stored, or hidden, behind the boxes of *Reader's Digests.*

Hosea had sat down on the cold cement floor. His eyes followed a crack that led to the drain hole. He remembered Tom telling him not to pee in it because he'd heard of some guy in Chicago or somewhere who had peed in his drain hole and had hit some electrical current that had travelled up the length of his stream of urine and then zap, his penis had been electrocuted and had turned black and shrivelled up right then and there. He must have been bullshitting me, thought Hosea. He sat there and no other thoughts came to mind other than the one he had been fighting off for the last minute or two.

She was drunk when she told me the Prime Minister was my father.

No, he thought, she couldn't have been. She was on her deathbed. She couldn't walk to the pantry in the basement to get a bottle, let alone lift her head to drink from it. "Her heart simply gave out on her, Hosea," the doctor had said after she died. Her heart or her liver? She wasn't very old. Had anybody known? Had the doctor known? Why was she drinking herself to death?

He had stared at the bottles for half an hour. He had never seen her drink, never seen her drunk. Had he just not known? She had always seemed content and in control. Did she drink only at night while he slept? During the day while he was at school? Is that what she did all day? Is that why she laughed and shrugged her shoulders at just about everything? Is that why she bought so many bags of scotch mints? Is that why she did handstands on the kitchen chairs?

Oh, Lord, it doesn't matter, Hosea told himself, and smiled. He thought about tempting fate and pissing in the drain hole. Who can blame her, after all? he thought. She was alone.

Is there something bad 'bout a lady drinking all alone in a room? A letter in your handwriting . . . hmmmm, he couldn't remember what the next words were.

Rye whiskey, thought Hosea. Had he picked fresh roses from Euphemia's garden that day after school for somebody who had never been there? Rye whiskey roses for a rye whiskey man. Well, thought Hosea, I'm real, anyway. "Mother," he said out loud, "was your life unbearable?" A letter in your handwriting and the scent of your perfume, I'm sorry, darling, so sorry, darling, I just assumed . . . is that how it went? Hosea hummed a little out of tune. "I'm sorry," he whispered. "I am."

He would tell Lorna about his plan. He would tell her she could move in with him after July first and do whatever she wanted with him and the house. Or maybe he wouldn't tell her about his plan, she might think he was crazy. He would tell her something else. Something that would make the July first date seem somehow prescient, significant, romantic, and well, just right.

On that same day that he had been cleaning, Hosea had found out from Jeannie that Tom was not doing well. Nor, for that matter, was Dory. Jeannie had said both were depressed and miserable and trying to fool themselves for the sake of their daughter and granddaughter. There was more but Hosea had suddenly feigned back pain and staggered into his house explaining to Jeannie that he needed some Tylenol and an ice pack.

Hosea sat in his clean house and wondered about his old buddy Tom. Expansive, humble, tolerant Tom. Feeling bad. And worse, depressed. Well, thought Hosea. He needs a friend and that friend is me.

Hosea looked outside and noticed Euphemia's rose bush blooming for the first time that spring. A dozen roses in a bottle of rye whiskey, thought Hosea. That would cheer him up. Hosea put on his windbreaker and Leander's hat and went outside and picked some roses and stuffed them inside one of Euphemia's empty whiskey bottles.

"Hosea! Roses! C'mon in!" Dory opened the door and took the bottle of roses. "Thank-you," she said. "That's very sweet of you, Hose." Hosea thought she looked like she'd been crying.

"Well, you're welcome," he said. "You know, I looked out the window and there they were. They're for Tom, too."

"Of course," said Dory, "of course they are." Had she sighed just then? wondered Hosea. "He's in the bedroom, Hose, if you want to say hello. He's not feeling well enough to get out of bed. Just walk in. Here, bring him these." She handed him the bottle of roses and said, "I'm leaving for a while. You keep him company. He's had his pills, he won't eat, and I'll be back in half an hour. Good-bye." She smiled. "If he wakes up and wonders where I am," she said, "tell him I'll be back in half an hour. He likes to know."

Hosea sat on top of Tom and Dory's laundry hamper and stared at Tom. He was sleeping. God, thought Hosea, he looks grey. What's wrong with him?

He did look grey. He looked like Euphemia did weeks before she died. Oh no, thought Hosea. He put the roses on the bedside table, next to several jars of pills, a glass of water, Tom's reading glasses, and a *Maclean's* magazine.

"Tom?" whispered Hosea. Nothing. "Tom?" he whispered louder. He picked up the whiskey bottle with the roses and held it to Tom's open mouth. He couldn't see any condensation on the bottle. Very gently, Hosea put his fingers on Tom's chest. For a second or two he couldn't feel anything moving. He panicked. But then he felt a little something. Tom was breathing. It was okay. Hosea glanced over at the magazine. He picked it up and turned it over to look at the front cover. There was the Prime Minister! It was a fuzzy shot of John Baert on top of a mountain, wearing skis, and kissing a woman who was not his wife. "More than a friend? PM says absolutely not," said the caption. At his age, thought Hosea. Could there be more children of his out there? Are we a little club? A big club? Hosea thought of the PM's beautiful wife at home in Ottawa. How would she feel about this photograph? Did she care? Was she willing to put up with a bit of hanky-panky just to be the PM's wife? Was she sad? Angry? Was she heartbroken? Had Euphemia been heartbroken? Perhaps he should send the Prime Minister's Office a bill for the cost of thousands of bottles of rye whiskey. Her heart simply gave out on her, the doctor had said. Is being kissed and stroked, impregnated and left, by this man

John Baert, a recipe for sorrow? Had he that much charisma, power, and sway? Could a man who broke women's hearts, led the country, inspired thousands, drank martinis with world leaders, and skied at the age of seventy really be my father? thought Hosea. Can the mind work when the heart is broken? Had Euphemia been telling the truth?

"Hosea," said Tom. "Hi." Hosea dropped the magazine and cleared his throat.

"Tom," he said. "Hi. How's it going?" He smiled at his old friend and Tom smiled back.

"Not so good. Did you bring those flowers?"

"Yup. They're roses. First batch this spring."

"They're beautiful, Hosea. Thank-you."

"You're welcome."

"Did you polish off that whiskey to make a vase?" Tom smiled.

"No, no," said Hosea. He tugged on the front of his windbreaker. "No."

Tom smiled. "I'm just kidding, Hosea," he said.

Hosea grinned. "Dory will be back in half an hour," he said.

"That's good."

"So . . ." said Hosea.

Tom smiled. His eyes were red and his hair was greasy. He needed to shave.

"It's quite nice outside these days," said Hosea. "Spring is here to stay, I'm quite sure."

Hosea remembered the two of them singing in school and getting sent home early. It was how they avoided the big boys.

Tom lay there, staring at the window.

"Knute's doing a terrific job. She's uh . . . a good worker."

Tom looked at Hosea and nodded his head.

"Say, Tom," said Hosea. "Would you mind if I borrowed your *Maclean's* for a day or two?"

"Just take it, Hose," said Tom. "Keep it."

Then the two men sat and lay in silence. Hosea shifted the roses around once or twice. He smoothed his trousers. He smiled at Tom and Tom smiled back. Then Tom fell asleep again. Hosea sat there for a minute or two, staring first at Tom and then at the picture of the Prime Minister. He wanted to hug Tom or at least talk about the old days. He would have liked to tell Tom about Lorna. He wondered how Tom talked to Dory. How he touched her, how he laughed with Knute and played with Summer Feelin'. He wondered how Tom did all that. He touched Tom's shoulder and whispered "good-bye" and tiptoed out of the room.

Back at his office Hosea pulled out his orange Hilroy scribbler from his drawer and entered Tom's name in the Dying and Potentially Dead column. Tom's voice in his head saying, Somebody die? And Hosea looking around saying, No, why? 'Cause, said Tom, your flag's flying at half mast. That was more than forty years ago but Hosea still looked down at his zipper every time he thought about it.

He pulled his chair up to the window and stared outside until all the shops on Main Street were closed and the kids hanging around Norm's had gone home and the sky was the colour of fresh liquid manure.

"Okay," said Hosea the next morning. "Okay. Places to go, people to see. Lorna can go to hell. No, I don't mean that, I take it back," he said.

One time he had said "places to go, people to see" to Lorna and she had said, "Don't ever say that to me again. I hate things like that."

"Me too!" he'd said. But hadn't meant it. He liked them, actually. Maybe later in the day he'd call Lorna and say, Hey, sweetheart, how about reconsidering me? You're a moron, she'd say. I know, I know, what's up, Lorna? he'd say. And she'd say, I don't know, stuff, and slowly they'd get back on track the way they always did.

He had to find out how Mrs. Cherniski was, see if it was true that Dr. François was thinking about leaving town, confirm that Max was back in town, and find out if Knute had done anything about that darn dog, Bill Quinn. Oh, and he had to put Johnny Dranger back in town limits so he could be crowned fire chief of Algren. Fair enough, thought Hosea.

Hosea straightened the framed picture of Lorna he had sitting on his couch, and then kissed it lightly. Soon, he thought, I'll carry you over the threshold. We'll ride off into the sunset, you and me. "I want to grow old with you, Lorna Garden," he said out loud. "Will you marry me?" Or, he thought, would she prefer, Marry me! It was hard to know. Hosea wondered how Tom had asked Dory to marry him. Or had Dory asked Tom? Or had they mutually, silently agreed to marry at precisely the same moment, opened their mouths, out of the blue, and said, "Yes!" in unison, knowing exactly what the other was saying yes to and falling into each other's arms, laughing, knowing, happy.

Probably, thought Hosea. Very likely.

He went out to his car and had a look at the tires. Years ago he'd attended a convention of mayors and town reeves in Sudbury, Ontario, and one of the conventioneers had warned him that hostile townspeople do things to their mayors like slash their tires and throw eggs at their houses. Since then he checked his tires every time he drove. Each time he found them intact and full of air, Hosea congratulated himself on the fine job he was doing keeping everybody in Algren happy—at least happy enough not to slash his tires. He took off his hat and put it on top of the car so he could bend down and have a real good look, from every angle, without his hat falling off his head and onto the dusty driveway.

Hosea was on his way to the hospital when he saw Max driving down Main Street with his little girl. What was her name? Summer Time? Summer Feelin', that was it. He and Max were stopped side by side at Algren's only traffic light. "Hello there," said Hosea through his open window. Max was wearing dark sunglasses and singing, and banging on the dashboard from time to time. Hosea thought he might also be pretending to play a guitar. An imaginary electric guitar hanging down low, on his hips. His fingers were moving very quickly and his left hand slid wildly up and down the neck of the imaginary guitar. His right hand yanked at imaginary strings like somebody trying to start a lawn mower.

Summer Feelin' was laughing and waving her hands around like a symphony conductor, but she noticed Hosea and smiled.

"Your dad likes to rock," said Hosea, smiling back at S.F.

"It's my grandma's car," said S.F. in response.

Hosea knew that but he said, "Oh, I see," and smiled again. Max's song was over and he looked at Hosea.

"Hey, hi," he said. "How are you?" Hosea nodded and smiled.

"Pretty good," Hosea said. "Welcome back to Algren."

"Thanks," said Max, grinning. "Taking your hat for a ride?" Hosea smiled and wondered what Max meant. The light had turned green and Hosea was moving ahead, slowly, through the intersection. He didn't hear Max yell, "Hey, your hat's on top of the car!" As he drove down Main Street, Hosea looked right into the sun and breathed deeply.

He turned his own tape deck up loud and sang along with Emmylou. He got to the chorus and said "Guitar" along with Emmylou to her band mate.

Hosea parked his car in the hospital parking lot and glanced at himself in the rearview mirror. Where was his hat? Damn, he thought, and Lorna says I look good in it. He got out of the car and began to laugh. "I am such an idiot," he muttered. He grabbed the hat from the top of the car and put it on his head. So, he thought to himself, I drive down Main Street singing and crying, with a hat on top of my car. He scratched his forehead and shook his leg a bit to realign his parts. "I could be senile," he said out loud.

Hosea walked through the front doors of the hospital. There was nobody around. He walked over to the front desk and peered at the posted list of patients. He was looking for the name Cherniski.

"Hello, Hosea, making your rounds?"

"Oh, oh, hello, Dr. Bonsoir." Hosea tugged viciously at his windbreaker and then stopped abruptly and stroked the brim of his hat. "How are you?" he said.

"Fine. Just fine. Call me Dr. Trèsbien, Hosea. How are you? How's the chest pain?"

"Oh, it's gone. It was nothing. Something I ate."

"Hmmm. So, Hosea, mind if I ask you a question?"

"Go ahead, shoot. What's on your mind?" Hosea coughed.

"What were you doing at the Cherniski residence the day she had her heart attack?"

"Me? Well, I was helping to rescue her dog."

"Yes, but how did you know her dog was in trouble? How is it that you just showed up at that exact moment when her dog needed rescuing?"

"Well, I don't know. Chance, I suppose. Coincidence? I was on my way to Johnny Dranger's."

"I see. Is he a friend of yours?"

"In a way. Yes."

"Hmmm . . ." said Dr. François.

"How is she?" said Hosea.

"Hard to say at this point."

Hosea told himself not to ask another single question. Why was the doctor acting this way? He stared hard at his shoes and tried to stop himself from opening his mouth. He put his hands in his pockets and felt the hard edge of his hips. He looked up and saw the doctor glance at his watch and then at something behind the desk.

"Do you think she'll make it?" he blurted out and cursed himself inside. The doctor stared at Hosea. He opened his mouth and closed it. He smiled.

"What would you say if I told you I was thinking of leaving Algren?" said the doctor. He began to pace back and forth, his hands behind his back.

"Leaving Algren," said Hosea. "But why?"

"For a better paying job in the States."

"The States! Why would you want to go to the States?"

"More money, like I said. And other reasons. Genvieve won't leave Montreal to live in a place like this."

"But what about us? We need you!"

"Well, don't worry, Hosea. I won't leave until you have another doctor. You organize a hiring committee, put an ad in papers across the country, and see how it goes. I'm sorry, Hosea, I need to live in a bigger place. I need to move on."

"It's because of the Epps, isn't it?"

"What about them?"

"Talking about suing you over the baby with the breathing problem."

"No, no, Hosea. That was unavoidable. Any doctor has to be prepared for potential lawsuits and disgruntled patients. That's not the problem. I'm a young man! I need a change! I want to practise in a large hospital and experience as much as I can. That's all."

Dr. François looked at Hosea. Hosea didn't know what to say. He needed to get rid of a few more people, but if the doctor left he'd have to replace him. He couldn't expect the Charlie Orson Memorial Hospital to function without a doctor. At least not for any length of time. Could he get away with not hiring a doctor just for, say, a month or two? Until after July first? The doctor put his hand on Hosea's shoulder. "Don't worry so much, Hosea. You'll kill yourself with worry."

"I hope you change your mind," said Hosea quietly.

"Well," said the doctor, "we'll see." He paused. "Hosea," he said, "I'll keep you posted on Mrs. Cherniski's condition." The doctor removed his hand from Hosea's shoulder and cocked his head. "Okay?" he said. Before Hosea could respond, three men came bursting through the front doors of the hospital. Two of them were helping Johnny Dranger walk and yelling at the doctor.

"He's not breathing hardly at all, Doc!" said one. "You gotta do something quick!"

The doctor was calm. He helped the men lay Johnny down on a stretcher in the hallway. By now Nurse Barnes had showed up and was already administering oxygen to Johnny.

"What happened to his inhaler?" the doctor asked the men. They all shrugged.

"We don't know," said one of them.

"Was he putting out fires again?" asked the doctor.

"Looks like," said one of the men. "He told us he'd just come from Whithers, some house fire he was helping on, his face was all full of ash and grit. He ordered a coffee, over at the Wagon Wheel, then started in on his coughing fit. Knocked his cup right off the table, and the gal over there, filling in for Cherniski, started yelling at him to get a grip. He started turning blue and he tried to talk but nothing came out, so the boys here and I stuck him in the back of the truck and brought him here. He's looking better, I can see."

Hosea stood beside Johnny, looking down at him and smiling. Johnny still couldn't talk but his colour was coming back and his breathing had settled down. "I'm putting you back in, John," whispered Hosea. Johnny blinked up at Hosea.

"Excuse me, Hosea," said the doctor. "I'll have to ask you to stand back a bit. He'll be fine in a while. He'll be out of here in an hour or two. Until the next time." The doctor was muttering, "An asthmatic firefighter, I don't understand . . ."

Hosea turned and walked towards the door. "Hey, Hosea," said one of the men. "Isn't that Leander Hamm's hat you got on? He gave it to you?" Hosea froze on the spot but the man went on. "Looks pretty good on you, Hosea, looks sharp. Doesn't it, Mel?" he said to the other man.

"Sure does," said Mel. "That's a bronc-bustin' hat you got there, Hosea, you know that? You could be a cowboy if you got yourself a horse."

Hosea smiled and said, "Well, maybe some day." But the men weren't listening. They were already making plans to get back to the Wagon Wheel and finish off their coffees, maybe find out more about the new gal taking over for Cherniski.

Hosea got into his car and backed out of his spot. He drove slowly down Main Street, nodding at the few people strolling along the sidewalk. Suddenly a dog stepped off the curb and sauntered across the street. Hosea slammed on his brakes and swore out loud. That damn Knute! She was supposed to get rid of that dog! Immediately Hosea felt bad about his outburst. He rolled down his window. "Uh, Bill Quinn?" he said. "Get off the road! Shoo! C'mon now, get going!" Bill Quinn turned his head to look at Hosea and then stopped in his tracks in the middle of the road. "C'mon now," said Hosea. "I said shoo."

Bill Quinn walked over to one of Hosea's tires and lifted his leg. "Hey!" shouted Hosea. "Cut that out!" He threw his car into reverse and slammed his foot down on the gas pedal. Bill Quinn looked behind him at the spot where the tire had just been, put his leg down and continued to cross the street. He found a square of sunlight and lay down in it. With his legs stretched out in front of him and behind him he took up the entire width of the sidewalk.

Hosea watched as a woman and her child gingerly stepped over the dog. The child bent down and scratched Bill Quinn between the ears. Bill Quinn licked the boy's face and the woman smiled. Hosea shook his head.

Well, thought Hosea, I'm really no further ahead than when I started. I've got three new babies and Max on my hands and nobody gone except Leander. I'm no further ahead. Hosea remembered raking leaves for Euphemia. As soon as he'd finished a patch of the lawn, the wind would blow and more leaves would fall from the trees directly onto his freshly raked patch. "C'mon in, Hosea," Euphemia would yell from the doorway, "don't worry about every single leaf." But he had worried about every single leaf. He'd stay outside until ten or eleven at night trying to rake up every leaf, trying to beat the wind. Sometimes Tom would help out for a while but eventually he'd get bored and wander off. "I'm going to bed, Hose," Euphemia would eventually call out into the darkness, "wherever you are, good night."

Hosea parked his car on the street in front of his office and got out. He said, "Hello, Peej," to a small stooped man who stood on the sidewalk gazing up at the sky. "Have you got seeding weather, Peej, or not?" Hosea smiled. "Let's hope," said Peej.

"Well, take 'er easy, Peej." A vicious jerk of Peej's chin by way of saying good-bye and Hosea had safely entered his office building.

He peered out the window of his office. He watched a couple getting out of their grey Subaru and going in to the Wagon Wheel. The woman glanced at Bill Quinn lying on the sidewalk and smiled. He thumped his fingers against the windowsill to a familiar tune. Waterloo, he thumped, my Waterloo. The couple took a table next to the large window in the front of the café.

Hosea watched as the man removed the woman's coat and then disappeared into the café, looking for a place to hang it. You'll have to hang it over the back of a chair, it's the Wagon Wheel you're sitting in, not the Ritz, thought Hosea. He stared at the woman and wondered if she was married to the man or was she his sister, his daughter? He thought of Lorna. The woman sat at the table, her legs crossed and sticking out to the side, and picked up a menu. She looked up at Hosea. Hosea looked up at the sky, to the right and to the left as if he'd just heard an airplane, and then quickly moved away from his window.

He noticed a note lying on his desk and picked it up.

Hi, Hosea, I let myself in with the key you gave me and I called the paint places in the city. It will cost, this is the cheapest, about $2,500 dollars to paint the water tower, without the horse. With the horse, about three grand. So . . . let me know what you think. Also, as you probably know, Bill Quinn is still in town, but I'm working on it. And I'll be buying the flowers later today with the money from that account. That's where I'm going now. Oh yeah, Lorna called. See ya, Knute.

P.S. Are you still interested in turning the old fred mill into a theatre because Jeannie, you know, your neighbour? said she's thinking about buying it and turning it into an aerobics/laundromat kind of place. She said she'd talk to you.

I'm sure she did, thought Hosea. "When?" said Hosea out loud. When, Knute? When did Lorna call, what did she say, how did she sound? Was she at work, at home? Why hadn't Knute just let the answering machine go? It would have been more helpful. At least he could have heard her voice. Hosea stood up and walked over to the window. He watched the couple for a while. The woman didn't look up at him again. A warm wind touched him. Knute's note fluttered off the desk and onto the floor. "You!" he shouted at Bill Quinn. The dog lifted one ear. "Get out of my town! Get the heck out of Algren!" Bill Quinn let his ear drop, yawned, and tried to get comfortable again. Combine Jo, who had been standing on the street with her back to Hosea, peering into the window of Willie Wiebe's Western Wear, turned around and looked up at him.

"Who the hell are you yelling at, Hosea? It's a little undignified, don't you think?" She was grinning. "Have you lost your mind, Hosea? Why the hell don't you come on out of your little tower and enjoy the sunshine. Summer's just around the corner! Did I mention S.F. and me are gonna be riding our bikes over on the dike? Hey, Hosea, you gotta bike?"

Hosea shook his head. "I was, uh, talking to Bill Quinn, to the dog," he said. "To that black dog there on the sidewalk."

"Oh him," shouted Combine Jo. "He looks harmless. Hey, wait a second, did you say his name is Bill Quinn? You mean from the original Bill Quinn? Is that one of his? Oh boy." Combine Jo shook her head.

"What do you mean, 'oh boy'?" shouted Hosea. "What's the story with the Quinns?"

"Oh, they're just wild, Hosea. They can't be trained. They can't be taught a thing. They do as they please. A few generations must have lived in Whithers or who knows where, 'cause you obviously missed out on it. Just ask Cherniski! She'll tell you all about it!" Combine Jo shook her head. "Christ," she said. She looked amused. "I guess they're back. Yell all you want, Hosea, that dog ain't gonna budge." She turned back to the display window of Wiebe's with a little wave over her shoulder. Hosea lifted his hand.

The phone rang.

"Lorna," said Hosea as he picked up the phone.

"How'd you know it was me?" said Lorna, laughing.

"Well, you know, if you want something bad enough . . ." Hosea coughed. "How are you?" he said.

"I'm fine. How are you?" she said.

"I'm okay," said Hosea, "I've . . ." Lorna interrupted.

"I've missed you, too," she said.

Hosea had been about to say I've been better.

"Yeah," he said. "How are you?" he asked again.

"I'm okay. Pretty good. Hosea, there's something we need to talk about."

"Yeah," he said. He wondered what it could be. "Yeah," he said again. "We should talk."

"Could I come out on the bus tonight?"

"Oh," said Hosea. "Of course you can, of course you can. I'll be there to pick you up. I love you. I'm sorry I'm such an idiot. I'm sorry I didn't call sooner. Lorna, I'm just really sorry."

She sighed. "You keep telling me that, Hosea, and nothing ever changes."

Hosea whispered, "I know. I'm sorry."

"Will you quit saying you're fucking sorry!" she said.

"Okay," said Hosea. "Yes I will, I love you."

"And stop saying that, too!" said Lorna.

"Why?" asked Hosea. "Why should I stop saying I love you when I do?"

"Because it makes me sad, Hosea, that's why. Because I wonder."

"Okay," said Hosea.

"Is that all you can say? Okay? So what does that mean, Hosea, that your love for me *is* a sad thing, that you don't even know if you mean it or not?"

Hosea put his hand on his forehead. "Tell me," she said again, softly. Was she crying?

"I have a plan, Lorna," he said. "It's a, well, it's just a plan. And if you'll just come here tonight I'll tell you everything and then you'll understand. My love for you is not a sad thing, Lorna. Please don't think it is."

"Just pick me up at seven, Hosea," she said. "And you know, whatever." She hung up.

Hosea closed his eyes. He could feel the warm wind blowing through his open window. He could smell the dust left over from last fall and he could hear Combine Jo laughing down on the street. He thought how much happier Leander Hamm's corpse would be now that the earth was drying up and the snow had gone. My blood, he thought. I'd sell my blood to buy her chocolate donuts. That had been the first line of a poem he'd written on a scrap of paper the day he had decided to become a poet. He'd changed it around a million times trying to get something to rhyme with donuts and then with blood. Nothing. Except flood, and that had seemed futile. Euphemia had found the scrap of paper in his pocket and had laughed out loud for twenty minutes, and then had broken her leg. Hosea had been in the basement and had seen a spider, and because he was frustrated with his poem had screamed at the top of his lungs, "SPIDER!" Euphemia had come running and falling down the stairs, saying, "Where where where's the fire" and her leg made a snapping noise and her femur poked off in the wrong direction, and Hosea had been quite happy about it. Even while Euphemia lay writhing on the basement floor, he had muttered sullenly, "I said *spider,* not *fire.*" Later that day he had written in his notebook that Vincent van Gogh and a lot of other great artists in the world didn't care what people thought of them, which was nothing.

Hosea opened his eyes. Everything was going to be all right. He and Lorna would work things out. He'd tell her the truth about his plan and she would understand. She would know why he wanted to see his father. She loved him and she would know. He would take the Prime Minister by the arm and they would stroll off a ways from the crowd, down Main Street towards where the sidewalk ends, and then up Town Line Road in the direction of the dike, and Hosea would smile and say, Mr. Prime Minister, do you remember meeting a girl named Euphemia Funk years ago right here in this town? Well, I'm her son. He would smile and look into the PM's face. And yours, he'd say. He wanted to show the Prime Minister his town, Canada's smallest, the place of his conception, his birth, and his whole life. He wanted the Prime Minister to see it and to like it and to think well of Euphemia and the place where she was from and the son that she had raised. Lorna would understand. It was simple. Hosea nodded his head and smoothed the shiny surface of his desk with his hand. He reached for the top drawer and then decided against opening it. He would find Knute and the two of them would plant the flowers along Main Street. He would help her. And then he would go to the bus depot and pick up Lorna and show her the flowers and take her home.

ten

"He doesn't go out at all?" Knute asked Dory.

"Nope," she said.

"What about when I'm at work?"

Dory shook her head. "Mm-mm."

"Does he get up to eat?" Knute asked.

"No. Not really, no," said Dory. She and Knute were in the kitchen drinking coffee and watching the sun go down. Dory leaned towards the open window, over the sink, and the warm breeze blew the hair off her forehead. Beyond Tom and Dory's big backyard was a field, plowed and ready for seeding, pitch-black and chunky, with a faint line of bushes towards the very end, and the giant orange sun was slipping down behind those bushes, round as a poker chip, and the purple sky covered everything. That was the view.

"You know what, Knutie?" said Dory. "Tom and I have lived here all our lives. In this town, every single day of our lives."

"Do you think that's what's making Dad so sad?" asked Knute. Dory looked at her and smiled.

"No, Knute," she said. "It's just the opposite. He loves this place, it's all he's known. He's afraid to say good-bye. He's afraid to leave it behind. He's afraid, Knutie."

"But he's been given a second chance," said Knute. "He's still alive."

"It's more mysterious than that," said Dory. "He wants his old life. He's not a stupid man. For him to get up and cheerfully make the most of each day, at this point . . . he would feel like a fool." Dory shook her head. Then she said, "He would be admitting to himself that life has suddenly become very short, very precious, that soon he'll no longer exist, that it'll be over. Of course he knew that, we know that, we say it, but to really, really know it, to be certain of it, is more than he can be right now. His bed is safe. Sleep is easy." Then she said again, "He's not a stupid man."

The sun had gone down right before their eyes. "Did you notice it disappear?" Dory asked Knute.

"Well, I noticed it was gone," said Knute. She put their coffee cups in the dishwasher and then stood with her hands on her hips and looked at Dory. "I'm going out," she said. "Don't worry about Summer Feelin', she won't wake up." Dory reached out her arms and put her hands over Knute's.

"I'm not worried," she said. "I think I can take care of one little girl well enough on my own."

"Yeah, well," said Knute, smiling, "I suppose you've managed before, more or less."

"What do you mean *you suppose*? What do you mean *more or less*?" Dory said, grabbing the tea towel from the fridge door and swatting Knute with it. "More or less," she growled. "My foot, more or less. Ingrate! Get out of here!" She snapped Knute with the towel. "Hey," she said, "where are you off to?"

"Oh," said Knute, grinning. "A little paperwork at the office."

"Really? I'm impressed."

"Nah," Knute said, "I'm going to check out my flowers. Hosea and I planted millions of them today, all along Main

Street. And they're all red and white. We planted them so they'd look like Canadian flags. It was his idea."

Dory began to laugh. "Really?" she said again.

"That's right," Knute said, lowering her voice and tugging at the front of her sweatshirt, "that's right. We can all be proud of Algren, Canada's smallest town. Well, Dory, I, uh, I, uh, I, uh, really better get going. You know how it is, places to go, people to see."

"Yes yes, Mayor Funk," said Dory. "Onward and upward. Don't let me stand in the way of progress. Carpe diem."

"Okey, dokey," said Knute. "And give my regards to Tom. And, uh, thanks for the coffee, Dory, you always did make a fine cup of coffee."

Dory shook her head. "Oh you," she said. "Go already." She was looking at the wall where the mirror used to be, before Combine Jo broke it. Hosea Funk, she sighed. Lord love him, what a funny man.

Knute walked out of the house and down the driveway. The night was warm and very dark. She felt like crying. She hadn't done a good job of helping Dory with Tom, and it was already June. She hadn't helped him get better or lightened Dory's load. He'd taken to his bed and Knute was concerned that Dory might be thinking of joining him. How much longer could she renovate one medium-sized house? Knute cut behind the feed mill and around by the bank and the post office and walked towards the flowers. She could smell them, they were beautiful, and they shone under the only streetlight. Something small and black jumped out from the middle of the flower bed and disappeared. Then another followed, and another. She bent over to see what they were and was almost hit in the face with another one. The Algren cockroach! The bastards were eating her flowers! She stood up and frowned at the flower bed and then picked up a few pebbles from the road and threw them into the flowers. About twenty of the cockroaches flew up and took off in different directions. She picked up another handful of gravel and threw it in the flowers and was about to do it again when she heard a voice say "Hey!" and she nearly fell over from fright.

"You're gonna kill them if you do that." She turned around and saw Max coming toward her, stepping into the white glow of the streetlight.

"Good," she said. "Damn it, I just planted these things this afternoon."

"And now you want to kill them?" asked Max.

"I don't want to kill the flowers, I want to kill the cockroaches. Look at them. They're eating the flowers."

"They're not eating the flowers, they're copulating in the fresh dirt you used for planting. They don't eat flowers. The Algren cockroach is conceived in dirt. They love dirt."

She picked up another handful of gravel and threw it at the flowers.

"And stop doing that, you'll just hurt the flowers."

Knute sighed.

"So this is your work, eh?" said Max.

"Part of it," said Knute.

"Do you enjoy it?" he said. He leaned against the streetlight and folded his arms.

She looked at him and smiled. "Max," she said, "were you with a lot of other women in Europe?"

He cleared his throat and took out a cigarette and lit it. He had a drag and exhaled dramatically and said, "I stopped counting." Knute threw a handful of gravel at him and he laughed.

"What do you mean *other women,* Knute?" he said. "Other than who?" They grinned at each other. Two little shapes moved towards them in the dark, making clicking noises on the pavement.

"Hey," said Knute, as the shapes came closer, "it's Bill Quinn."

"And a friend," said Max. He moved his foot out of the way so the dogs could pass.

"I'm supposed to get rid of him," said Knute. "He gave Mrs. Cherniski a heart attack."

"You're doing a great job," said Max.

"Yeah, well, you would know." Knute looked at her flowers and up at the sky. It would be nice if it rained. She knew Max was looking at her watching the sky. She knew he was leaning against the streetlight smoking a cigarette with nothing to do and nowhere to do it. She picked up another handful of gravel to throw at the cockroaches in her flower bed, and Max said softly, "Is there a place we can go?"

"Um . . ." she said quietly, "there's . . ."

"You know what I mean," he said, looking at his big boots, blowing smoke at them, and waiting for Knute to rescue him.

She still had Hosea's office key in her back pocket. She could feel the outline of it through her jeans. "Well," she said, "I don't know." Max looked up and opened his mouth but didn't say anything. He put his hands up in front of him, palms outward, as if to ward off an assault. He smiled.

"I can ask," he whispered. Knute reached out and took his hand. He closed his eyes for a second or two and put his arms around her. They stood that way for a while in the dark, on the deserted main street of their hometown. He smelled like hay and cigarette smoke and the back of his neck was as soft as Summer Feelin's. He pulled his T-shirt out of his jeans and put Knute's hands on his bare back.

She moved his hand to her back pocket and he took out the key and said, "Where's the door for this thing?"

"Right here," said Knute. "We're leaning against it. It's my office." She smiled.

"Your office," Max breathed. "You have an office?"

"It's Hosea's office." Max had already opened the door and was pulling Knute up the stairs.

They made love on the top of Hosea's shiny desk, and on the floor, and when they were finished they lay there naked, smoking cigarettes and talking. "I love you," said Max. And she said, "You don't really know me anymore." And he said, "Well, there's that." And they laughed and acted casual about everything and tried not to make any promises or plans. They could never go back to where they'd been. And nothing seemed to be waiting for them down the road. So they were free. It was a sad kind of freedom but at least they knew it. They didn't say it but they both knew Summer Feelin' was the best thing either of them would ever have. They got dressed and stood beside each other, leaning on the windowsill and looking out at the purple sky. "Eggplant," said Knute.

And Max said, "Just what I was gonna say." Every few minutes he stuck out his lower lip and blew the hair away from his eyes.

"Remember that time you cut my hair outside that bar?" he said. "Remember that grey sweater dress you had on?" They took turns kissing each other gently and touching each other and then they went back to leaning on the windowsill and looking out. Neither of them wanted to go home.

"So, let's see, what's new . . . hmmmm," said Hosea. He had picked Lorna up from the bus depot and now they were sitting at his kitchen table drinking herbal tea and trying to get to a spot in their conversation where they could feel natural with each other. "Well," Hosea cleared his throat, "Max is back in town."

"Max?" said Lorna.

"Knute's old boyfriend," said Hosea. "Summer Feelin's dad."

"Oh yeah," said Lorna. "You told me about Knute and Summer Feelin'. What a great name, Summer Feelin'."

Hosea smiled.

"It's okay," he said.

"It's a great name," said Lorna again.

"Okay," said Hosea. "She's a sweet kid, too."

"Yeah?" said Lorna. "It's nice for her to have her dad back, I guess."

Hosea nodded. "They get along," he said. "He takes care of her while Knute works in the office."

Lorna nodded and sipped her tea. "Hmmm," said Lorna, looking at her watch. "It's June sixth today, D-Day."

"Is that right?" said Hosea. Oh my God, he thought.

Lorna shrugged.

"Yeah," he said, "I guess it is."

He stared at Lorna while she fiddled with her watch. He was trying to work up the nerve to tell her his plan. *Isthmus* rhymes with *Christmas,* he told himself. Her eyes, two oceans of blue, and a skinny isthmus of a nose running in-between. Her mouth, the Bermuda Triangle, no, that's wrong. Dehumanize your audience. Hosea could hear the voice of Mr. Flett, his old speech arts teacher. Pretend your audience is a brick fence, a body of water, an ancient land mass. And then say what you have to say. A field of wheat won't think you're ridiculous. A small continent won't get up and leave. Tell her right now, Hosea told himself, tell her. You love her, you need her, you deserve her, tell her right now or kill yourself.

"Lorna!" he said loudly, scaring himself and making her jump.

"What?" said Lorna. "Are you nuts? I'm not deaf."

"We should do that talking now, the talking we talked about before," said Hosea, "on the phone."

"Okay," said Lorna, taking a big breath. "You're right." She smiled. "It's very weird."

Hosea was confused. What was weird? What did she think was weird? He hadn't told her yet. He hadn't said anything about the plan.

"What is weird?" he said.

"Weird," she said slowly, smiling, "weird is that . . ." She stopped and moved her chair closer to Hosea, leaned across the corner of the table, cupped his face in her hands, put her lips against his forehead, and whispered " . . . is that I'm pregnant."

Mr. Flett had never mentioned the possibility of a land mass getting pregnant. Pregnant. Pregnant. Lorna's lips were still fastened to his forehead. He could stick out his tongue and lick her neck if he wanted to. He put his arms around her and said, "That's amazing, Lorna. That's amazing."

She sat back down in her chair, folded her arms, and said, "I know it is." She looked at Hosea. "Please smile," she said, "oh, please smile."

"I am," said Hosea, frowning, "I am."

Lorna laughed. "Are you happy?" she asked. He was happy, he was thrilled. It had never occurred to him that he could make a woman pregnant, especially not a beautiful woman he really loved and wanted to live with for the rest of his life. He was happy, all right.

"Yes, Lorna, I'm happy," he said, smiling. Trying to smile. "I'm happy." And then he added, "Are you?"

Lorna nodded. "I think so," she said. "I'm pretty sure I am."

"Amazing," he said.

"The doctor told me it's the size of my thumbnail," said Lorna.

"Really, wow," said Hosea. "Let me see your thumb." She held it up and he looked at it closely. He pulled her thumb to his lips and kissed it.

"But the thing is," she said, holding out her thumb, "the thing is, Hosea, it's got to be different."

"How do you mean?" Hosea stopped kissing her thumb and held her hand in his lap.

"I'm just not gonna fool around anymore, Hosea. I'm too old for that and so are you. I'm not gonna date you like a teenager or have some kind of long-distance love affair with you when I'm pregnant with your kid. Forget it."

"Okay," said Hosea, "I know. I know what you mean, and things will change. You're going to move in with me and we'll be happy, we'll be a family, we'll all live together right here in Algren. We have a school, there's a park, okay? Okay, Lorna?" Hosea smiled and opened his eyes wide.

"Today, Hosea," said Lorna. "As of today I'm living here. If you can't make that commitment, knowing we're having a baby, and everything else—you know we're not kids, you know we're not getting any younger—then I don't know. Then I just don't know. Basically, I think, it would just be over. I'm not gonna raise a kid with you if you can't make one commitment. Then I might not even have it."

Hosea let go of Lorna's hand and reached for the front of his shirt.

"Don't," said Lorna. "Don't do that. Just deal with this, okay? I don't mean for this to be an ultimatum, Hosea, I hate ultimatums, but it's just at that point where we have to, where you have to, make a decision. Maybe I'm just an idiot, but I thought that when you said you had stuff to talk to me about, on the phone before, that you were gonna pop the big question, ask me to marry you or whatever, at least move in with you. That's what I thought you were going to say. So what? Were you? What did you want to talk about?"

"I just need you to trust me," said Hosea.

"You need me to trust you?" said Lorna.

"Yes," he whispered.

"No," said Lorna. "You need to trust me, you need to trust yourself. I do trust you. Why the hell do you think I'm here right now? Why the hell do you think I keep coming back to you time after time? Why are you so afraid of living with me? Because it might not work out? Because I'll become more real to you? Because you'll not have a reason to feel sorry for yourself, all alone? Why? I don't understand, Hosea. Is there somebody else? Are you seeing somebody else?"

"God, no," said Hosea. "I have a plan, and it's very important to me, and if you just wait for three weeks, it'll be over, and my life, my whole life, will be yours, and the baby's. Please understand, Lorna, please don't leave me . . ."

"Tell me what your plan is," said Lorna. "Tell me what it is, and we'll see." She moved behind Hosea and stroked his hair and rubbed his back. "Tell me," she said. "C'mon, Hosea."

Hosea turned around to face her and he put his hands on her waist. "I want to see my father," he said. "I want to see what he looks like. I want to talk to him. I want to see if I'm like him at all. I want him to see my town."

"Hosea," said Lorna, "who is your father?"

Hosea cleared his throat. "John Baert, I think. My mother told me that, anyway."

"You don't mean the Prime Minister, do you?" Lorna smiled.

Hosea nodded. "Yeah," he said. "That's the one."

Max and Knute said good-bye on the street with a high-five in slow motion, their hands clasped together for a couple of seconds reaching for the sky and everything else unattainable, and then they smiled at each other and went their separate ways.

When Knute got home, Dory was still up. She had her SoHo T-shirt on and Tom's sweats and she was steaming the wallpaper in the dining room with a kettle and tearing at it with a plastic scraper.

"Mom," Knute whispered. "What are you doing? It's the middle of the night."

"Yes, Knutie," she said, "I made that observation myself. What does it look like I'm doing?" She hadn't taken her eyes off the wallpaper.

"You're gonna take out the whole wall, not just the paper, if you keep banging at it like that," said Knute.

"Thank-you for that," Dory said. "It might be a good idea."

"Well," Knute yawned, "this is kind of strange. Why don't you go to bed and finish it in the morning? Or I could help you after work tomorrow."

"Where were you?" asked Dory, her eyes still fixed on the wall. Knute paused and thought, To hell with it, she already knows.

"With Max," she said. She moved the kettle closer to the wall.

"I see," said Dory. Her lower lip started to tremble.

"Oh, Mom," said Knute. "It's not that big a deal." Dory nodded and blinked a few times. "It's really not."

"I don't . . ." Dory began.

"I know," said Knute. "Don't worry." Dory looked at her and smiled, sadly, and wiped the sweat off her nose with the bottom of her T-shirt.

"Do you remember Candace Wheeler?" she asked.

"Candace Wheeler," said Knute. "Candace Wheeler. No, I don't. Why?" Knute already knew it would be something terrible, maybe a pitchfork through her cheek or flesh-eating disease.

"She had to have a C-section in the city," said Dory.

"That's too bad," said Knute, thinking it could have been a lot worse. She wanted to go to bed. She wanted to dream of Max and their nowhere relationship before the sun rose and ruined everything.

"The baby was totally, you know, totally . . . stressed out," Dory continued.

Knute smiled. "Stressed out?"

"Well, whatever," Dory said. "Under stress, I guess is what it was, or duress. Apparently Candace's pelvis wouldn't open up far enough for the baby to go through, but they only discovered this after eighteen hours of hard labour. So Candace was just about dead from the pain, and then suddenly they decide to do the C-section. They thought they had given her enough anesthetic, but because they were in such a hurry to save the baby, they made a mistake with the levels and she wasn't entirely, you know, frozen, you know, the area, and so she could feel the knife cutting her open. She was only slightly numb. She was far too weak to object, though, and, oh, Knute, it was awful. A large flap of skin, the stomach skin, was pushed aside, sort of draped up over her breasts and then it took two doctors to pry her rib cage open far enough to get the baby out. And she's feeling all of th—"

"Mom," Knute said. "Please stop." Dory began to cry, and moved her finger through the condensation on the kettle and shook her head. "It's okay," said Knute. She sat down on the floor next to Dory and put her arms around her. Dory put her head on Knute's shoulder and wept.

"Oh, Knutie," she sobbed, "I don't know what to do. I don't know how to make him live. I don't know how to make him talk."

"It's okay, Mom." Knute stroked Dory's hair the way Dory used to stroke hers when she was sad or sick.

"He doesn't talk to me, Knute. He just lies there."

"I know." Knute nodded her head. She didn't know what to say.

"I don't want him to die, sweetheart," said Dory. She had stopped sobbing but tears were still streaming down her cheeks.

"I know," Knute said again. She kissed her mother's forehead.

"But sometimes I do," said Dory.

"Yeah." Knute nodded quickly.

"Then I would know, you know?" Dory continued. "Then I would know what to do. I don't know what to do now. I don't know if I should force him out of his bed or if I should sit by his side or talk to him and just be patient and let him get up when he's ready or if I should tell him I'll leave if he doesn't try, at least, but that's so cruel and I don't want to leave him. How could I? I just don't know. And it's not his fault. But he could at least sit down for meals or go on a little drive with me or just talk to me. Uncle Jack called earlier this evening and I couldn't stop crying on the phone. You know how much Jack's always loved Tom. He said he'd try to talk to him, but I don't know . . ."

Knute didn't know, either. "Maybe . . ."

"He can't think straight, Knute, and it's getting worse. The neurologist thinks that he's had a series of small strokes, not big enough for anybody to really notice, except he knows it and he can't do things, you know, like he used to. He can't read anymore. When he said he was reading his journals in the garage while I worked, he wasn't, you know, he just pretended to. His handwriting is illegible. His short-term memory is gone. Sometimes he forgets where he is, he gets dizzy. He can't drive. And, Knute, he's not affectionate like he used to be, he's not funny, with the jokes and laughing, he's just not the same guy . . ."

Knute closed her eyes and leaned her head against the damp wall.

"I'm sorry," Dory said. "I don't want to upset you. I just needed to talk to someone. I don't know what to do. I want you to be happy, and now with Max back, I don't know what's going to happen, will he leave you again? Pregnant? Will he break Summer Feelin's heart, too, this time? How many times is this going to happen?"

"Mom," said Knute, "I'm not going to get pregnant. Don't worry. Max and I aren't even in a relationship. I can't help it if he leaves again, but Summer Feelin' is better off knowing him, having seen him, and having had fun with him. She'll miss him but she'll be fine. If he leaves again, I'm sure he'll be back to see her. He won't be able to stay away for long. He's crazy about her. His mom lives here, I'm here for the time being, and this is his town. Don't worry about me and Summer Feelin' on top of everything else. Let's just go to sleep and in the morning I want to hear about Dad and you and we'll talk about it, and figure out what we can do, how we can live with it. It's gonna be okay."

Dory began to cry again.

"I love you, Mom," said Knute. "I love you very much."

Dory whispered, "I know you do, Knutie," and stared at her ravaged wall.

Later, after Dory was asleep, Knute went to the garage and looked at Tom's veterinarian journals. She skimmed over an article on ringworm and one on pregnant-mare urine, and then went inside the house and had a quick peek at Summer Feelin'. Her mouth was open, and her arms and legs were spread apart like a starfish. Knute moved her right arm and leg to make some room and then curled up beside her. "The sun's coming up," she whispered. She didn't think S.F. had ever seen a sunrise, except for when she was a baby, and had woken up hungry and crying. She whispered it again.

"Okay," said S.F. in her sleep, "that's okay." And she stretched out her right arm and leg again, on top of Knute.

"So, let me get this straight," said Lorna. "You think Baert is your dad, but you're not sure. Euphemia told you on her deathbed, and you believe she was lucid enough to know what she was talking about. That was three years ago. Since then you haven't called him or even tried to get—"

Hosea interrupted. "Well, Lorna," he said, "I can't just call up the Prime Minister and say, Hey, I'm your son, you know, about fifty some years ago you rode through this small prairie town on a horse and—"

"Okay, okay," said Lorna. "Fine, I understand. So then you get a letter from the Prime Minister saying he's going to visit Canada's smallest town on July first as a way of showing the country he's interested in, well, small towns, I guess."

"Right," said Hosea.

"Hmmm," said Lorna. "Interesting publicity stunt."

"It's not a publicity stunt," said Hosea. "It's a way of reaching out to rural Canadians, to show them that he cares."

"Yeah," said Lorna, "about their votes."

"Well even so," said Hosea, "it's my chance."

"Okay," said Lorna. "It's your chance. So, you want to make sure Algren is Canada's smallest town on July first so you get a chance to see your dad, and show him what you've accomplished in your life."

"Well," Hosea smiled. "I guess—"

Lorna interrupted again. "Well, that's basically it, isn't it?" She smiled. "God, you're an idiot, Hose."

"Am I?" he said. "But do you love me?"

"Yeah," she said, "because I'm an idiot, too, and now we'll have a kid who's an idiot, because how could it not be, with two idiot parents like us?"

Hosea smiled and for a second worried that she might be right.

"Okay," she sighed. "Max and three babies. Four too many. Right?"

Hosea nodded. "Right," he said. "Fifteen hundred is the number I need."

"I know," said Lorna. "You told me that. Okay, anybody else pregnant?" she asked.

"Just you," he said.

"I mean anybody else in Algren due to give birth before July first?"

"Not that I know of," said Hosea.

"Okay," said Lorna again. She tapped her finger against her forehead.

"Look," said Hosea, "the sun's coming up."

"Hmmm," said Lorna. "You sound surprised. Now, Leander Hamm's dead, so that's one. Three left to get rid of."

"Don't say that," said Hosea.

"Okay, not get rid of," she said. "Three to, well, whatever."

"Okay, get rid of," said Hosea, smiling and rubbing Lorna's stomach.

"Stop that, I'm trying to help you here. Cherniski's in the hospital, because of Whatsisname the dog—"

"Bill Quinn," said Hosea.

"But," said Lorna, "who knows where that'll go? If she makes it, she might go and live with her daughter in the city, which would be good. If she dies . . . well . . . I don't want her to die. I'm just saying *if* she does, that would work out."

Hosea frowned. "Well . . ." he said, "that's not exactly how I—"

"I know, I know," said Lorna. "Let's just say Cherniski's up in the air. Okay, then there's the doctor. He says he might leave. But only after another doctor's been hired and trained and et cetera et cetera and there's no way that can happen before July first, so don't even think of him as an option. You know, I can't believe I'm doing this."

"I'm sorry," said Hosea. "It's like I can't stop, I can't stop until—"

"Okay," said Lorna, yawning and holding up her hand. "Stop. Then, um, who's this Johnny guy?"

"Johnny Dranger," said Hosea.

"Right," said Lorna. "The guy who could be in or out?"

"Yup," said Hosea. "But he has to be in, because he needs to be the fire chief."

Lorna looked at Hosea for a second. "Needs to be the fire chief?" she asked. "Like he needs to eat and sleep?"

"Exactly," said Hosea. "Just like that. He has to stay in, to be the fire chief. He loves to put out fires. He has to put out fires. I'll explain another time."

Lorna raised her eyebrows and let her head fall to her chest, in a dramatic gesture of defeat and exhaustion. "Make me some coffee," she said. "No wait . . . no caffeine . . ." She had her head resting on her arms, on the table.

Hosea thought of Caroline Russo, pregnant with Johnny's baby, and dying in the fire while Johnny was passed out in the yard. He nodded his head and stroked Lorna's hair. "He needs to put out fires," he murmured softly. "He really does." Hosea understood perfectly. "You see, Lorna, it's like this," he said. "Years ago . . . Lorna?" said Hosea. "Lorna?" Lorna made a purring sound but didn't move. She loves me, thought Hosea. She will help me meet my father, and then she'll have our baby. Carefully, he picked Lorna up from the kitchen chair and carried her to the bed. As he bent over to remove her socks he noticed they didn't match. One was pink and fleecy and had a little ball on it that poked out from behind Lorna's ankle like a spur, and the other one was a kneesock, plain and white. Hosea gently pulled the socks off Lorna's wide feet and laid them over the back of the chair so she would find them when she woke up. He stared at Lorna's bare feet for a minute or two. He considered lifting her T-shirt slightly just to see her stomach and to imagine the thumbnail-sized embryo that was inside it that he had helped to create—but instead he moved her hair away from her face and covered her up with the blanket. He went back to the kitchen table and sat down and stared outside at the sky. The colour of Knutie's cigarette filters, he thought to himself. He saw the water tower sticking up into the orange sky and imagined the white horse racing round its bulbous top. If he could paint the water tower the colour the sky was right then, the colour of Knute's filters, thought Hosea, then the water tower would become one with the sky and the white horse would look like it was flying through the air. At least at those times of the day when the sky was orange. Like right now, thought Hosea, looking at the time on his VCR. 5:20, it said. Well, that's quite early, thought Hosea. But how else to achieve this effect? When the baby was grown up a bit, thought Hosea, he could choose the colour of sky he liked best and Hosea would find a paint to match, maybe dark blue or pink, and Hosea could pass on his flying horse to his son. Or his daughter. "Or my daughter," said Hosea out loud, smiling. Now close your eyes, honey, and stand over here and look way up and when I say open your eyes you will see a horse flying. But, thought Hosea, for now it will be filter orange. I've got to get on it. I'm running out of time. Will I be guaranteed an orange sky and a flying horse when the Prime Minister is in town? Not necessarily, he thought. But you never know. Hosea banged his scarred palm against the side of the table but felt no pain. Hmph, he thought, it must come and go. He did it again and still nothing, not a twinge, not one jot of tenderness, no pain. Hosea walked over to the bedroom and took off his clothes and lay down next to Lorna. She opened her eyes for a second and put her arm over his chest and her head on his shoulder.

Dory had asked Tom's Uncle Jack to pay him a visit. Uncle Jack lived in the States, just on the other side of the border in Fargo, North Dakota. He was a part-time magician and a full-time auctioneer and even when he wasn't working he spoke really fast, in entire paragraphs, a hundred miles an hour, like the telling of his stories was a timed Olympic event. Tom loved the guy, and Dory was sure that if anyone could jar Tom from his depressive stupor, at least for a minute or two, it would be Uncle Jack.

All right, I'm here, but not for long, you son of a bitch, what gives? Lost your sea legs, Tom? You're down, you're not beat, not yet, listen to me, I had a cancer of the groin not once but twice, not a fuckin' picnic, I'll tell ya, though it hasn't, I repeat, has not affected my performance, the girls'll attest to that much, what are you smiling at, two weeks after the chemotherapy gets rid of that mess in my groin, my prostate explodes in my ass, hadda have it hoovered out through my backdoor, eh? eh? still smiling? I shit you not, my friend, it's true, Doc told me not to ride my horse for four goddamn months, I was on her in a week, scuze me? Less than a week, that's right, four days it was, but then, Jesus Christ, that shit for a horse falls on top of me, breaks fifteen of my ribs, that's all, but what? four? five? still, my pelvis, my arms, both of 'em, and my goddamn tailbone—that's when I quit smoking, in the hospital, too much damn work going down the hall, down the elevator, out the front doors. When you can't smoke in a hospital—that's where you really need one. I don't know, I don't know, what's that? Nah, forget about it. I went to Vancouver to visit my daughter and her husband, find out the guy's a woman, she never told me it was her husband, she said, never ever, she said, Partner, partner, I said partner, Dad, she says to me, partner, Tom? What is that? Partner! But never mind, last summer I hooked my eyeball with the end of a bungee cord, pierced the retina, the iris, the cornea, the works, the hook stuck in my eye socket like it was plugged into a wall, the bungee cord dangling there like this, and I'm thinking, though of course I'm in excruciating pain, excuse me, do I look like a source of power, my eye holds no electrical current, under fifty watts in this cash register at all times, please unplug this hook from my eye, somebody, and then wouldn't you know it, the neighbour's cat spies the cord dangling and makes a running leap for it, I can just see it out of my good eye, the one without a hook stuck in the middle of it, and I'm thinking, No way, don't do it, don't do it, don't, but forget about it, he does it, and I'm thinking good-bye, right or left or whatever eye, depends of course on how you're looking at it, good-bye it was nice seeing you or seeing with you as the case may be, because as soon as this damn cat, it's a fat son of a bitch—looks like a small pony, makes contact with the bungee cord he'll yank the entire eye unit out of its hole, and I'll be Mr. One-Eye, Mr. Cyclops, the life of every boring party as I drop the glassy job they give me in the hospital into the punch bowl, and drag my foot around behind me, I'm thinking, you know, of how I can work this unfortunate loss of mine to my advantage when the damn thing falls right out onto the ground, the hook, that is, along with the cord, not my eye, the cat's miffed and leaves, blood squirts from my eye, from the hole where until then the hook had been, blocking the blood from leaving, you know, like a knife in the back, you leave it in until you get to the hospital, so you don't bleed to death, and so there I am, at emergency I didn't have to wait, of course, nobody likes to sit in a waiting room next to some guy projectile bleeding from one eye and trying to read a magazine with his other, Doc slaps a patch over my pierced eye, the slimy tissue grows over the hole, leaving a faint scar, and everybody's happy. Eh, Tom? Tom?

"Jesus Christ, man, a heart attack, not a death sentence. . . . Can you not look at me? I'm cracking a beer here and now I am pouring it—ahhhhhhh, good—down my throat. Cold, familiar beer. Want one? . . . Okay, I'll drink it all myself. And when I'm done I'll have fortified myself enough to give you a proper burial because this, this is not a life, pal. All I gotta do is get rid of this bed, pry away the carpet and the floorboards, not to mention the underlay and linoleum, then lower myself a few feet, jackhammer the concrete basement floor, drop you into the dirt, bed 'n' all, and you're in your bloody grave, man, say a few Hail Marys, remember the laughs, hope it doesn't happen to me anytime soon, and Uncle Jack bids a fond farewell to Tom McCloud, good-bye, Kid Fun, good-bye, my favourite nephew . . . good-bye. Jesus Christ."

"Well," said Tom's Uncle Jack, "Lord knows I tried." He stood by the front door wrapped in what looked like a groundsheet, fumbling with a bottle of extra-strength Tylenol. "Like Cheerios I eat these," he said to Dory. He turned to Summer Feelin' and said, "You're perfect, you are a perfect little girl."

"She's a perfect little girl," he said to Knute.

And then to Summer Feelin' he said, "I was born the day the *Titanic* sank." Summer Feelin' smiled. "That's right, two disasters in one day," said Uncle Jack. "But never mind, have you got a pumpkin?" Summer Feelin' shook her head. "That's too bad," said Uncle Jack. "If you had a pumpkin I could show you my card trick. Do you know that I can throw an ordinary playing card right through a pumpkin and have the damn thing come out the other side with not one, I shit you not, not one shred of pumpkin flesh hanging from it, and the slit from the card entering and exiting barely visible on either side of the pumpkin?"

"Can you do it with a cantaloupe?" asked Summer Feelin'. Or somebody's head? Knute wondered. "Absolutely not," said Uncle Jack. "It must be a pumpkin. But listen to me, have you got a ten-story building anywhere around here, anywhere in this town?"

"A tall one, you mean a tall, tall building?" said Summer Feelin' standing on her tiptoes and holding her arms up over her head.

"That's right, it's gotta be ten stories, not nine, not eleven, but ten, ten stories tall."

"No, we don't have one of those," said Summer Feelin'.

"Well, that is too bad, that's really a shame, because if you had a ten-story building I could show you another card trick. There are only two men in the whole world who can do this trick, me and my brother, your Uncle Skylar."

Dory cleared her throat. "Jack," she said gently, "Sky's been dead for . . ."

"Never mind," said Uncle Jack, "that's what you think."

Dory shook her head and tried not to laugh, not because she didn't want to offend Uncle Jack, but because she didn't want to encourage him.

"Now listen to me, Hooked on a Feelin' or whatever your—"

"Summer Feelin'!" said Summer Feelin'.

"That's right," said Uncle Jack, "and some aren't. Listen! I can take an ordinary playing card and, on the very first try, with just the right wind conditions, of course, throw that playing card onto the top of a ten-story building. Standing on the ground, me standing on the ground, of course. What do you think of that, Summer-Time Feelin'?"

Summer Feelin' began to flap and hum. "What are you doing?" said Uncle Jack. "What's she doing?" he said to Knute.

"She's excited," said Knute. "Don't worry. She likes the idea of that card trick."

"Really?" said Uncle Jack. "You find me a ten-story building, an ordinary playing card, get me out there, bring the kid, and I'll do the trick for her, it'll knock her socks off. I'm serious. Bring a pumpkin, I'll do that trick, too, no charge. I mean it. Tell Tom to crawl out of his coffin and come along, he's seen me do it, I'm better at it than Skylar ever was, or is—"

"Good-bye, Uncle Jack," they all said in unison.

"Find me that building, Knutie!" he yelled just before getting into his car. "I'll do the trick, I promise! Good-bye! A rivederci! So long, Knutie! Keep your knees together . . ." his voice trailed off as he drove away.

eleven

"Areola is a nice name for a girl," said Hosea. "Don't you think?"

Lorna started to laugh. "Areola?" she spluttered. "God, you kill me—" Lorna was laughing hard. "Hey, Hose," she said, "what do you think—?"

"Oops, watch your step, my dear."

"Stop telling me to be careful, please. If you don't let me move around normally my body will think I'm dead and reject the baby. I'll end up aborting, Hosea, if you keep—"

"Well, every name means something, doesn't it?"

"Areola Garden Funk, lovely. Sure. I love it. Can we walk a little faster, Hosea?"

"I never walk, you know, never, beats me why, I just—"

"Well, you're fat and lazy, that's why, I'm only pregnant, I can walk."

"I prefer Funk Garden . . . isn't that a band?"

"No, you're thinking of Sound Garden."

"Am I? Hey, wait a second . . ."

"Look," said Hosea. "Shit. Shit, shit."

"What's wrong?" asked Lorna, looking around, pushing her sunglasses to the top of her head for a better view.

"Over there! Behind the Wagon Wheel. It's Mrs. Cherniski,

oh shit, that means she's back, she's okay. She's already working, for Christ's sake, some kind of feeble heart attack that must have been—"

"Hosea!" said Lorna, trying to unscramble her sunglasses from her hair. "I promised you I wouldn't laugh, I promised you I wouldn't move to Algren until after July first, I promised you I would keep your crazy plan a secret. But you promised me that you wouldn't act like a nutcase, like some kind of grim reaper rubbing your hands together, sniffing the air for the scent of decaying flesh—"

"Lorna! I am not a grim reaper, sniffing the air for . . . I just thought if Cherniski had gone to live with her daughter in the city, then—"

"Oh, bullshit, you just wanted her gone. Even if she'd croaked, you wouldn't have minded."

"Lorna, that is not true, and don't get all mad at me, it's bad for the baby, and it's—"

"Now listen to you, Hosea. In one breath you're pissed off that Cherniski's heart attack didn't kill her, in the next you're all concerned for the baby and admonishing me for, well, for basically reacting the way any normal person would to your bizarre plan, getting your father—"

"Hello, Mrs. Cherniski," said Hosea, looking at Lorna and casually slicing his index finger across his throat in an attempt to shut her up. "It's good to see you up and around, and back at work so soon, my God, you're a lucky woman."

Mrs. Cherniski glared at Hosea like she'd just been hit with a pitch, and was preparing to storm the mound. "Lucky? Lucky, my foot," she said. "Lucky to be back slaving over a hot stove for a bunch of greasy, gap-toothed men in overalls and rubber boots who wouldn't know a decent meal from a poke in the eye . . ." Mrs. Cherniski heaved a black garbage bag into the giant bin outside the Wagon Wheel and stomped back inside.

"I'll tell you what, though, Hosea," she yelled through the screen door. "Lucky is that my daughter is coming to Algren to help me out. She's moving here, the whole kit and caboodle, and I'm gonna get myself some long overdue help from that girl. By the way, I hope to heck you've managed to get rid of that bastard Bill Quinn, you know he was the one who put me in the hospital, and if I see his scrawny butt ever again you're the one who'll be in the hospital, Hosea Funk."

Hosea smiled and nodded. "Uh, when? When is she, are they, coming?"

"Can't hear you, Hosea! What'd you say?"

Hosea's hand flew to the front of his shirt. "I said when? When—"

Lorna grabbed Hosea by the arm and hissed, "Forget it, Hosea, don't be so obvious, just let it go . . . say good-bye."

"But . . ." said Hosea.

"Good-bye, Mrs. Cherniski," said Lorna cheerfully, "don't work too hard!"

Hosea and Lorna walked around to the front of the Wagon Wheel and nearly tripped over Bill Quinn, who was strolling down the sidewalk, tick tick tick, with his overgrown toenails clicking on the concrete and a new goatee-ish tuft of mangled hair on his chin and his soft wet eyes ringed by dark circles as if he'd spent all night smoking Gitanes in a waterfront speakeasy.

"Dammit," said Hosea, "it's Bill Quinn." Hosea lunged for the dog and missed while Lorna put her hands to her face like Munch's model in *The Scream,* except she was laughing, and Bill Quinn kept walking. Tick tick tick tick. No problem. Enjoy your trip, Mr. Mayor? See you in the fall, har har.

"It's okay, Hosea," said Lorna. "He's crossing the street, Cherniski won't be able to see him. Don't worry." She crouched down and touched Hosea's shoulder.

"All right, up you go now, old man," said Lorna.

"Hey! Whatcha doin', Hose?" said Combine Jo, who had just pulled up next to the sidewalk Hosea was lying on. "Listening for hoofbeats? Are we in for a raid? Whoah, girl," she said, as she turned off the ignition. "How much time do we have, Sheriff Funk?"

Hosea cleared his throat. "Actually, I was trying to catch Bill Quinn, but he got away and I tripped over him." Lorna and Combine Jo exchanged grins.

"Hah!" said Combine Jo, "serves you right, padre, nobody catches a Quinn. Hello, Lorna, nice seeing you, you oughtta hang a sign around Mr. Loverboy here's neck saying so and so many accident-free days—you wouldn't get past eight or nine. You know he's a magnet for trouble, Cherniski will attest to that, strange things happen when he's around, ask the doc, when Hosea goes to the hospital the Earth moves. People die, babies are born . . ."

"Oh, Jo, that's not true," said Hosea, stretching his mouth into the shape of a smile, more painful than vaginal tearing during childbirth, he thought, remembering the lurid chapter of the pregnant woman book he was currently reading. Not true at all, heh, heh, stretch those lips, push the teeth to the fore and chuckle confidently, now he felt his mouth was at least forty centimetres dilated, don't forget to breathe and—

"She's gone, Hosea," said Lorna. "Are you okay?"

"I'm fine," said Hosea, massaging his cheeks, returning them to their original position, expecting to taste blood and pass out at any moment. "Just fine. Shall we?" he said. Hosea and Lorna walked slowly to the bus depot. Hosea didn't want to say good-bye. He hated saying good-bye. Lorna was sighing in that way people do after laughing, shaking her head, "Ooohhhh God, Hosea," wiping at her eyes, emitting a few remaining snorts and guffaws. Hosea nodded his head and grimaced amicably. "Ha ha," he said, "go ahead and laugh. It's good for the baby."

"Good-bye, Hosea," said Lorna, dropping her sunglasses and her bus ticket and holding her arms out for a hug.

"Oops, I'll get those," said Hosea. "Good-bye, Lorna, don't take your love to town."

"Excuse me?" said Lorna, starting to laugh all over again. "Okay, Hosea, I won't. . . . don't you take your love to town, either. . . ." And then she was gone, laughing, dropping her sunglasses, waving good-bye. Hosea popped a Frisk into his mouth and stood watching while the bus disappeared. He headed back to the Wagon Wheel, hoping, as he always did, for an answer to his question. Man's life's a vapour, full of woes . . . Oh, Mrs. Cherniski, he rehearsed in his mind, you know how I like to pay a visit to new residents of Algren, just to make them feel welcome and all that, so I'm just wondering . . . (Hosea cocked his head in an attempt to appear sincere) when did you say your daughter was coming to town? Hosea looked over his shoulder, half expecting Lorna to be trailing him, like a probation officer. Aha, she'd say, I told you not to go near Mrs. Cherniski, I told you to leave her alone, you've breached the conditions of your probation, Hosea, and now you must be punished. Hosea practised his delivery one more time, "Oh, Mrs. Cherniski . . . just to make them feel welcome and all that." He saw Lawrence Hamm pulling up to the feed mill in his silver pickup and immediately Hosea felt the top of his head, was it there? No, thank God, no hat . . . he'd left it at home. Well, thought Hosea, that will have to do. He nodded at Lawrence across the street, had a quick look around for Bill Quinn, and opened the front door of the Wagon Wheel Café.

In the evenings after Summer Feelin' went to bed, Max and Knute would sit on top of Johnny Dranger's pile of hay and smoke and talk and make love. It seemed like maybe they could be a real couple again. They talked about their childhoods. They were okay, pretty good. Knute's was better. Max told her that he felt his mother loved him. That she loved a lot of things, a lot of people, and that hers was a hard way to go, a potentially disastrous way of living. Knute listened to him talk a lot about Combine Jo. She had got used to hating her, so she didn't know what to say. Knute talked a bit about Tom and Dory, and Max shook his head. "I wonder what he wants," he said about Tom. They talked about what Summer Feelin' got from Max and what she got from Knute. They laughed a lot. The purple sky and warm breeze and the smell of dirt and fresh seed inspired them. Even if they couldn't quite see a future together they could remember a past, and that was enough to build on. Dusk on the prairie in June, that's where they were. Enough light to see what's in your face, too much darkness to see what lies beyond.

"It's good to be back," said Max. "I missed you, Nudie. And I love being a dad, although it is weird. . . ."

"That would explain all those hundreds of letters and long-distance phone calls," said Knute. They were lying on top of their pile of hay, in Johnny's field.

"Yeah," he said. "Okay, I didn't call or write or whatever, but I was fucked up. So you can't resent the fact, or you can, whatever, but you can't be justifiably pissed that I had a brain problem and left when I was told to. And as for Summer Feelin', I was scared to death of finding out about her. That was a major deal for me and don't you think for a second I didn't care about her. I figured I was doing her and you a favour by just disappearing. Okay, it's a cliché, whatever, and you probably don't believe me, but it's true. I didn't have a fucking clue what to do about her or you or myself or anything."

"Well," said Knute, "didn't your mother tell you to leave so you wouldn't get stuck being a father at your age, and with some girl who you maybe weren't totally sure about and you just said, 'Yes, Mother, good idea, Mother . . . '"

"No. That didn't happen. I just told you that at the time. I was pissed off at you for telling me to fuck off just because I wasn't initially thrilled at the prospect of having a kid. I mean, you know, were you thrilled? At the time? I was worried that you'd just leave me out of the whole thing, think of me as a totally useless parent. I was mad that we couldn't just deal with it openly, I was pissed off that I couldn't express doubt about having a baby without being thought of as a total shit. . . . So, whatever, for some stupid reason, I guess I was just scared, or confused, or whatever, I said my mother had encouraged me to leave, which, in hindsight, made me look like a total fucking spineless little kid, Mommy told me to leave, et cetera, et cetera, and made you hate me, and my mother, who really is just a harmless drunk, not a bad one, and she can't figure out why you hate her, except that she assumed you'd hate me, for leaving, and . . . you know, hate her by proxy. I don't know, whatever, it was a lie and I had a major brain problem. Okay? I'm sorry."

"It's okay," said Knute. "Okay?" She took Max's hand.

Max took a deep breath. "Fine," he said.

Knute looked at his face. She tried to see it the way Combine Jo would have. She tried to look at it with love only. And concern.

They lay there quietly for a long time and watched the purple fade from the sky. They saw some lights go on in town and saw Johnny Dranger's yard light go on and they heard his dog bark a couple of times and the slam of a car door and Johnny yelling at the dog. If they hadn't lived in Algren most of their lives they would have smelled the liquid fertilizer on the fields. They were used to the smell of shit.

Max lay next to Knute, propped up on his elbows. His smooth white butt, surrounded by the brownish straw of the bales, shone like a giant egg in a dark nest. "Why didn't you tan your bum in the South of France?" Knute asked him.

"Shut up," said Max, laughing.

She gave him a big push with her foot and she heard him yell and then he disappeared entirely and there was a dull thud. Max had fallen overboard into the field. "Oh my God, are you okay?" she shrieked, scrambling to put her clothes on and peer over the side at the same time.

"Fucking hell," said Max, "I think I broke my leg. You're gonna have to go get Johnny, Knute, for fuck's sakes . . ."

Knute landed on the ground beside him and leaned over to have a look.

"Did you bring my clothes?" he asked.

"No," said Knute, "sorry."

"Oh fuck, oh God, my leg is fucking killing me . . ."

"I'll go get Johnny!" she yelled, already running through the field towards Johnny's little house.

"Hurry, I'm dying!" Max yelled. "I'll rot in this fucking field!"

Johnny brought them to the hospital in his truck. Max lay stretched out on the seat with his head on Johnny's lap, moaning. He was naked except for a gunny sack thrown over his loins. Johnny sat and drove, and laughed. And Tiny, Johnny's dog, and Knute rode in the back of the truck with the warm wind in their faces.

When they got to the hospital they had to wait for the doctor to show up. By then it was around midnight, and the only person on duty was Nurse Barnes, who shook her head when Knute told her what had happened to Max. "I see," she said. "I see." It didn't look like she saw. If she had seen she would have been nodding her head, not shaking it. "Can you put any weight on it?" she asked Max.

"No!" he said. Johnny laughed at that point and so did Knute. Max was lying on a gurney in the reception area, dressed in his gunny sack and staring up at the ceiling. "What the hell is so hilarious over there?" he said. He cursed under his breath. "Can I smoke in here?"

Nurse Barnes said, "No, I'm sorry." And she added, "I'm afraid Dr. François is having some car trouble, it may be a few minutes before he arrives." So Johnny wheeled Max outside and they all had a cigarette on the front steps of the hospital. Nurse Barnes passed by the open front door pushing an X-ray machine or microwave oven or something and said, "Johnny, I'm surprised at you, with your asthma."

Johnny shrugged and Max said, "What the hell does that mean?"

"Sorry," Knute said to Johnny, "for dragging you around like this. Sorry Max is naked. It was a very warm evening, you know, and . . ." She was smiling and Johnny nodded.

"Sorry?" yelled Max. "Why the hell are you saying sorry to *him*? I'm the one you booted off the bales. I'm the one with the fucking broken leg here!"

"And I'm sorry, Johnny," said Knute, "that Max isn't more grateful . . ."

"You guys are so lucky," said Johnny out of the blue. He was staring at the moon. "You really are—"

Max interrupted him. "Lucky!" he said. "Lucky? Jesus, Johnny, are you warped?"

"Shut up, Max," said Knute.

"Or what? You'll break my other leg? . . . Johnny," he said, "are you there?"

"Yeah," said Johnny.

Nurse Barnes poked her head outside and waved her hand in front of her face. "Smoky," she said. Max said "fuck off" in a very low voice, and then Nurse Barnes said, "The doctor's here now, c'mon back inside."

"I'll race you to the front desk," said Max, and Johnny wheeled him back inside.

The next morning Combine Jo drove Max over to Tom and Dory's place. Summer Feelin' saw them drive up and went running out to help Max with his crutches. She was looking forward to drawing all over his cast with her markers. Combine Jo made sure Max made it to the front door and then gave him a reassuring pat on the back. She picked up Summer Feelin' and kissed her. "See you later, aviator," she said to S.F. who grinned and shook her head. "See you later, hot potater?"

S.F. laughed and said, "No, no, no."

Combine Jo tried again. "See you later, elevator?"

S.F. shrieked, "Alligator! Alligator!"

Combine Jo, all 250 pounds of her, jumped back and waved her arms in the air. "Where? Where?" she screamed. "Where's the alligator?"

By now S.F. was flapping wildly with delight. "Over there!" She pointed to a spot behind Combine Jo, who jumped to the side. "No, no, over there!" S.F. said, and Combine Jo screamed and jumped again.

"Hey, Jo," said Knute. Jo stopped jumping and put S.F. back down on the ground.

"Yes, ma'am?" she said, laughing and out of breath.

"Do you want to come in for a cup of coffee?"

"Oh no," she said. "Thanks anyway, Knuter, but I have some shopping to do, and a few errands to run, another time, though, eh?" She smiled and looked at S.F. "See you soon, you big balloon. Bye, Knute, see ya, Max! Dory!" she yelled into the house. "Give my regards to Tom!" Max had already hobbled into the kitchen and was sitting at the table with Dory, reading the morning paper.

Dory said, "Will do, Jo."

And Max said, "Don't forget, king-size! Not lights! And thanks," he added.

This was the situation. Dory and Knute had had a long talk about Tom, about Max, about Summer Feelin' and about themselves. They agreed that the most frustrating thing was that they didn't know what to do. That is, they didn't know how to make Tom happy, how to get him out of his bed. The doctors said there wasn't much they could do, either. If a grown man decides to stay in bed for the rest of his life, what can you do? His headaches and his confusion and memory loss and depression, all of that was real. And his heart was weaker than it had been before his heart attack, but not strong enough yet to have open-heart surgery. He had been diagnosed as clinically depressed by his psychiatrist, but he had refused to talk to the doctor about his life, his family, his hopes, his dreams, the world, his sadness, anything. Then he had refused to go altogether. So Dory had started going to his appointments instead and discussing her life with Tom. Tom was on medication for all of his illnesses but nothing seemed to change. His medication had been increased, decreased, changed entirely, stopped altogether, and then prescribed again. The doctors said he should be able to do some light work, go for walks, travel, socialize with friends, stuff like that, without too much discomfort, or none at all. Staying in bed, they said, was not going to make him well. But what do you do when a grown man takes to his bed and won't budge? Tom was lying at the bottom of his own mysterious black hole and they could do nothing to help. All they could do was wait for him to make a decision on his own, or for his sadness to lift. "Can you die from being sad?" S.F. had asked. And what could Knute say?

In the meantime, Dory would get on with her life. She decided that she would stop with the home renovations for a while, and go back to work full time at the labour pool, and join a support group in the city for people like her—women who love men who love beds, or something like that. Actually, it was cryptically called Friends of Houdini. They met every Tuesday night. And she thought she might try a couple of university courses in the fall.

It was also evident that Max and Knute had rekindled the old flame and Dory wasn't happy about it. She wanted to be happy about it, but she wasn't. "I need some time to process this," she'd told Knute. She was still worried that Max would disappear any time and leave Knute and S.F. heartbroken once again. But Max and Knute were fine. They were in love, still, and having fun. They had plans for the future, to move to the city, to find work, and to raise their daughter together. "People can change, Dory," Knute said. "People can grow up."

"Yes, Knutie," Dory said, "that's true."

But for now, Knute still had her job with Hosea, Dory was back at the labour pool and Max, they had decided, would look after S.F. at Tom and Dory's place so that Tom would have some company while Dory and Knute were gone. Neither Max nor Tom was looking forward to spending their days together. When Dory had casually mentioned the plan to Tom, he spoke for the first time in days. He rolled over and said, "Preposterous. That boy has the constitution of an Oxo cube. Not to mention the resolve. Put him in a situation requiring responsibility and he'll dissolve at once. He's unfit to look after himself, let alone a child and an old man who happens to hate his guts."

Dory had said, "Tom, Max is not a boy, the child is his own and they get along beautifully, and you are not an old man, although you're acting like one. And, furthermore, since when do you use the expression to hate someone's guts? Really, Tom. People change, people grow up. If you haven't noticed, I'm not a big fan of Max's, either, but right now he's all we have, so get used to it."

Or that's how Dory told it, anyway. She was proud of her firm response to Tom's indignation. She would have loved him to have gone on about it, to argue and rant, to jump up and down on the bed, to refuse to have Max in the house, to have said anything more at all, but he didn't. He rolled over and didn't say another word. When Knute told Max about the plan he responded, initially, with laughter. "Tom hates me," he said.

"We all do, Max," said Knute, "you're a parasite."

"I know, I know," he said. "But, Knute, it'll be pure hell, I have to take care of him? *And* Summer Feelin'?"

"Yes," said Knute. "That's correct."

And now he had a broken leg, too. But that was the situation. Dory and Knute were confident they would manage somehow.

That morning, before Max showed up with his cast and crutches, Knute called Marilyn. She told her all about the night before and they had a good laugh. Then she told her all about Tom. "Are we young or old, do you think, Marilyn?" she asked.

"Oh, for fuck's sake, Knutie," said Marilyn. "We're young, sort of. Young enough. Tell me what you said when S.F. asked if you can die from sadness."

"I didn't say anything," said Knute. "I didn't know what to say. If I had said 'yes,' she would have worried about Tom, and also would have felt she could never feel sad about something without risking her life."

"So why didn't you say 'no,' then?" asked Marilyn.

"I don't know," said Knute. "It wouldn't have been the truth, really, I don't think. To say 'Of course you can't die from sadness' would be a terribly clinical thing to say, Marilyn. To say, 'Well, technically, the heart stops beating, the brain stops sending signals, the internal organs shut down and that's how a person dies. End of story,' she'd grow up to be a cynic. I just think it's more mysterious than that. I think you can die from sadness."

"Well," said Marilyn, "it's like a passive form of suicide, just letting go, checking out. Though I still think it takes more than one botched response to your kid to turn her into a cynic."

"Okay," said Knute, "whatever. It's not his fault. It's not a lack of willpower."

"I know," said Marilyn. "Drugs might help Tom, but then again they might not."

"They don't," said Knute. "They don't seem to, anyway. And you know, this sadness . . . as far as I know, Tom's had a happy life, except for his heart attack and now the mental lapses . . ."

"Well, that's enough, isn't it?" asked Marilyn. "Sometimes it's just the fucking sadness in the world, from the beginning of time, and no end to it in sight that begins to eat away at some people. A lot of people, I think. But a lot of people do things about it, like drink too much, or work too hard, or sleep around too much . . ."

"Tom just floats on it," said Knute, "and it takes him out to sea. He gets lost."

"How do you get him back?" asked Marilyn.

"I don't know . . ."

Knute had to go to work, and Marilyn had to answer the door so they said good-bye. Marilyn said it would be a while before they could all get together again because Josh had the chicken pox and she had met a nice guy who was fixing the street in front of her place, so maybe her social life would pick up. But they agreed to talk again soon.

twelve

Hosea stood at his window and watched as Knute watered the flowers along Main Street. Red and white petunias, thought Hosea. Yes, that will work. He watched Knute turn around and say hello to a young woman about her age. She was smiling and nodding her head vigorously. Then she pointed to the flowers and laughed. She looks so much like Tom, thought Hosea. She really does. For a second or two Hosea thought about his own child residing within Lorna's womb and he wondered, would he or she look like him? He watched Knute say good-bye to the other woman and light up a cigarette. She smokes too much, he thought. She'll end up having a heart attack like Tom. But then Hosea remembered that Tom had never smoked, except for a couple of cigarettes one summer night up on the dike when he was a kid, because Peej had forced him to. Actually Peej had tried to force Hosea to smoke the cigarettes, but Tom had told Peej that Hosea was asthmatic and could die if he inhaled. "Here," Tom had said, "gimme those damn things, I'll smoke 'em myself."

Hosea opened his office window and wedged a fat felt-tipped marker under it to keep it up. He tried to make out the emblem on the front of Knute's baseball cap. He thought it was the Brooklyn Dodgers. Tom's cap, he thought. That's Tom's old cap.

Peej had always wanted to fight Hosea. He knew he would win and he knew Hosea wouldn't tell Euphemia, and even if she found out she'd probably just shrug it off or make a joke. And Hosea had no father to defend him.

Hosea remembered watching the baseball game from the relative safety of the dike. He'd known Peej was there waiting for him. Hosea rode his bike around and around the dike. All the boys playing baseball could see him up on the dike and from time to time one of them would wave. Peej wasn't going to go up there to fight Hosea because he wanted an audience. He wanted Hosea to come down to the field where all the boys were. Finally Tom couldn't stand it any longer and he threw his baseball glove in the grass and walked over to where Peej stood. "C'mon, you stupid piece of shit, I'll fight you."

This made Peej laugh. "Go back to your little game, you jam tart, you're not the girl I'm looking for." Tom looked up at the dike. Hosea had stopped riding and stood straddling his bike, watching.

"C'mon," said Tom, "you big chickenshit. Fight me. If I win, you leave Hosea alone. You never touch him, ever."

Peej laughed. "Okay," he said. "And if I win?" Tom flew at him. He didn't have an answer for that question. He just knew he had to win.

Tom didn't really know how to fight. He didn't know how to punch and kick and ward off blows, hook and jab, all that stuff. In fact, he fought like a girl. He clawed P.J.'s face with his fingernails. He pulled P.J.'s hair until his head snapped back and his tongue stuck out and that's when he bit half of it off and spit it back into P.J.'s face. And that's when P.J. went down and the fight was over. Tom was sobbing and trembling and he fell to his knees beside P.J. who was bleeding into the dirt and whimpering like a newborn calf. Tom looked up and saw Hosea way off in the distance, riding his bike around the dike, and disappearing. He was free.

Knute was watering the petunias along Main Street, having a cigarette and keeping a lookout for the painters from Whithers. She had hired them to paint the water tower and put the horse decal on it and they had guaranteed the job would be finished by July first, when the Prime Minister might be coming for a visit. They were coming with a few truckloads of paint called eldorado, a kind of filter-orange, Hosea had said, a colour that would blend with the fiery hues of the sunrise and make it look like the white horse was racing through the sky and not plastered onto the side of a water tower. Whatever, she had thought to herself when Hosea told her that. She figured it must have been his girlfriend Lorna's idea. Anyway, she was watering the flowers when Hosea opened his window and called out, "Hey, Knutie, who was that woman you were just talking to? I haven't seen her around town before!"

"It's Iris!" she yelled back. "Iris Cherniski! She's moved here to help her mom at the Wagon Wheel!" And then Hosea slammed his window shut, just like that—end of conversation.

Hosea put his head on his desk. Well, he thought, she's here. Those damn Cherniski women don't waste any time, do they? Now I've got Max, the triplets, and Iris Cherniski, that's five over fifteen hundred. Hosea opened his top drawer and pulled out his orange Hilroy scribbler. Under the column New Citizens of Algren, he added the name Iris Cherniski. He put his scribbler back in the top drawer and closed it. Then he opened the middle drawer and pulled out the tattered copy of the letter from the Prime Minister, promising to visit Canada's smallest town on July first. It has to be, thought Hosea, it just has to be. He thought of the boxes of empty bottles in his basement and of Euphemia's dying words, "Your father is John Baert, the Prime Minister." He didn't want to think about it. He re-folded the letter and put it back into the middle drawer. Wait a second, he thought. Today's my birthday! Today's my friggin' birthday. He knew he'd have to remind Lorna. She often had trouble remembering her own. God, I'm ancient, he thought. People will think I'm my baby's grandfather. Hosea flipped his hands over and checked for liver spots and any type of trembling. Had his left hand quivered? He decided to go home and make himself some lunch. He would call Lorna and have a quick nap, and on his way back to the office he would check on the painters and also on the progress of the carpenters who were busy transforming the old feed mill into a theatre. Then he would talk to Knute about Bill Quinn, and also drive out to the Welcome to Algren, Canada's Smallest Town sign, and think about how to jazz it up.

Hosea drove home and pulled into his driveway. He imagined himself reaching over and unbuckling the seatbelt that would be securely fastened around his infant son or daughter's car seat. Or, he wondered, does the baby ride in the back seat? From now on, he decided, he would closely observe parents interacting with their children. He made a mental note to remind Lorna to do the same. Hosea had his screen door open and was almost in his house when Jeannie appeared from between their houses. Hosea was afraid she'd bring up the subject of turning the feed mill into an aerobics/laundromat and he was about to tell her he already had plans for it, but he didn't get the chance. "Oh, Hosea," said Jeannie, "thank God I caught you, is this a bad time?"

"Uh," said Hosea, "for what?" He knew for what, and yes, he thought, it was a bad time. Every time was a bad time as far as Jeannie was concerned.

"Well, I'll just be a second," she said. "Listen to this. Veronica, you know, Veronica Epp? With all the kids? She's leaving her husband. Apparently, he's being a jerk and not helping out with the triplets at all, he says they're probably not his, excuse me? Not his? I don't think so. It's not like Veronica has any time to have affairs on the side. But he says triplets don't run in his family, and they don't run in hers, so in whose do they run? Veronica says, Well for Pete's sake, they don't really run in most families. So anyway, she's had enough. She's leaving. And she's taking the triplets with her. She was going to take all the kids, but they don't want to go, you know, they're older and all that, and Gord's nice to them because he can see the resemblance, et cetera, et cetera, so—"

"Wait!" said Hosea. "Veronica's leaving? With the triplets? You mean all three of them?"

"Well, yes, Hosea, all three of them," she said. "Triplets, three, get it?"

"I can't believe it," said Hosea, "that's fabulous, well not fabulous, I mean, as in good, I mean, you know, fabulous, as in like a fable, it's so strange, can it be true? That kind of fabulous . . ." Hosea's hand flew to his shirt.

Jeannie shook her head. "Well, I don't know, Gord may be a jerk, but he was probably more help than she realized. It won't be easy for her to be alone with three babies, not to mention being separated from her other kids, and who knows what strange ideas Gord will put in their heads about their mother and their three baby brothers?"

"So," said Hosea, "where is she moving to?" A quick horrible thought came to him. Maybe she was moving into the next block, in with her sister who lived in Algren, in which case it would make no difference to the number of citizens, she'd still be in the same town.

"Winnipeg," said Jeannie. "She's moving into public housing in Winnipeg and she's gonna go on welfare until she can get her act together. Right at the beginning she'll be at her sister's. They call it a trial separation, you know, they're not getting a divorce or anything, but as far as I'm concerned, those trial separations never work, that's it, it's over, people don't get back together again, they just call it a trial separation 'cause it's not so, you know, conclusive, and, of course, for the sake of the kids, who probably don't want their parents to split up and for her parents, who will probably be devastated, they're so conventional, and Gord's parents, who think the sun rises from his you-know-what and—"

"Do you know when they're leaving?" Hosea asked Jeannie.

"Yeah, sometime on the weekend. She's fed up."

"Oh, you know what?" said Hosea. "I think I hear my phone ringing. I'd better go." Hosea had heard all that he needed to hear. This was wonderful news. And on his birthday! Four people leaving, that would leave only one person too many for Canada's smallest town. There was some hope, there was a chance Hosea's dream might come true. He threw Leander's hat down on the sofa and rushed to the phone to call Lorna.

"Do you know anything about the Algren cockroach?" Knute asked Tom. No answer. "Do you know anything about petunias?" No answer. "Do you know anything about polite conversation?"

"Plenty," said Tom. "Too much."

"Then tell me about the Algren cockroach," said Knute. No answer. She sat down on the bed next to him. "Did you know that cockroaches are responsible for producing 85 percent of the world's methane gas?"

"No," said Tom, sadly, "I didn't."

"Well, it's true, it's their flatulence that does it. Have you ever delivered a two-headed calf?"

"No."

"A two-headed horse?"

"No."

"A two-headed anything?" No answer. She sat and stared at her hands. She yanked a few bits of material dangling from her cutoffs and rolled them into a ball and flicked it to the floor.

"Do you miss being a vet?" she asked.

"No," he said. Silence for a while. S.F. was playing in her room and Knute could hear her softly singing. She looked at the sky through the window. It would be a very hot day. It was time to leave for work. She got up and Tom said, "I never loved being a vet."

"No?" said Knute.

"I wanted to take care of people," said Tom. "I would have liked to have become a doctor."

"Really? Why didn't you?"

Tom sighed and smiled at her. "I was afraid I'd make a mistake." They heard S.F. running down the hall and yelling, "Daddy's here, Daddy's here!"

"Well," said Knute, "S.F. needs a lot of attention and Max has a broken leg . . ."

Tom smiled. "Think that'll keep him from running away again?" he asked.

Knute reached around to feel her cigarettes in her back pocket.

"Gotta go," she said.

"Hey, Knutie," said Tom, "how's Hosea doing?"

"Fine, fine," Knute said. "He's kind of strange, he's okay."

Tom smiled. "Say hi to him, will you?"

Knute nodded. "You were afraid to make a mistake because . . . why?"

Tom sighed again.

"I know why," said Knute. "Because you wouldn't want to be responsible for screwing somebody's life up, or for cutting it short. You wouldn't want to kill anybody. Right?"

"Yes," said Tom, "that's part of it."

"But then again, you might have saved somebody's life. Or made it better."

Tom was quiet.

"You know," he said finally, "horses gather in clusters when they know it's going to rain. Isn't that smart? So if you want to know when it's going to rain, go for a drive in the country and look at the horses. They always know." He closed his eyes and smiled. Knute could hear Dory giving instructions to Max. ". . . and a chicken casserole in the freezer if you're interested . . . and his tablets are on the kitchen table, S.F. likes to bring them to him in an egg cup . . ."

"Tablets?" said Max.

"Pills," said S.F. "Tablets are pills."

"Okay," said Max, "fine. Do you know how many he gets and how many times, all that?"

"She knows," said Dory. "If he doesn't wake up or respond when she goes in, she just leaves them on the bedside table. He takes them eventually. Or so we think, anyway . . . is that a skirt you're wearing?"

Knute looked at Tom. Did he listen to their conversations all day? Did he care? His eyes were closed and his feet stuck out from beneath his blanket. They were big, strong-looking feet with blue veins all over them and they looked ridiculous poking out from under the soft, yellow cover.

"Yeah, it's a skirt," Knute heard Max say. "I'm not going to cut my jeans to get them over this stupid cast, and I refuse, on principle, to wear sweat pants or baggy shorts, so for now I'm wearing dresses. They're cooler." Knute heard Dory and S.F. begin to laugh and she left Tom to join them. Sure enough, Max had a skirt on and a wide leather belt. The skirt was a green suede mini with pockets that had outer stitching on them. He had one big black boot on, with a hockey sock, a baseball cap on backwards that said And? on the front of it, and no shirt. She noticed a few scratches on his shoulder that she had probably given him. His cast was covered with S.F.'s drawings of hearts and flowers and crooked houses with smoke coming out of their chimneys. She had painted the toenails poking out of the cast a light pink. "It's one of my mom's," he explained to us. "It was too big, of course, so I just cinched it here with this tool belt, like this, and . . . what do you think?" S.F. nodded her head and said, "It's cute," and Dory said, "Nice legs."

thirteen

Richard? thought Hosea. No. Tobias? No, no. Magnolia? Scarlet? Or just Jane? Emmylou? No, he couldn't. How about Lorna? She'd hate it. Not another Lorna Garden, she'd groan. Euphemia? Hmmmmm . . . too bad Summer Feelin's taken, he thought, and smiled. He was on his way to Gord and Veronica Epp's place. On the way he'd survey his town and note the progress Knute was making with the flowers, the painters were making with the water tower, and the renovation people with the old feed mill.

It was a beautiful hot mid-June day and Hosea was wearing shorts for the first time that year. He also had on a tomato-red T-shirt with white letters spelling Canada, a woven belt he'd bought at a Native American craft shop in Denver when he'd been trying to impress Lorna at the auctioneers' convention, white tube socks, and his L.A. Gear runners. And, of course, his hat, Leander's hat, which was the same shade of beige as his shorts. He looked down at himself, for a second, while driving, and thought he might look like Indiana Jones's dad. Oh well, he didn't care. Things were good, only one person too many in his town, a woman who loved him, an almost guaranteed visit from the man who must be his father, a bun in the oven—sorry, he thought, a baby on the way—and, to top it off, he'd lost six and a half pounds.

He drove down First Street and turned left onto Main, towards the feed mill. On the sunny side of the street he saw Knute, who had been taking care of the flowers, suddenly drench herself with the water in her watering can, and the doctor standing beside her wearing cycling shorts and a tight T-shirt and laughing. Hosea smiled. Nothing wrong with that, he thought. He watched as Knute shook her head and sprayed water all over the doctor.

Hosea wiped his brow and rubbed his sweaty hand on his shorts. "Gad, it's hat," he said out loud like an American in a sauna somewhere in Texas. Knutie and Bonsoir can't be having a, a thing, can they? he thought to himself, remembering the young men in the city Lorna hugged and cracked jokes with. If I wasn't so old, he thought, if I wasn't Indiana Jones's pappy, I'd understand. Hosea quickly tugged at his shirt front and dropped his shoulders in an attempt to appear relaxed. No, can't be, he thought. He knew Max and Knute were a happy couple these days . . . he'd been hoping Max would leave town again, mysteriously disappear like before, in fact he was sure it would happen, and now . . . it wasn't happening. But of course he was happy for Max and Knute and Summer Feelin', he just, dammit, he just needed Max to leave. He needed somebody to leave, anybody really, he had thought Max would be the natural choice. But S.F. loves him, she knows him now, how could he hope Max would disappear . . ."Fucking hell!" said Hosea. He looked down at the neatly ironed crease in his shorts and his pale legs and thought about the Prime Minister, about Lorna, Euphemia, his own unborn child, and what a doofus he was. To hope that a child's father would disappear so that he, an adult, a responsible mayor and soon-to-be father, could have one afternoon with his own dad, alleged dad, not even . . ."Oh for fuck's sakes," Hosea said again. He waved to Knute and then to the doctor who had left Knute standing, soaked, in the sunlight, and was now walking east down Main towards the hospital. And was that, dammit, it was, thought Hosea, it was Bill Quinn trotting along beside the doctor like a self-righteous St. Bernard on a life-saving mountain trek. Hosea slowed down and drove up beside the doctor and the dog.

"Hello there," he said. "I've been trying to get rid of that dog for weeks now, and here he is again . . ."

"Ah, Hosea," said the doctor, ignoring his comments, "I've been wanting to talk to you." Hosea stopped his car and the doctor came over and leaned in through Hosea's open window. "Oh, nice belt," said the doctor. Hosea was about to say "Thanks, it's a Native American blah blah blah," but the doctor said, "So, this is the thing. I've had an offer from a big hospital in Indianapolis, it's a teaching hospital with a good reputation, it's in a great neighbourhood, it's altogether a great offer, and the money, of course, is much better, not that that's your fault or anybody's, it's just fact."

Hosea cleared his throat and nodded, "And?" he said. He smiled and glanced for a second at Bill Quinn, who was lying on the hot sidewalk licking his balls. Bill Quinn lifted his head for a moment, winked at Hosea, and then resumed his position, head bowed and bobbing, back leg sticking straight up in the air.

"And," said the doctor, "I don't know what to do."

"Hmmm," said Hosea. "I can understand that." Leave! he thought to himself, Go to Indianapolis! Take Bill Quinn with you!

"I kind of like Algren," said the doctor. "Especially now that summer is here, it's an easy place to live, you know, an easy place to practise. I wish I could take on a few more challenges professionally, but then again, that may be overrated. I think people like me here, maybe—"

"Oh no, for sure, Doctor," said Hosea. "They like you for sure. I know I do . . ." and he really did, he always had. He admired the doctor's easy ways and his unfailing professionalism and dedication. And they will in Indianapolis, too, he thought sadly, and happily at the same time. This could be the one. The one to leave and make Algren's population a perfect fifteen hundred. He could easily get another doctor immediately after July first, or so he hoped. The doctor and Hosea smiled at each other like a couple of kids.

"Thanks, Hosea," said the doctor. "I like you, too." He patted Hosea on the shoulder and Hosea smoothed down the front of his Canada T-shirt. He nodded.

"Good," he said. He looked down at his white tube socks and back up at the doctor's smiling face. "Good," he said again, awkwardly patting the hand the doctor had rested on Hosea's shoulder for the time being. Is this a French thing? he thought. He might kiss me.

"So, anyway," said the doctor, much to Hosea's relief, "I don't know what to do." A few drops of water fell from the doctor's hair onto Hosea's lap. How soon would this happen? thought Hosea, trying to remember what highway you take from Algren to Indianapolis. "At least," the doctor continued, "I didn't know what to do until this morning."

"Oh," said Hosea, "what happened this morning?" He used the heel of his right hand to smooth the drops of water into his shorts and immediately felt a sharp pain from the scar on his palm.

"Genvieve called and told me she'd be willing to move here if she could set up a darkroom and do her photography. I told her I had this offer to go to Indianapolis and she said if I did I could just, how do you say that, get out of her life . . ."

Of course she did, thought Hosea, hating all women for a split second and feeling intensely ashamed of himself. "Well," he said, "does she want you to move back to Montreal?" The doctor shook his head and more drops of water fell onto Hosea's shorts.

"No, no," said the doctor. "That's the thing. Now she wants to get out of Montreal, she's tired of all this yes, no, yes, no business, so she's decided to marry me and move to Algren." The doctor was beaming. Hosea willed himself to smile back.

"That's great," he said meekly. "Wonderful. Wonderful news." Hosea shook his head slowly as if to indicate the wonder of life and all its sudden glory.

"Well," he cleared his throat, "I'm very happy that you'll be staying in Algren. Your services have been . . . impeccable. And I'm really looking forward to meeting Genvieve." Hosea stuck his hand out the window. "Put her there, Doc. Congratulations."

The doctor put both his hands over Hosea's and said warmly, "Thank-you, Mayor Funk." Bill Quinn had stopped licking his balls and was fast asleep in the middle of the sidewalk. Hosea heard the faraway sound of a child laughing and a mother calling, "Come here right now and put your sun hat on. I mean it. Come here right now."

"Well," said the doctor, "I'd better be getting to work. Care to join me on my rounds today, Hosea? I know how much you enjoy visiting the hospital—"

"No, no," said Hosea, smiling. "I'll leave it to you. Say, when is your girlfriend coming?" He glanced at Bill Quinn. Had that damn dog cocked his ear just then? Was he listening to everything Hosea said? Hosea wiped his brow. I may need medication, he thought.

"Oh, in the fall," said the doctor. "She has some loose ends to tie up over there, you know . . ."

"In the fall," Hosea repeated. Thank the Good Lord Jesus Christ Almighty, amen, he thought. "Well," he said, "in the fall. Lovely. That's lovely."

The doctor nodded. "I'm happy," he said. "I love her." Hosea was about to say, me too, but said instead, "I'm sure you do."

The doctor whistled at Bill Quinn and said, "C'mon, boy, I'll give you some leftover tuna casserole from the cafeteria . . . See ya, Hosea." Bill Quinn leapt from the sidewalk, had a quick piss on one of Hosea's tires, and left with the doctor. Hosea stayed where he was and looked at the position of his hands on the steering wheel. Ten to two, he thought. He remembered that stupid joke Tom had told him: "Hey, Hose, when's it time for you to use a rubber? Ten to two, get it? Get it? The arms on the clock are the girl's legs, get it?" Hosea had hated that joke. He hadn't got it at first but when he did get it, he hated it. He hadn't known what a rubber was and he'd never had sex in his life. At least, he hadn't thought he had. Hosea moved his hands on the steering wheel to six o'clock. "And keep it on," he heard the woman's voice coming from far away. "If I see that sun hat lying on the ground you're coming in for the rest of the day. And I mean it."

Hosea drove away slowly from the curb. He felt his pulse and wondered if his heart was racing. "Relax, Hosea," he said out loud. "Calm yourself." He turned onto Second Street towards the water tower. *That's it, sweetheart,* he heard the voice of Euphemia, *that's it. Find a peaceful place inside yourself and go there, Hosie, don't worry anymore.*

When Hosea was about five or six, he had insisted that Euphemia warm up his bed for him while he was in the tub, having a bath. *Is it ready?* he'd screech from the bathroom, *is it ready?* Warm as toast, Hosea, she'd yell from his bed, make a beeline for it! And Hosea would leap from the tub, grab a towel and run for his preheated bed. At just the right moment Euphemia would lift the blanket and Hosea would dive in. Ladies and gentlemen, we have a new record, Euphemia would always say and make up a time less than the one before. Hank

Williams would be singing in the living room and Euphemia would read a *Reader's Digest* or a novel and Hosea would curl up next to her and fall asleep.

Well, thought Hosea as he drove down Second Street, that was a peaceful place. He tugged on his shirt and cleared his throat.

He drove into the tiny parking lot at the base of the water tower and got out of his car. That's a beautiful thing, he thought to himself. The workers at the top waved down at him from their scaffolding and gave him the thumbs-up sign. Not one of them was wearing a shirt. Hosea cleared his throat again and returned the gesture. "Nice," he yelled up at the men.

"What's that?" one of them yelled back.

"Nice!" said Hosea. "Nice work!"

"Okay," said the guy at the top, and went back to his painting. It was perfect, thought Hosea. It was exactly the colour of the sky at five o'clock on a June morning, the colour of Knutie's cigarette filters, and now all it needed was the giant decal of the flying white horse and it would be complete. A week to go, he thought, and the paint needs two days to dry completely, hopefully it won't rain, the painters will be done painting today, they promised, which means the decal goes on on Thursday and then . . . then it's time, thought Hosea, then it's the day. He remembered a recent Associated Press photograph of the Prime Minister avoiding a scrum of reporters and holding his briefcase high over his head, the way a soldier holds his gun up in the air when he wades through a stream. It looked like a backgammon game, thought Hosea. In fact, all those politicians look like they're hurrying to important backgammon tournaments all over the country. Hosea thought about his own briefcase and frowned. He wondered for a split second if he could get away with carrying around his old backgammon game on the first when the Prime Minister came to town, but quickly thought better of it. No, he'd have to get Lorna to buy him a sleek, hard-edged briefcase in the city. He waved good-bye to the backs of the painters on the water tower and got back into his car, reminding himself to make that call to Lorna as soon as he got home.

The Epps lived on the edge of town in an old house with a few modern additions built on. They had hay bales around the old part for insulation, and a swimming pool in the backyard. Their cars were rusted-out beaters and their farming equipment was brand new. Their silo had had skulls and crossbones spray-painted on it by one of their teenage sons, and a homemade wooden sign that dangled from their mailbox said Welcome to the Epps.

Hosea drove up the driveway and parked in front of the two-car garage. He hoped Gord wouldn't be home. He and Gord had never really spoken to each other. They knew each other, of course, like everybody in Algren, but they'd never had much to say to one another. Hosea wasn't sure if he could entirely believe what Jeannie had said about Gord accusing Veronica of having an affair, and him not being the father of the triplets, and all that stuff, but he could believe that Gord wasn't much of a help around the house because he spent most of his spare time in the Wagon Wheel drinking coffee and chatting with the boys. Hosea got out of his car and straightened his hat. Where was everyone? he thought. Where were all the kids? Hosea walked to the front door and rang the bell. He peered in through one of the glass panes and saw Gord lying on the couch in the living room, apparently asleep. He saw a baby swing set up in the living room, next to a giant TV that was on, but no babies, no Veronica, just Gord. Hosea looked at Gord asleep on the couch. His bare stomach hung over the couch like a pillow-case half full of Halloween treats, and one arm covered his head and face. Gord's work boots were placed neatly beside the couch. Hosea could see tiny streaks of sweat on the back of Gord's neck. He decided to go home and call Lorna about the backgammon briefcase. If Veronica hadn't already left with the triplets, she would by the weekend. Or so Jeannie had said, anyway. Hosea had just about reached his car, when the Epps' front door swung open and there was Gord. "What's up, Funk?" he said, looking tired and pissed off. "What's the problem?"

"Oh," said Hosea, "Gord, hi, I hope I didn't wake you up, there's no problem, it's just—"

"How'd you know I was sleepin'?" asked Gord.

"Oh," said Hosea again, "well, I, uh, I could see you through the window on the door, you were sleeping on the couch—"

"I wasn't sleeping on the couch, I was lying on the couch. Thinking," said Gord.

"Okay," said Hosea nodding his head. "I hope I didn't, I hope you weren't, um—"

"She's gone, Hosea," said Gord. "I don't know what to do about it. I wish I did." Gord sat down on the front step and stared off towards the road. "And here it is," he said sadly, "a beautiful day."

"I'm sorry, Gord," said Hosea.

"She just, you know, left," said Gord. "Just left. She said I wasn't doing what I should be doing and if I didn't know what that was, then that was it, she wasn't gonna tell me. That was it. You know, I had bought these diapers, these Huggies, expensive ones, for her, and that perry natal care stuff like the doctor said, you know, and I was trying to keep all the other kids from mauling the babies and giving her a break and, well, I thought I was, we were, okay, it was hell, but we were okay, we were managing."

Hosea walked over to where Gord was sitting. He put his hand on Gord's shoulder and kept it there for a while, the way the doctor had. "I'm sorry, Gord," he said again.

"When the kids come home from school, I have to tell 'em," said Gord. "Veronica said and tell 'em why, just before she left. But fuck me if I know why . . . we were doing okay . . . I don't know what to tell 'em."

"She might come back," said Hosea. "She probably just needs a break."

"I was givin' her breaks," said Gord. "I was. I was trying to. We needed a break together, that's what we needed. Go somewhere, drink champagne, go on a tour or something. That place we went to once. We needed a break together, that's for sure." Hosea took his hand off Gord's shoulder. One Veronica, three babies, that makes four gone. Hurray, hurray, Hosea thought bitterly. And one broken man. Right here, right beside me.

"It'll just take a little time to get used to, probably," said Hosea.

"I don't want to get used to it," said Gord. "I want her back. I want my babies back, too." Gord shook his head and stared off at the road some more. "I never thought this would happen," he said. "Not in a million years." Hosea stared at the road too and tried not to cry. He wanted to leave the Epps' sad farm and call Lorna and tell her how much he loved her. He hadn't made Veronica go away and take the babies. No, he hadn't. Gord had. Or maybe he hadn't. Who knows why Veronica left? He wished she'd come back, for Gord's sake. There was still a week left. Maybe a different family would leave before July first, all together and for a good reason.

"When I see that school bus come down the road with my kids in it, all happy and innocent, I'm gonna cry," said Gord. "I'm just gonna sit here and cry and my older boys are gonna despise me and the little ones will just be scared of me crying. And I don't even know what happened. And even if I did, it's too late. I waited too long and now I'm screwed."

"Why don't you call her at her sister's?" said Hosea.

"Ah, so I guess Jeannie told you where she went, eh?" said Gord.

"Do you want me to call her?" said Hosea. He didn't have a clue what he would say, but he'd call if Gord wanted him to. "Gord?" said Hosea. Gord put his hands over his face and shook his head.

"I can't talk to her, Hosea," he said through his tears. "I don't know what to say. I've never known what to say to her, that's been my problem. A long time ago, I figured it out that I didn't ever know what to say to her to make her happy, so I just tried to do things to make her happy, and not worry about the talking, and then somewhere along the way even that stopped, the doing stuff, and then—" Gord cried. Hosea sat down beside Gord and put his arm around his shoulders. Finally Gord spoke again. "I just love her, I want her back. And the babies, too." Hosea nodded and both men stared off at the long road and the empty sky above it. After a while Gord said, "Do you listen to Lightnin' Hopkins ever?"

And Hosea said, "Country's my thing, really."

Gord nodded and then said, "You know what the names of my babies are?"

"What are they?" said Hosea, vaguely remembering.

Gord took a breath. "Indigo," he said, "and Callemachus, and Finbar. He's the one with a little lung problem, Finbar is. But the doctor said it would heal." Gord looked at Hosea. "Do you like those names at all?" he asked.

"Yeah," said Hosea, "you know, I do. I really do. They're names of, well, of distinction."

Gord stared at the road. "The bus is comin'," he said. "I can hear it."

"I guess I'd better be going," said Hosea.

"Yup," said Gord, getting to his feet. "That's an Impala?" he asked, pointing to Hosea's car.

"That's right," said Hosea.

Gord nodded. "Nice lines," he said. "Good mileage?"

"Pretty good," said Hosea. "I don't go very far."

Gord opened his front door. "Well," he said, "that bus is comin'."

"Bye, Gord," said Hosea. Gord nodded and walked into his house.

What the hell is this? thought Knute. She'd gone up to Hosea's office to call Max and see how things were going and she saw a note addressed to her on Hosea's desk.

Dear Knutie, here's twenty dollars to buy yourself a regular pair of shorts and some nice sandals, for the festivities on the first. Hope you don't mind.
Regards, Hosea Funk.

Nice sandals? She didn't think so. She didn't think Baert would care what she wore, that is if he even showed up. She flipped the note over and wrote *Will Do, Cheers, K.* and pocketed the twenty. She could wear some of Dory's regular shorts on the Big Day and buy Summer Feelin' some new ones. She called home but it was busy. She stared out the window for a while and watched three guys and two women renovating the old feed mill into a theatre. Hosea thought he'd get Jeannie or someone to organize a production of *Arsenic and Old Lace* or *The Music Man* and get it running over the summer. Right now the only thing that would make anybody think it was a theatre and not a feed mill was a huge sign that read Future Home of the Feed Mill Summer Theatre of Algren. Which reminded her, she was supposed to give the Welcome to Algren, Canada's Smallest Town sign a fresh coat of red paint and mow the grass around it so it stood out properly. She decided to make a quick call to Marilyn first.

"How the hell are you?" asked Marilyn. "Are you in the city?"

"No, I'm at work, in Hosea's office."

"You're working in the office now?"

"No, I'm calling from the office. I have to go and paint a sign."

"The one in the ditch? The smallest town in the world?"

"In Canada. Yeah."

Marilyn laughed and said, "Well, you still have the job, that's a record, isn't it?"

"Yeah. I think so. I think it is, actually."

"How's the domestic situation?" she asked.

"Weird. How's yours?"

"Stupid."

"I figured. So, hey, do you and Josh want to come out here for Canada Day? There'll be a little midway and fireworks, Baert might even show up."

"What? The Prime Minister? Really?"

"Yeah, that's the plan. It was in the paper a while ago. He promised to visit Canada's smallest town on the first. And we might be it. I have to wear nice sandals."

Marilyn was laughing. "Herod's idea?" she asked.

"Hosea's. Yeah. I know, I know."

"You know, I'd like to meet the Prime Minister, I've got a couple of questions for him. What's he gonna do, operate the ferris wheel? He's pretty ancient, isn't he?"

"He'll just walk around, I guess, and check things out, make a speech. You know, the usual."

They talked for a while and Marilyn told Knute she'd try to make it out on the first, and then Knute had to go and paint the sign. On the way to the ditch she decided to stop in at home and see how things were going. Everything was quiet when she got there. She looked around thinking maybe Max and S.F.

would jump out at any second and scare the shit out of her. She looked into Tom's bedroom and he appeared to be fast asleep. Then she heard some murmuring coming from the basement and she snuck down the stairs as quietly as she could.

"Yeah," she heard Max say. "I miss you, too. Yeah. Yeah. No, not really."

He was on the phone. Who does he miss? she wondered. And then she knew. He missed a woman. Some woman she didn't know. Some woman he had met in Europe or somewhere. She sat on the bottom stair looking at his bare back and listening to him talking to this woman. "No," he said, "I'm not, either. Yeah, I still do. I love you, too. What? Yeah, sometimes. Summer Feelin'. I know. My old girlfriend. She has blond hair, yeah, she's four. Five? No, she's four."

Yeah, she's fucking four, Knute thought to herself. Get it straight, asshole.

"Yeah, I broke it," Max said. "Oh, I fell. Nah."

"Tell her how you fell!" Knute yelled and she ran for the phone and grabbed it from him and threw it against the wall as hard as she could. Max sat there with his mouth hanging open for a few seconds and then he started yelling.

"What the hell are you doing? Where'd you come from?" That sort of thing and Knute was yelling, "What the hell are *you* doing, you fucking asshole!" That sort of thing. That sort of very typical thing. She yanked the cord out of the wall and then threw the phone at Max, both of them screaming the whole time. He ducked and the phone knocked over a lamp and the bulb shattered all over the rug. "Where the hell is S.F.?" she yelled. By now she was sobbing and yelling, "I thought I could trust you!" And mixed in with "Where's S.F.?" and "Who was that?" and "I can't fucking believe it." Then back to "I thought I could fucking trust you!" Over and over. Max was trying to get to her, to hold her and calm her down, but his cast hooked onto the phone cord and he fell into the broken light bulb, and he cut his back and started to bleed, and just lay there, saying, "Calm the fuck down, Jesus Christ, calm the fuck down, please. She's playing in the back, she's playing in the backyard with Madison. Shut the fuck up and let me talk to you."

Knute could hear Tom yelling from his bed, "What in the Sam Hill is going on down there? What broke?!"

And then she left. She ran out of the house and out of the town and past the sign she was supposed to be painting and she just kept running down the highway.

"Hello, sweetheart," said Hosea from his desk. He saw Knute's note and smiled. "How are you?"

"Oh, you know, fat," said Lorna over the phone. "And green."

"Fat and green?" asked Hosea.

"Pretty much, yeah. I'm hideous."

"No, you're not."

"I feel hideous," said Lorna. "How are you?"

"Well, I'm fat, too," said Hosea. "Fat and white. I'm wearing shorts."

"Well, it's hot enough," said Lorna.

"What are you wearing?" asked Hosea.

"Nothing," said Lorna.

Hosea smiled. "Really?"

"No," said Lorna, "I'm wearing shorts, too, with a panel."

"A panel?" asked Hosea.

"Stretchy stuff in the front, maternity shorts."

"Oh," said Hosea, "I should get a pair."

Lorna laughed. "I don't really need them yet, I'm just trying them out. How's the plan?"

Hosea cleared his throat. "Remember when I told you that Veronica Epp had left with her triplets?"

"Yeah," said Lorna.

"That's actually a shitty thing," said Hosea.

"But it brings it down to one person, doesn't it?" she asked.

"Yeah, but it's shitty for Gord and her other children."

"I guess it would be," said Lorna. "But, you know, it might be good for Veronica. Anyway, Hosea, it's not your fault, you know."

"I wish I didn't feel so happy about it."

"You're not happy about that," said Lorna. "About her leaving, specifically. You're happy that the numbers have gone down enough so that Algren might be the smallest town and you'll get to meet your dad."

Lorna was quiet.

"You're laughing, aren't you?" asked Hosea.

"No, of course not."

"Lorna!" said Hosea.

"Well, okay, I am, but c'mon, Hosea, what do you expect?"

Hosea thought for a second. "I don't know," he said. He wanted to beg Lorna never to leave him. He wanted her to promise she would never leave him sitting heartbroken on the front step. He wanted her to promise she would never take their baby away from him. "The water tower looks great, though," he said. "It's perfect."

"Is the horse on yet?" asked Lorna.

"Almost. Hey," he said, remembering the favour he needed to ask of Lorna. "Do you think you could buy one of those backgammon-type briefcases for me and bring it out when you come on the thirtieth?"

All right, okay, thought Hosea as he popped an Emmylou Harris tape into his car deck. That's taken care of. They'd made arrangements that Lorna would come out on the thirtieth with a bag of clothes and the backgammon briefcase, and after the first they'd move the rest of her stuff into Hosea's place. Their place. "Huhhhhhhh," said Hosea, expelling a giant breath of relief. One more's gotta go. Just one more. I'm happy, thought Hosea. He thought of Gord on his front step. Am I happy or am I sad? he thought. I don't know which to choose.

He pressed play on his tape deck. Then he changed his mind and pushed the eject button.

Knute ran until she was too tired to run, and then she walked. She thought maybe she'd walk to Winnipeg, to Marilyn's, or maybe all the way down the Trans-Canada Highway to Vancouver. She walked into the ditch and up to a barbed-wire fence surrounding a field. She lifted the top wire and climbed through the fence and then she walked to a little tuft of bluish long grass in the middle of the dirt and lay down.

Caroline Russo, thought Hosea. Caroline Russo was pregnant with Johnny's baby. Wild Caroline Russo with the eldorado-coloured lunch kit and the leather flask full of Dr. Pepper. If she and the baby were still alive, they'd be the kind of family that would sail around the world on a homemade boat, and let the kids go naked, and Johnny would have a beard . . . they'd laugh a lot . . . Hosea pulled into Johnny's driveway. Johnny was standing there in his doorway smiling and holding two bottles of beer, like he'd been expecting Hosea. "Am I out?" he asked Hosea.

Hosea smiled. "No, no," he said. "You're still in. Soon you'll be Algren's new fire chief."

"Hmmmm," said Johnny.

"It's a paid position," said Hosea. "No more of this volunteering."

"Yeah, I know," said Johnny. "Want a beer?"

Johnny and Hosea moved the picnic table into a shady part of the yard and sat down to drink their beer. "I'm glad you stopped by, Hosea," said Johnny. "'Cause I'm leaving this place day after tomorrow."

"For how long?" asked Hosea.

"For good. I don't want to die here."

"But you're not that old," said Hosea.

"I know," said Johnny. "I don't want to die here, you know, I don't want to live here like I'm. Dead I don't mind dying here, I just don't want to *die.* Here do you know what I mean?"

"I think so," said Hosea. "I didn't know you hated it here."

"I don't," said Johnny. "I don't hate. It it's fine."

"You might not find another place you like any better," said Hosea.

"That's true," said Johnny. "But I can have a look around anyway and. Besides, I can just keep. Moving I don't have to stay put in one. Place there's no reason for me to. Oh, don't look so. Sad, Hose, it's a good. Thing I'm excited about moving. On I'm looking forward to it."

"But what are you going to do while you move around?" asked Hosea. "What about your farm?"

"I'm gonna put out fires," said Johnny. "There are fires burning out of control all over the. World I'll get fed, and put up in some place, and I'll just fight fires all over, until I've had. Enough or until my lungs give out." Hosea stared at Johnny. "And there'll be other things to do, too, Hosea, don't. Worry can I tell you something?"

"Yeah," said Hosea. "Of course."

"I want to sleep with women," said Johnny. "Women from all. Over I want to have. Sex, you know? Just a lot of good, happy. Sex I'm tired of Caroline's memory hanging over. Me I want to remember her, but I don't want it to stop me from doing stuff anymore."

Hosea cleared his throat and looked at Johnny gravely. "Do you really think you'll be happy just moving around and screwing all sorts of women?" At that point both Johnny and Hosea began to laugh.

"Yeah," said Johnny, "I really do." Hosea was shaking with laughter now and Johnny could barely speak. "Yeah," he managed to say, "I think I will be very happy doing that for a while." Hosea was laughing too hard to say anything but he lifted his beer up to Johnny's, against the pink sky, and they clanked their bottles together, and he thought he heard Johnny say, "To Caroline." Or maybe he had said something else entirely and Hosea had only imagined that Johnny had said her name.

Eventually Knute woke up and decided to go home. First she sat in that blue tuft and examined the grass marks on her bare legs and then she wondered is it better to try to understand life or is it better not to? Which makes you happier? She remembered a book of Dory's that said the mystery of life is one with the clarity and she thought, Yeah, okay, makes sense. Fighting and anger don't necessarily drive a person away. And love and friendship don't necessarily keep a person from going away. She had S.F. but she was losing Max. She knew she would in the end. She just knew it.

fourteen

"Are you drunk?" asked Lorna.

"Maybe," said Hosea. "I was drinking beer with Johnny. In the sun. A lot of beer, I don't know how many, but a lot. Good beer, though, very good beer. We had a good time, just sitting there at his little picnic table and—"

"Hey, Hosea!" shouted Lorna over the phone. "Snap out of it. I get the picture."

"Okay," said Hosea. He was writing the name Johnny Dranger in the Soon To Be Leaving Algren column and Veronica Epp and three babies in the Moved Away column. "Okay," he said again to Lorna. He slapped a hand over his right eye and tried to focus on the page. "I wanted to tell you what we were doing."

"You were drinking beer in the sun, you already told me that. Call me when you're sober, Hose, and please don't make a habit of getting hammered with losers like Johnny Dranger. You're going to be a father soon."

"That's right," said Hosea, slurring his words.

"Man, that beer should have been mine," Lorna continued. "I wouldn't mind having a cold beer, it's so fucking hot, and I'm so itchy, do you think one would hurt? Hosea? Hosea!"

"We were celebrating, Lorna," said Hosea. He'd put his head

down on the desk and had the phone resting on the side of his head so he could still hear her. His eyes were closed. His hands dangled down by the floor. "I'm so happy. Everything's just . . . so good. I've got fifteen hundred. I've got it right."

"Really?" asked Lorna. "How?"

"Johnny's leaving," Hosea said. "He wants to meet women."

"Really?" asked Lorna.

"Yup," said Hosea happily. "And fight fires all over the world." Hosea could hear Lorna laughing at the other end. His lips slid into a kind of half smile. "Do you love me?" he whispered, and the phone fell off his head and onto the desk, and Hosea was sound asleep.

Knute went home. The sky was a beautiful shade of blue, dark and soft and warm, and she could hear people talking in their houses because all the windows were open, and she could smell barbecues, and maybe a bit of rain on its way, and she could hear a lawn mower off in the distance and a car with no muffler tearing down deserted Main Street, looking for a race, and the crickets were starting up but sounded a bit rusty, and in front of her house, on the road, was a small woollen mitten covered in dust. It was S.F.'s so she picked it up and took it in.

Dory and Summer Feelin' were playing Junior Monopoly and eating ice cream. They didn't think anything was wrong. "Hi, Mommy!" said S.F.

"Oh, Knute," said Dory, "Max said you'd be late. There's some pizza left on the counter if you're hungry."

She gave S.F. a kiss and said thanks to Dory. Then she walked into Tom's room. He knew she was coming. He was awake and was wearing his glasses. Knute closed the door quietly and sat on the edge of his bed and began to cry. "I didn't tell them," said Tom. "They don't know what happened."

"Do you?" she asked.

"Yes," he said.

"How do you know?"

"Max told me."

"He told you? Max came in here and talked to you?"

"No. I got up and went down and helped him clean up the glass and I put some hydrogen peroxide on his cuts. S.F. played outside the whole time with the neighbour kids."

"So," said Knute, "aren't you going to tell me you told me so, about Max being the same old Max?"

"He was talking to a girl. A little girl. He had a job taking care of her in London, her and her baby brother, and he was calling her to tell her he wouldn't be back. When he left he had told her he might be, and now he just wanted to tell her the truth."

Knute looked at Tom. "He told you that?" she said. "And you believe it?"

"Yes, I do. He called her back after you had, well, interrupted him, and he apologized, and then he told her what he wanted to tell her."

"That he wasn't coming back," said Knute.

"Right," said Tom. "That he wasn't coming back."

"Because he wants to stay here?"

"Yes."

"So where is he?"

"I don't know."

"Was he going home?"

"No, Combine Jo called here looking for him."

"Oh God," Knute said, and put her head in her hands.

"He can't have gone too far," said Tom. "He's got a cast on his leg, and no car. Looks like Helen Keller dressed him this morning . . ."

"Oh God."

"You know, Knutie," said Tom, closing his eyes. "If you have fun with the guy . . ." Tom took a deep breath ". . . I hate advice," he said. "But why don't—if you have what you want—Why don't—"

"Knutie!" Dory yelled from the kitchen. "It's Jo on the phone. She's wondering if you have any idea where Max could be."

Hosea woke up from his nap with a stiff neck and a dry mouth. The room was much darker than it had been. He put the phone back where it belonged and put his notebook in the drawer. "I've got my fifteen hundred," he whispered. "I've got the smallest town." He sat at his desk with his hands folded in his lap and wondered, Was I coming or going? Well, he thought. I'm here now so I must be going. He stood up and walked to the open window and stared out at Main Street. It was completely deserted except for two small girls. They sat on the curb in the yellow light under the streetlight, playing a clapping game, and taking time out for sips from a Coke they were sharing. "Con-cen-tray-shun," Hosea heard them chanting, "Concentration must begin-keep-in-rhyth-UM!" One of the girls slapped her thighs at the wrong time and both of them put their heads back and roared with laughter. "Okay, start again. Start again," one girl said. "Okay, okay, hang on, okay, no, wait, okay," said the other, and began to laugh again.

Hosea didn't feel like going home. Tom, he thought. I'll visit Tom. He was about to leave a note reminding Knute to spray the petunias with cockroach killer one more time, before July first, but then remembered that he'd be seeing her at Tom's. Or, if she was out, he could leave the message there and she'd get it in the morning. Hosea left his office and his car, which he could barely remember parking, and set off for Tom and Dory's. "Hello," he said as he passed the girls on the curb.

"Lovely summer evening, isn't it?" The girl who'd been having a hard time concentrating was trying not to laugh, and nodded her head, and the other one said, "Mm hmmm." She made a face at Hosea as soon as he had passed, and both girls burst into laughter yet again.

"C'mon, Summer Feelin'," said Knute, "we're going to find Max. Hurry up, let's go."

"Is he lost?" she asked.

"We'll see," said Knute. "You can go barefoot, c'mon. We're taking the car."

Dory stood up from the table. "What's going on?" she asked.

"Ask Tom," Knute said. "He knows."

"Tom knows?" asked Dory, as Knute and S.F. ran out the door.

"Ask him!" Knute yelled. "Wake him up!"

"Oh, Hosea," said Dory, answering the door. "Is something wrong?"

"No, no," said Hosea, "I was just wondering how Tom was. I thought I'd come visit for a while."

"Oh. Well," said Dory. "You know, Hosea, we're having a little, well . . . oh, for heaven's sake, just come in, then. Go and talk to him. My goodness, it's hot out here." Dory shook her head and peered off into the night. "Do you want a beer?" she asked suddenly.

"Oh no," said Hosea. "No thank-you. Well, all right," he said, and thought, hair o' the dog, after all.

"Go on in," said Dory, "I'll bring you one. The only reason why I have a beer to offer you is because of Max. He's looking after S.F. and Tom, while Knutie and I are off at work."

"Well," said Hosea, "that's a nice arrangement."

Dory frowned and stared off into the darkness again. "Go on in," she said. "I'll be right there."

"Um, I could just get it myself, Dory," said Hosea. "I know where the fridge is."

"Fine," said Dory. "Help yourself."

"Sure thing," said Hosea. "Thank-you." He went to the fridge and got himself a beer and then went over and knocked on Tom's door. No answer.

"For heaven's sake, Hosea, just walk in," Dory yelled. "He won't answer. Just go in."

Well, thought Hosea. Dory's acting very strangely. "Thanks, okay," he called out.

Hosea sat down on the laundry hamper and crossed and uncrossed his legs. He put his beer on the dresser next to the laundry hamper, and cleared his throat and tugged at his Canada T-shirt. All he could see of Tom was the back of his ruffled head poking out from under the blanket. *Whooooo,* Hosea kind of breathed out loud. It was a hot day all right. Hosea stared at the back of Tom's head, willing it to swivel around and face him. Hosea could hear the crickets and the hum of the refrigerator. Dory must have stepped outside to have a good long look at the dark sky, he thought. "So," said Hosea, "what's new?" He stared at the back of Tom's head and said to himself, Move, move, your damn head. Look at me. He drank some of his beer and did a mental tally of the number of beers he had had that day. This was his eighth. And last, he told himself. He thought briefly of Lorna, and of the baby-to-be, and of his father, the Prime Minister. And then he thought of Euphemia. "So," he said again, "how are you feeling, Tom?" He finished off his bottle of beer and longed for another. I'll just get one, he thought. He wanted to talk about his fifteen hundred, his smallest town, so badly, he wanted to tell someone about it. He got up and went to the kitchen for another beer. Nine, he thought. No more. He went back to Tom's room and sat down on the laundry hamper again. Tom's head was in the same position. Nice head, he felt like saying. Needs combing. Hosea leaned over so his head was close to Tom's. He could hear Tom breathing. He reached over and put his hand on Tom's chest. Up and down, up and down, good sign. Like a baby, thought Hosea. Well. "So, Tom," he said, "something is happening. To me. Something good." He leaned over and pulled gently on Tom's blanket. "Something good, Tom," he whispered. Hosea looked around the room. "Hey, Tom," he said. "You know something? I'll tell you a secret. My father is the Prime Minister of Canada." Hosea stared at the back of Tom's head. He thought for sure that remark would get it to move, or at least make a sound. Nothing. He's asleep, then, thought Hosea. He's not hearing a word I say. Hosea had a sip of his beer. "And he's coming to visit me on July first," he said. Hosea told Tom all about the smallest town contest and about all the comings and goings of the people of Algren, about the triplets and Veronica Epp, about Leander Hamm, and Iris Cherniski, about the doctor's girlfriend, and Max, and Johnny Dranger, about Lorna, and the baby, and how, finally, Algren had fifteen hundred people exactly, which was just the right number to make it the smallest town, and on and on. "So," he said, "I'm going to meet my dad, Tom. I'll see him for the first time, and I'll tell him who I am, and I'll show him my town."

Tom's head didn't move. "What do you think of that, Tom?" said Hosea. "What the hell do you think of that, Tom!" he said. "This is my dream, you bastard, now what the hell do you think? Aren't you my fucking friend, Tom?"

Still, Tom's head didn't move. "I'm sorry, Tom," said Hosea. "I'm sorry for yelling. I need a friend, Tom, that's all, really. I'm sorry," he said. "Okay? I'm sorry." Hosea pulled on Tom's blanket again, and then got up and left.

Knute knew exactly where to find Max, except that when she and S.F. got to that place he wasn't there. If he wasn't at the hay bales and he wasn't at Jo's and he had a cast on his leg and no car, then where was he? Bill Quinn was at the bales, though, looking kind of lost, so Summer Feelin' coaxed him into the car and they took him with them. "You know," Knute said to her, "I'm supposed to be getting rid of that dog."

"Why?" S.F. asked. She asked why a few times, but Knute didn't really hear her because she was so worried that Max had left for good, again. And she was so mad because why couldn't she just get mad and yell and run away for a couple of hours, without having to worry about him leaving, too, on top of everything else? Why couldn't they be a normal couple? Get mad, get misunderstood, act stupidly, know the other's not going to run away, come home, make up, have fun, you know, until the next shitty time comes up, and they'd just ride that wave then.

"Why, Mom?" asked Summer Feelin'.

"Why what?" said Knute. She was driving around the four streets of Algren now, around and around, trying to come up with a plan.

"Why do you have to get rid of him?"

"I don't know," said Knute. "Well, because Hosea asked me to."

"So?" said S.F. She had begun to flap and Bill Quinn sat there on the back seat staring at her. Knute looked at him in the rearview mirror.

"I'm going to crawl over and sit with Bill Quinn," S.F. said.

"Fine," answered Knute. And added, "I don't know."

"You don't know what?" asked S.F.

"I don't know why Hosea wants me to get rid of him."

"Can I keep him?" asked S.F.

"No!"

Bill Quinn looked out the window politely like he was pretending not to hear the conversation. Then S.F. started up with "Why not? Why not? Please, please, please."

"Okay, you can," said Knute. This was just fucked, she thought to herself. Where the hell was that jerk?

"Yippeeeee!" yelled S.F. "You're my dog!" She put her arms around him and he barked and licked her face. "You're so cute, Bill Quinn," she said, rubbing her nose against his.

All right, Knute thought to herself, maybe he's at Jo's. Maybe she's drunk and he's hiding out in his room, pissed off at the world, or just at me, really, and it's a big house, maybe she doesn't even know he's there. Whatever, I'll try it.

She sped up near the dike road and S.F. toppled over onto the dog. "Put your seatbelt on," said Knute. She just wanted to say sorry and get back on track, and not lose him. Just because he was the one who went away for four years didn't mean that she couldn't say sorry every once in a while.

Then she saw Hosea. He was up on the dike, walking in the dark, all alone, like some kind of sentry who hadn't heard the war was over. She slowed down and stopped on the road, below him. "Hey," she yelled through her open window "Hi, Hosea!"

He stopped and looked at her and waved. Then he came down from the dike and walked over to the car. Shit, she thought, Bill Quinn.

"Hello, Knutie," he said, "is that Summer . . ." His voice trailed off.

"Feelin'," said Knute.

"That's it. Summer Feelin'," he said. "Hello there, Summer Feelin'. You've got a dog?"

"It's Bill Quinn," said Knute. It was dark and she knew there was a chance Hosea wouldn't recognize him, but Hosea had a look on his face, a faraway look, and it didn't seem right, for some reason, to lie to him.

"Is it?" he said. He shook his head and smiled. "They come," he said, "and they go."

"I'm trying to find Max," said Knute. "Have you seen him?"

"No, I haven't," said Hosea. "Not recently. Why? Where'd he go?"

"Well, I don't know exactly, that's why I'm trying to find him."

"You don't think he's left . . ." Hosea glanced at S.F., who was busy playing with Bill Quinn " . . . left Algren?"

"No," said Knute, "I don't think so. I'm going to check at his house. Jo hasn't seen him, but you know . . . he might be there."

Hosea looked like a ghost in the moonlight. His face was as white as the letters spelling Canada on his red shirt. "What if he's gone?" he said. Knute looked back at Summer Feelin'. She didn't want to get into this with her listening.

"I'm going to find him. I'm pretty sure he's around."

Hosea looked like he was about to cry. Why she was trying to reassure him that Max was around, when Max was her boyfriend, and the father of her child, who was sitting right there, was beyond her.

"Don't worry, Hosea," she said. "It'll be okay. I'll find him. He's got a broken leg." She started driving away slowly. "Okay, see ya, Hosea, see ya at work tomorrow. Don't worry!" she yelled out the window, "I'll find him!"

Hosea walked home and sat on his front steps for a while. He could see part of the white horse decal on the water tower, sort of shimmering in the black sky and he looked forward to seeing the whole thing against the filter-orange sky of early morning. "I hope you find him," he said out loud, remembering S.F.'s smiling face in the back seat. It was a pure thought, a simple wish, with no strings attached. He truly did not care about his fifteen hundred at this point. He hoped on every star and flying horse in the universe that S.F. would find her dad. He thought of calling Lorna to tell her that everything was, once again, up in the air. Max was missing. He'd yelled at his buddy Tom, and made a fool of himself. Why would he want to tell Lorna that? he asked himself. He went inside and lay down on his bed and wept.

When Knute and S.F. got to Jo's house, Jo came lumbering out to the driveway and said, "No, he's not here, Knutie, I don't know where he is." It was really late by then, after midnight, and Knute told S.F. to lie down on the back seat with Bill Quinn, and try to go to sleep. She got out of the car and lit a cigarette and Jo said, "What happened, anyway? Why'd he take off?" So Knute leaned against the car and told her exactly what had happened, and she said, "Oh for Christ's sake, Knutie, he loves you, it's so fucking simple. Let it be! He hasn't run away from you. It's the goddamn guilt that's killing him."

"Oh," said Knute, "he's running away from the guilt of running away?"

"Yeah," said Jo, "and all the work in front of him trying to rebuild your trust, which he wants, and S.F.'s, and all that very difficult shit. And believe me, it's difficult. He hasn't run away from you!"

"Okay," Knute said. "Then where do I find him?"

"How the hell should I know?" said Jo. "Wouldn't I have found him myself if I knew? The poor kid has a broken leg, after all, he can't have gone far."

"If he was walking," said Knute.

"Right," said Jo, "and I'm sure he was. His private helicopter is in the shop and it's his chauffeur's day off. Don't be ridiculous,

Knute. Even if he'd have tried hitchhiking to God knows where, do you honestly think anybody would pick up a guy in a cast and a skirt and a ballcap? No shirt, no suitcase? Trust me, he walked."

Knute threw her cigarette down and ground it out with the heel of her boot.

"Listen," said Jo, "why don't we have a drink and then I'll come looking with you?"

"Just bring it along, Jo. Let's go."

They decided to drive along the country roads around Algren, circling farther and farther out for a few miles, and then circling back in, going over the same ground again. It seemed as logical a plan as any. They'd been driving for a while when Knute decided to ask Jo about her habit of blasting down Main Street on her combine and sharing a drink with her dead husband over at the cemetery. "That combine thing, Jo, do you ever . . . ?"

Jo looked at her and sighed. "I don't do it anymore," she said. Knute nodded and they kept driving. "You know," said Jo, sitting in the front with Knute, and resting her arm on the windowsill, "when Max was nine I took him to Cooperstown."

"Oh yeah?" said Knute. "What's that?" She thought Jo had been too drunk and fat to get out of the house all those years. That's how the story had gone, anyway. She wondered how much she really knew about her little town and the people living in it.

"Cooperstown," she said. "Cooperstown, New York. The Baseball Hall of Fame is there."

"Oh," said Knute, "keep looking out your side." S.F. and Bill Quinn were fast asleep in the back seat.

"Max was so excited," continued Jo. "He'd say, oh, four days 'til we get there, and then, you know, two days, one day, six hours, three hours, like that. And, you know, we had driven for days and days and finally we got there, to Cooperstown, and

Max didn't want to go to the museum! We had gone all that way for him, you know, he loved baseball and this was a dream come true for him, the livin' end, and then he balked. The little fucker, I thought then. What's going on? So I said 'Okay then, let's have something to eat' and he chose a restaurant a little way down the street from the hall of fame, so we could just sort of see the flagpost that was in front of it, but not the actual building. And then he just farted around in that damn café for an hour and a half, making up excuses not to go to the g.d. hall of fame! So, you know, we took a little trolley ride around the town, it's a really pretty little place, just up this windy road from Woodstock, actually. Anyway, a fun little trolley ride packed with other tourists and some local people. And finally I thought, Okay, we have to go to that hall of fame now. We just have to. So I told Max, 'Okay, we're getting off this trolley at the next stop and we are going into that hall of fame. End of story. You know, the damn thing's gonna close for the day before we get in.' So we get off and we walk up to the front steps of the building and Max stops. He just stops and stands there staring at it. And I take his hand, you know, c'mon, c'mon. But he stands there and he starts to cry. Now I'm totally fed up, but, you know, a little concerned, and I say 'Max sweetheart, what is the problem here?' And he says, 'If I go in now, it'll soon all be over, like a dream. And I don't want it to end.'"

Jo shook her head and laughed. "Crazy little fucker, eh?"

"Well," asked Knute, "did you eventually go in?"

"Oh yeah," she said. "We did."

"Was it . . . did it work out okay?"

"Yeah," said Jo. "We went over every single square inch of that place. I followed Max around and he covered it all, we were there for hours and hours, they had to kick us out at closing time. He was in heaven, that's for sure."

"Did he cry when you had to go?" asked Knute.

"No," said Jo. "No, I don't think he did. He was perfectly content, as I recall."

"I thought you never left the house when you were, uh, when Max was little."

"That's just another lie, Knutie," said Jo. "Don't believe everything you hear."

"Well," Jo said a little later, "we're not finding him, are we?" She passed Knute her bottle of bourbon.

"Maybe he's in Cooperstown," said Knute. Jo laughed and yawned.

"Are you okay to drive, Knutie?" she asked. "Not too sleepy?" She put her head back and shifted her large body around on the seat.

"I'm fine," Knute answered.

"I'll just have a quick catnap, then, if you don't mind," said Jo, and closed her eyes.

Knute was worried. She was already circling back the way she'd come and if she hadn't seen him on the way out of town, she didn't know why she should expect to see him on the way in. Besides, he wouldn't necessarily be on the road, he might have walked into somebody's field and fallen asleep or gone into an open silo, a barn, anything. She passed the Hamms' farm on the left. It had a giant yard light on that lit up the entire area for what seemed like miles. A million moths and bugs flew around the light and a couple of dogs were walking around in the yard. No lights were on in the house. Then Knute had an idea! She stepped on the gas and drove straight into town and out the other side, back onto the dike road and headed for Johnny Dranger's house.

She peeled into the driveway, pulled right up to Johnny's front door and left Jo, S.F., and Bill Quinn asleep in the car. She could hear music coming from the house and laughter and low voices and she knew she had her man. She just walked right in and said, "Hello, Max, hello, Johnny, what's up?" They both stood there, smiling and staring at her, and instead of yelling she smiled and stared back. Johnny said, "Have a seat, Knute."

"You're mad at me, aren't you, Knutie?" said Max.

"Nah," she said, "I'm here to apologize." Johnny disappeared into the kitchen then and Knutie whispered, "But why do you keep running away?"

"You ran away, Knute, this time. I didn't."

"You ran away after I ran away," she said.

"No I didn't," said Max. "I stayed at your place until Dory came home, like I was supposed to, then I offered to take S.F. back to my house but she said no, she was gonna make pizza with Dory, so fine, no problem, then I left and—"

"And didn't tell anybody where you were going," interrupted Knute.

"Why should I have?" said Max. "I'm an adult, Knutie, I'm twenty-four years old. If a twenty-four-year-old doesn't go straight home after work, is that a problem?"

"I know," she said, "it's not, but can't you understand how I might have worried? You know it's happened before."

"Yeah," said Max. "Okay, whatever, I'm not going to argue anymore, I have too fucking much at stake now, okay? You want me to understand all this stuff about you, fine, why don't you try to understand some stuff about me?"

Knute didn't say anything then. What was there to say? Then she thought of something. "Okay," she said. Silence.

"Well, thank-you," said Max. He smiled.

"You're welcome." Silence. "How's your leg?"

"Fine, thank-you," said Max. "How's yours?" Knute smiled. Silence.

"I know about the phone call," she said.

"I assumed," said Max. "Tom told you?"

"Yeah." Silence.

"I have something to ask you, Knute," said Max.

"Do you think you and S.F. would like to live here with me? You know, just try it out, see how it goes, we could fight on a more regular basis, you know . . ."

It was the first time Knute had seen Max looking unsure of himself.

"What do you mean?" she asked. "Where?"

Max took a cigarette out of his pack and lit it. "Right here," he said, blowing out smoke.

Knute pointed to the kitchen. "With Johnny?" she whispered.

"No, no, he's leaving," said Max. "That's the thing. And he's offered me his place. Us his place. If you want it."

"Well, sure," said Knute, "okay," and then they laughed for a while thinking of themselves as farmers and Johnny came back into the living room with some snacks. Eventually Knute remembered that S.F. and Jo and Bill Quinn were sleeping in the car. Johnny threw them out at four in the morning, said he had to pack. Knute drove Max and Jo home. Bill Quinn went with them. And then S.F. woke up and said she was going with the dog, so that night she slept over at Max's. And Knute went home alone.

fifteen

Knute slept until noon the next day without S.F. around to wake her up, and when she went into the kitchen there was a note that said:

> *Dear Knutie, S.F. will stay over at Max and Jo's for the day. Tom says he doesn't mind staying alone for the afternoon while we're at work. And Hosea called, would like you to pick up more cockroach spray and give the petunias one more squirt on your way into the office. Love, D.*
>
> *P.S. I know about yesterday, so relax. And what's this about S.F. having a dog? I'm having a few people from Friends of Houdini over tonight.*

She had written something else about someone in town stepping on a rusty nail and having a strange reaction to the tetanus shot, but she had crossed most of it out, and written "Oh never mind" underneath.

Knute peeked into Tom's room and asked him if there was anything he needed before she left. He shook his head and smiled. She told him about Max and her and S.F. moving into Johnny's house and looking after his farm, and he gave her the thumbs-up sign and said, "That's great." He seemed short of breath and she asked him if he was okay and he nodded. She kissed him good-bye and left for work.

When Knute got to the office Hosea was there and he said, "Did you find him?"

"Yup," answered Knute. "At Johnny's house." And then she told him about the plan to move in with Max and he, too, was very happy about it.

"How's Tom doing today?" he asked, and Knute said she didn't know.

"It's hard to know anything about him these days," she said. Hosea told her that they had the smallest town, they had fifteen hundred people, as soon as Johnny left, anyway. The count would happen in the next day or two and that would be that. The Prime Minister would be coming to Algren on July first.

"Well then," said Knute, "all is well."

"Quite," said Hosea, formally, and kind of sadly, and Knute put up her hand for him to slap, you know, high-five, but he said, "Oh, you're going?" And he waved back.

Which was one of the funnier things that had happened to Knute in a while.

Hosea sat at his desk and felt the warm midday sun on his back. As randomly as I was conceived, he thought, as randomly as I was named, as randomly as . . . he heard a horn honking under his window and he got up and walked over to have a look. "Hey, Hosea!" shouted Johnny Dranger. "I'm leaving! I'm gone!" Hosea waved and yelled, "Good luck! Come back alive! And send me a postcard from time to time!"

"I will!" yelled Johnny. "So long!" And he was gone.

The phone rang and Hosea hoped it would be Lorna. "Hello?" he said.

"May I speak to Mayor Hosea Funk, please?" said the voice on the other end of the line.

"Speaking," said Hosea.

"Ah," said the woman, "I'm calling from the Prime Minister's Office. Your town, as you know, is one of Canada's smallest and is one of the contestants in our smallest town competition."

"Yeah, yes, I know that," said Hosea, and added, "thanks."

"One of our census people will be in your town tomorrow to do an official, uh, count, and who shall we tell her will be the person to contact when she arrives?"

"Oh," said Hosea, "that could be me."

"Yourself?" said the woman.

"Yes," said Hosea. He coughed. "Yes, myself."

"Very good then," said the woman. "And the address of your office being?"

"Office being?" said Hosea.

"Yes," said the woman.

"Oh," said Hosea, "okay." And he gave her the address.

"Our counter should be there at ten o'clock, Mayor Funk, is that convenient for you? Mayor Funk? Hello, Mayor Funk? Mayor Funk!"

"Oh yes," said Hosea. "Sure thing. Thank-you."

Hosea hung up the phone and two seconds later heard the scream of Algren's one and only ambulance as it ripped through the torpor of the day. Before Hosea could make it to the window, the ambulance had passed and the street was, once again, as dead as a ghost town.

Hosea ran out of his office and towards the hospital. The siren had stopped and Hosea could hear birds singing and an airplane flying directly behind him, maybe it was a crop duster, why was it following him? And a stampede of horses. Or was it his heart? One kid stopped playing in his yard and looked up at the strange sight of Hosea Funk sprinting down the sidewalk like an escaped parolee, and a couple of women visiting outside stared at him and shook their heads. "That Hosea Funk," one said, but Hosea, by that time, was nearing the hospital, and then he was there, running up the stairs, then through the front door, towards the emergency room, and shouting, "No! No! No!"

Tom lay on the stretcher surrounded by machines and cords. Dr. François was pounding on his chest and checking levels on one of the machines. Nurse Barnes was injecting Tom with something and another nurse was standing next to the doctor, watching a machine and opening up a small package. A third nurse was on the phone to another hospital and Hosea heard her say, " . . . massive cardiac . . ." and then some numbers. Then the doctor speaking to the nurse beside him, softly, and . . . Tom, just lying there. The doctor turned around and saw Hosea standing in the doorway and said, "For God's sake . . ." and turned back to Tom. After a few seconds, the doctor said to Hosea, "Find Dory," and then he and the nurses surrounded Tom, and Tom disappeared inside them.

Twenty minutes later, Dory and Knute stood in the waiting room, waiting for the news. The doctor was sure Tom was going to die, there was no way he could survive that much trauma to the heart, and, in fact, Tom had been dead for a minute or so, but came back to life.

"If he'd been taken to Winnipeg right off the bat would he survive?" asked Dory.

"He wouldn't have made it to Winnipeg," the doctor answered. He told them that Tom had called the hospital himself before he had the heart attack, saying he was feeling very strange, and when they got to him he had been dead, for that minute.

So, there they were. Tom was on a lot of morphine and lay there with his eyes closed, but Dory and Knute squeezed his hands and kissed him and said good-bye. They were in shock, complete shock. Hosea came in for about a minute, that's all the doctor would allow him, and he touched Tom's arm and looked at Tom. "I'm so sorry," he said. "I'm so sorry." Then he was asked to leave the room.

But then things got weird. Tom wasn't dying. Knute and Dory could tell Dr. François was getting sort of nervous because he probably figured he should have transferred him to Winnipeg after all. Not that the doctor wanted Tom to die, he just seemed a little confused. So Tom remained alive and eventually Knute even left to get some coffee for herself and Dory. The doctor came in and by then a few doctors had come from other towns, and one from Winnipeg, and they huddled around Tom, speaking in hushed tones, telling Knute and Dory that they had to admit they were puzzled. That the heart had sustained so much damage, they didn't know how it was capable of functioning. Knute and Dory were still so overwhelmed that they just nodded and stared at Tom and, well, just waited.

Hosea tried to make himself comfortable in the waiting room. The doctor gave him updates on Tom's condition, but mostly Tom was just still alive. "Still alive?" Hosea would ask, and the doctor would nod and go back into Tom's room. At one point Dory came out and asked Hosea if he would sit with Tom while she went to the cafeteria to get some more coffee. Knute had left to get Max and Summer Feelin' and bring them to the hospital. Hosea sat down next to Tom. Suddenly, without opening his eyes, Tom whispered, "What time is the count?" Hosea, startled, grabbed at the front of his shirt and cleared his throat. He looked at Tom, and said, "What? What did you say, Tom?"

Tom, exhausted by the effort he had made to speak, began again. "What . . . time . . ." He took a deep breath, and then was quiet for a long time.

Hosea held his hand and squeezed. " . . . Is the count?" he whispered in Tom's ear. Tom nodded once.

"At ten o'clock tomorrow morning," said Hosea. "They called me today from Ottawa . . . but how did you know . . . how do you know about the count?" Tom didn't say anything. He'd heard it all the other night, every word, thought Hosea. He knows the Prime Minister is my father. He knows what's going on.

"Tom," he whispered, "you don't—"

Just then the doctor came into the room with Dory and said to Hosea, "Okay, Hose, let's not tire him out," and Hosea nodded and went back to the waiting room.

Tom stayed alive all night, although he had developed a fever. Dory sat in a chair beside his bed, and held his hand and put small flakes of ice between his lips from time to time. Knutie slept on another bed in Tom's room, Max took S.F. home and tried to console her, doctors and nurses walked in and out quietly, adjusting levels, writing down information, and Hosea curled up as best he could on a sweaty vinyl couch in the lobby of the hospital, where he spent the night alone and dreaming.

He was dead. Right after he died, he said, "I don't want to be put into a box and buried in the dirt," so they pumped him full of helium and tied a steel cable to his ankle and cranked him up into the sky so he could float around the world and check things out, without getting lost, and losing Algren. He checked out a Mexican circus and New York City and lost tribes and a few hundred wars and a housing project in New Orleans. And then he felt a gentle touch, a hand on his shoulder. He had a short-wave radio with him, propped up on his stomach, and he lay on his back and floated for a while over mountains somewhere in the world and listened to police calls on his radio, and then Knutie's voice on the other end saying, "We need you here in Algren, we're bringing you back," and the cable jerked on his ankle and the short-wave radio fell off his stomach and they started cranking him back down to earth. Iris Cherniski was squirting a little WD-40 into the crank machine and saying, "That's it, that's it, easy does it," and Max was there with a microphone and holding S.F. in his arms, saying, "Perfect two-point landing, ladies and gentlemen, thank you for flying with CorpseAir, we hope you enjoyed your flight." And there were Peej and Euphemia playing concentration on the curb, smiling shyly at each other and ignoring Hosea entirely, and then there was John Baert, standing beside Euphemia, asking if he could play, and Hosea tried to undo the steel cable from his ankle and go over there, "Those're my folks," he said to Max. "I gotta get this thing off. Today's the day. Help me get this thing off."

"But, Hosea," said his Aunt Minty, who had just showed up, "you're still pumped full of helium, if we take it off you'll float away."

"Then empty me!" yelled Hosea. "C'mon, help me, Minty!"

"Oh, Hosie," said Euphemia, finally looking up, "relax, sweetheart, you're dead." She smiled sweetly at Peej and John Baert and said, "He's so dead . . ."

"Tough shit!" yelled Hosea. "So are you, get this damn thing off me!"

And Minty said, "Well, we could take the head off and let some of the pressure out, but I don't know . . ." and she disappeared, and in her place was Lorna. She put her hand out to Hosea to touch him and she said, "You're so round, you're so bloated, like me, look," and Dory brought coffee out for everyone and Hosea could hear Dory say, "I like my stories happy, the sadness comes creeping out of the cracks in the story like blood, happy stories are the saddest." And then it began to snow and Max said, "Excellent, Dory! Excellent!"

In the morning Hosea asked if he could see Tom. Dory was asleep in the other bed now and Knutie had gone into the hall to make some phone calls to friends and relatives of Tom. Hosea passed Knute in the hallway, at the payphone, and he was about to say something, but Knute smiled wearily and put her hand up to stop him. "Hello?" she said. "Uncle Jack?" Hosea smiled back and nodded. He pointed to Tom's room, but Knute had turned her back to him and was talking to Uncle Jack. Hosea went into Tom's room and stood beside him. He wanted to tell Tom he didn't have to stay alive if he didn't want to, if it was too hard, but he knew he couldn't say these words out loud, not with Dory there, not with the way things were. That is, the way life was, the way life was that precluded us from saying things like that out loud. And besides, what he meant was that Tom didn't have to do this for him, for his cockeyed plan to see his father. But instead, he leaned over and whispered, "Tom, I'm going to my office now." He'd wanted to say something more, something poignant and earth-shattering, words that conveyed the love he felt for Tom, and the gratitude. Instead he said, "So long, Tom," and turned to go. But then he heard Tom's voice. "Time," he said, not moving his lips so it sounded like *tie.* Hosea stopped and looked at Tom. "Tie," he said again.

"Time?" said Hosea. "Well, uh, the time is 9:45, Tom." He cleared his throat and looked over at Dory who was waking up in the other bed. "It's 9:45," he said again.

"Okay, thanks," said Dory. "My goodness, I slept too long. How is he?" Hosea was about to answer her, then noticed that she was talking to the doctor who had come into the room and was standing behind him, writing something again, and so he mumbled a garbled good-bye and left Dory and the doctor to discuss Tom's condition.

Hosea walked out into the beautiful day to meet his census-taker, and do the count. The counter's name was Anita and she told Hosea she had a sister who was also an official counter and was doing a count somewhere in Nova Scotia as they spoke. "A contender," she said. The two of them walked the dusty streets of Algren, knocking on doors, getting information from the neighbours of people who weren't home, and referring to Hosea's notebook. Anita raised her eyebrows when she saw the orange Hilroy scribbler and said, "Geez, Mr. Funk, you want this bad, don't you?"

You don't know the half of it, lady, were words that came to Hosea's mind, but he smiled and said, "Well, we'd all love to see the Prime Minister come to Algren. It would be a special day for all of us."

"Well, then," said Anita, "let's hope this one's a promise he keeps." She laughed and said, "I'm kidding."

And Hosea laughed, too, and said, "Good one."

That evening it was on the news. Algren was the winner with an uncanny fifteen hundred exactly. How did it happen? It doesn't matter, it did. It was the last item on the news, the feel-good piece to put people to bed with, to leave them with the impression that not all was as bad as it seemed.

Tom died that night, too. His last words were, "Where is . . ." and something Dory couldn't understand, but sounded like " . . . horses."

Max said he'd heard Tom say "Damn ticker" once just before he died, but Dory said he wouldn't have used either of those words.

S.F. was sure he'd been trying to sing, and Knute was sure he'd told her he loved her.

At 5 A.M. on July first, anyone floating over Algren would have been impressed. All along Main Street, Canadian flags in the form of red and white petunias sparkled with dew and reflected the sun, which was beginning to rise. The new Algren Feed Mill Summer Theatre, at least the outside of it, really looked like a theatre, and over at the edge of town a white horse flew through the sky. For a few minutes, anyway, until the colour of the sky changed and the water tower became visible and the horse was revealed as a decal. But it was an interesting few minutes of optical illusion, and why not? Surrounding the little town were fields of yellow and blue so that if you were floating over you could pretend you were on a sandy beach in Rio. Nobody was out and about in Algren at that time except a black dog who stood next to a farmhouse on the edge of town, jumping up from time to time and snapping at a few bugs, and a little girl who sat on the front step of that farmhouse, stretching and yawning and laughing at the dog, and waiting for her mom and dad to get out of bed.

Hosea didn't hear the phone ring because he was fast asleep, too, with his arms around Lorna and his face buried in her hair. He slept until the sun was well up and so bright that the white horse on the water tower was all but obliterated by its rays. Later in the day he returned the phone message from Ottawa with one of his own.

"Hosea Funk here, not to worry, things come up, maybe next year. Please wish him a Happy Canada Day from the mayor of Algren."

MIRIAM TOEWS is the author of three novels: *Summer of My Amazing Luck* (nominated for the Stephen Leacock Award and winner of the John Hirsch Award), *A Boy of Good Breeding* (winner of the McNally Robinson Book of the Year Award) and *A Complicated Kindness* (winner of the Governor General's Award for Fiction, and finalist for the Giller Prize) and one work of non-fiction: *Swing Low: A Life* (winner of the McNally Robinson Book of the Year Award and the Alexander Kennedy Isbister Award for Non-Fiction). She has written for CBC, *This American Life* (NPR), *Saturday Night, Geist, Canadian Geographic, Open Letters,* and *The New York Times Magazine,* and received the National Magazine Awards Gold Medal for Humour. Miriam Toews lives in Winnipeg, Manitoba.